From the Ashes

 The fire crackled and popped in the fireplace of the old tavern on the edge of town. It glistened in the blue eyes of a young woman sitting at a table in the corner as she scanned the crowd as a jungle cat would; alert for any possible threats. Her copper hair flowed down her back in waves. Her simple cotton dress helped to enhance those looks while allowing for free movement.

The bench faced the entire tavern, giving her a good view of the all that happened during her meeting while affording the protection of having a wall at her back. Two tankards of ale sat on the table, waiting to be sampled.

"I'm honored you came to meet with me." Her voice was steady as she looked her new possible employer in the eye. "I will be honest, sir, I am looking for the protection your name would bring me. There are rumors starting to fly that would ruin me."

A man sat across from her, his own brown eyes scrutinizing every inch of the beautiful woman he was to interview as his new employee. He was dressed very plainly with his dark hair cut short in a very utilitarian fashion. He had obviously experienced a lot in his life. An observer might think he was in the army or worked as a city builder. Getting a read on him was very difficult.

He seemed to have no reaction to what this girl said but she noticed a flicker of concern cross his slightly wrinkled face for a fraction of a second. He made it his business to know the business of others and was interviewing her for an open position as his aid. His green eyes didn't give any indication of his emotions, which is why he was still alive.

"What kind of work could you do for me? After all, protection does not come for free." he stated gently, in an even tone, so as not to get her angry. He carefully assessed her while picking lint off of his very ordinary workman's shirt of coarse fabrics as he waited for her answer. The girl was young, perhaps twenty years of age. She had copper hair that flowed over her shoulders in waves. Her almond shaped eyes were of a very deep blue, almost purple, in the shadowy light of the tavern.

"I have many different skills, sir. I play music, as you have never heard it, but do not have the disposition most look for in performers. I am able to gather information from the slightest twitch of the head. I live by my own rules rather than those imposed on me by men who know nothing of the real world. The strong rule the weak, but I refuse to be weak and bow to the wishes of others simply because they feel their blood is purer than mine. It is not about the blood in your veins. We would all be better off if the smarter men, not the richer men, ruled the common folk." she paused and took a deep breath cringing inwardly as she realized she'd been rambling. "If you are the man I have been looking for, you will see the value in hiring me." She fell silent once more and fingered her phoenix shaped necklace. Very carefully she slowed her breathing waiting for any reaction out of this potential employer.

There was a long pause as the man waved a server over to fill his now empty wine glass. When the server was out of earshot he asked, "If you refuse to follow the order of law, how can I expect you to follow what I say? Why should I bring you into my household? What would hiring you do to benefit me?" He knew he was taking a risk with the questions but it could not be avoided. He needed to know if she could be the very person he had been looking for.

"I am as human as you or anyone who works with you. I get angry, sad, hungry, hurt, and happy. I eat the same as anyone else. I walk around for work and money in order to keep myself healthy and in good condition. I can protect myself. I can lift a purse without any effort and break a lock without leaving any evidence. The only true difference between you and me is that I am a woman." She paused.

"I also know about every person in this room. You are of noble birth. It's in your speech, no matter the pains you take to hide it. And your clothes might be of the standard cheap cut, but there are special pockets sewn in and slits for knives and the cloth is of a finer quality. You spend more time reading reports than in the field, judging by the impatient tapping you were doing while I watched before coming to the table. You also have a bigger secret than your job." She held his gaze.

The man started to rise.

"Wait, please don't go. I'm desperate. Will you help me? I can help you and you wouldn't feel sorry." The girl fell to her knees and reached out to grab his sleeve. "Please don't leave. My family has been in this business for generations," his eyebrows rose a fraction at that, "which is how I was able to find you. I have skills already. Please." Her plea reached her eyes which was surprising because she usually had such control over her emotions.

The man slowly eased back down onto his bench. "I can't protect you, so I can't hire you."

"Are you saying that so you don't have to hire a thief, or are you telling the truth?" The girl seemed to be on the verge of tears. That same pleading look in her eyes made the man rethink his decision. *Could this girl really help me? Could she be the answer that I seek? Do I tell her that I know who she is and who her family is? What do I do?*

"You have to prove to me that you can keep up and after a trial period, I will decide if you are good enough to help me. If you are caught and sent away from my service I can't protect you. If you *are* caught in one of the many assignments given you, you will not mention you work for me or we will both be killed. These are the rules you are to follow beginning now. There are many rules that will be added to these but start there." He said this so briskly that he seemed to want to leave in that instant and remove himself from the situation. "Tomorrow, you must report to twenty-four Wood Lane for your first day at one hour after dawn. Remember that if you mention what has happened here, you will not only be hunted down by the authorities but by me as well, and I have far more resources than they do." He smiled thinking; *a creature like this girl will never survive in this world. Even with her family heritage, she is too weak. A leaf caught in a breeze that's about to be dashed against a wall. She won't last because it is in her nature to fail.* He smiled and nodded a farewell. He glanced at her pendant that she had been fiddling with and turned back. "Oh, you will be called Phoenix. I am the only one who knows your name. You will only call me Sir or the Shadow Man." With that he left.

The newly dubbed Phoenix remained in her seat hardly willing to breathe. *He took me on. I'm going to work for the best spymaster in the world. I'm not going to be exiled from my city.* She took a long sip of her draught. *Here's to you granddad. I'm working in the business that killed you.*

Her new employer had left coin to pay for the table and she would not let that go to waste. It had been days since her last true, belly filling meal, rather than scraps. She waved over the serving girl. "Could I trouble you for a bowl of the stew I smell and a bit of bread, please?" she asked. The girl saw the glint of precious metal on the table and hurried off.

Thick chunks of venison floated in the viscous gravy in the company of potatoes and carrots. The smell floating above the bowl was intoxicating. Very slowly, her stomach protesting the strictly controlled pace, the newly dubbed Phoenix began to eat the hearty stew. After fifteen minutes of savoring the stew, she mopped up the last of the gravy with a hunk of the bread, drained her tankard, and sat back with a sigh. Her stomach was no longer complaining, it was warm and full for the first time in a long while.

Suddenly, Phoenix's senses went on the alert. A large muscular man slid onto the bench opposite hers. He was clearly a soldier, probably with the city guard or he'd be at a finer tavern. "You look like you enjoyed that stew," he said.

"Yes, I did," she responded warily. Phoenix could only think of a couple of reasons why this man would have approached her and none of them were good.

"I haven't seen you here before, sweetheart," he said with a slight slur on the last word.

"I am just passing through today," she replied. *He's drunk which doesn't bode well.* Phoenix rose from her bench and started to turn away. She did not want this man to get any ideas.

"That's it?" he demanded.

"Your friends are waiting for you by the fireplace," she said. "If I were you, I would return to them and not make a fool of yourself by pursuing me." As the words tumbled from her tongue, she cringed. *That's done it. Time to make my escape,* she thought as the guard's face turned scarlet from rage.

"No wench talks to me like that!" he roared and lunged to grab her.

Phoenix twisted away and danced out of reach, right into another patron. The new man's face went right into his steaming bowl of stew. He reared out of his seat with a yelp and swung his arm around to catch whoever it was who disturbed his meal. Phoenix once again dodged the grasping arm of a man and ducked out the door.

As she carefully made her way down the street, she heard the crash of men being thrown out the door of the tavern. She quickly ducked around the corner into the shadows of an alleyway. The sound of pounding feet approached her hiding place, so Phoenix pressed herself as far into the shadows as possible.

The guardsman rushed past the hidden form of his quarry. His face was bruised and his lips were cut, evidence that the tavern owner tried to teach the man to leave his other patrons to their meals and not cause a ruckus in another person's place of business. Phoenix waited five minutes before carefully checking the area and melting out of the shadows to make her journey home.

***

The Shadow Man carefully moved out of the alley across from the tavern where he had been watching Phoenix since he had left. He knew that it wouldn't take long before one of the drunken toughs would wander over to her and he wanted to see how the new girl would handle herself. She had done quite well staying out of physical danger and blending into her surroundings to avoid the man after she left. There was quite a bit of potential.

What caught his attention, and caused his gaze to linger on the woman, was the rather curious birthmark on her right shoulder. While she had been dodging the men, Phoenix's sleeve had slipped down her shoulder, revealing the curious shape of a bird on fire. He had given her the codename "Phoenix" for the pendant she wore, but now it seemed much more appropriate and significant. It seemed he had found exactly the woman he was looking for. *I need to confirm this in the archives,* he thought as he carefully made his way home. If he had been a whistling man, a merry tune would have been playing across his lips but he was a cautious man instead. There was however a small smile lightening up an otherwise serious face.

The next day she left her homely, drab apartment on Wall Street and headed to the inner city towards Wood Lane. On her way to number twenty-four she could not help but study the new surroundings. Every step took her past buildings far more elaborate than the last. Phoenix had never been in this part of the city. Usually she avoided it because people would assume she was a thief. She was wearing very common, dingy, dirty, old clothes, the best of what she owned, and this area of the city was the home of high ranking officials and merchants who lived in huge mansions to proclaim their worth to the world. These mansions were at least three stories high with perfectly sculpted gardens and large statues depicting every image and person imaginable. The design of many mansions suggested that the owners also had courtyards of their own to host stunning summer galas. Her eyes were finally drawn to number twenty-four. Although the facade of the mansion was relatively simple it was obvious that all other residents in the area fell short of the wealth and influence of her new employer. The workmanship was magnificent. There was not a single blemish on the outer wall. Not a stone was out of place or crumbling and the windows were covered with glass and flanked by oak shutters. A thief would have his work cut out for him if he tried to enter this impenetrable stronghold. *A man of worth,* she thought as she walked up to the house. *I wonder how a man of means could have found himself involved in such a trade as information gathering.*

Before she could make any move to knock on the beautifully carved oak door, someone opened it. Phoenix found herself looking into the eyes of a middle-aged woman who obviously served as a maid of the household. The maid sniffed in an unconcerned sort of way. "Probably just a slut for hire," she mumbled. Phoenix paid her no attention; she had heard it all before. She stepped inside and heard the door shut behind her. A shuffle of feet announced the maid returning to her duties. Not knowing what else she could do, Phoenix stood still and took in her surroundings. She carefully took deep breaths, listening to the quiet stillness of the morning and slowing the beat of her heart.

"Ah, you are here." Phoenix spun around at the sound of the voice and assumed a casual looking defensive stance. "Good reflexes. But there is no preparation. We must teach you to use knives and your fists." There was a man leaning against the wall. Phoenix hadn't seen him when he came in. He was tall and muscular in a willowy sort of way. His face bore the arching eyebrows of a man who questions everything and a slim nose. The man may have been a year or two older than her, but Arlaya didn't think he was much older than that. He came over to her and started to feel the muscles on her arms. His brown eyes were intelligent under their strong brows. "Your arms are workable but I suggest you strengthen them up if you want to stay in this line of work. We have exercises which should help with that"

"I am a woman please do not treat me like a horse. You haven't even introduced yourself." Phoenix jerked her arms back as the man's eyes glittered with amusement and he raised his hands in surrender. "If you don't stop touching me, I might have to hurt you."

The man laughed. "I think it might be a while before you could even touch me." All the same he dropped his hands. Crossing his arms over his chest, he studied her for a few more seconds. "I am Tiger. I have the pleasure of showing you the ropes." He began to walk toward a large wooden door. He pulled out a large brass key, inserted it into the lock, and then whispered something so softly it was barely perceptible even to Phoenix who has exceptional hearing. Phoenix had to rush to keep up with his long stride as he stepped through the door and walked down the hall toward the sunlight at the other end.

"First we arrange for a few lessons in hand to hand combat. This is Hawk, our master fighter." He indicated a delicate looking woman standing in the sunlit courtyard. "Mother Hawk!" he called, "I have a new child for you to adopt into your class." Hawk looked at Phoenix for a long moment, taking a quick analysis of what she saw.

"You better not be trying one of your 'famous' practical jokes on me. This weakling wouldn't last more than a day on the streets. You might as well send her back where she came from." Hawk turned away. The derision in the woman's voice stung and Phoenix felt her face grow hot.

"Madame Hawk, I am Phoenix. All I wish is to be able to defend myself in this line of work. I do not ask you to like me but I do ask you to give me the tools to let me reach my goal and that of the Shadow Man." She stopped and waited.

"Only one of the agents and recruits would know of the Shadow Man." Hawk turned toward the pair and looked long and hard at Phoenix.

Phoenix just glared back. She had begun to tire of this game of insults. It was time that these people look at her like a comrade in arms rather than a tool to be wielded with no regard for its own well being. "If that is not proof enough that I am who I say I am, then allow me to demonstrate. I will not hesitate to do anything you deem necessary to prove that this is where I belong." Phoenix held Hawk's gaze, daring her to say anything. This was her last chance at the life she wanted and she wasn't going to give it up so easily.

"I do not know what he saw in you, however, I will teach you. If only because good help is hard to come by. In fact, any help is hard to come by. Come back tomorrow at dawn." Her eyes flashed as if threatening the girl to argue. "I warn you, if you are late, even by a second, you will not get anything from me that day, so I suggest you be on time. Of course, if you are on assignment exceptions can be made. Now go, you are beginning to annoy me."

Phoenix turned to find that Tiger was no longer standing beside her. She walked to the door that she had entered the courtyard through and found Tiger in a fit of silent laughter. Phoenix punched him hard in the gut so he was gasping in air. When he had recovered enough to stand straight again, she stabbed her finger at him. "You knew she wouldn't want to teach me. You knew she would need convincing and you didn't warn me." She swiped at him again but he managed to dodge the blow.

"You did well enough on your own. I have not seen her accept a pupil as quickly as she accepted you. Oh, a word of advice, don't throw the Shadow Man's code name around; it can get you killed in a very slow and painful way." Phoenix felt like she had just blundered her way through some form of testing and had come out on the proper side of things, if only just.

"Where to next, Oh Master of Practical Jokes?" Phoenix smiled at Tiger and found him grinning shamelessly back.

"You shouldn't always believe what you hear." He cocked his head to one side. "Actually, you should make a habit of deciphering through all the useless junk you might hear while on assignment, and most of what you will hear about me is junk." He winked and started down the hall before she could respond. "I wouldn't get on Hawk's bad side, by the way. I suggest being here on time every morning that you can. Her training has saved more than one life in the past. Besides when she gets mad the pain lasts for a long time." He winced. Phoenix guessed that he had experienced Hawk's temper first hand.

As they were passing a large wooden door on the left side of the hall, Tiger suddenly stopped and grabbed Phoenix's elbow. "I am starving. This is the kitchen. Let us see if Mistress Mole and Master

Wolf have anything we can beg off. They are the most wonderful cooks I have ever met." Phoenix imagined him licking his chops as he slid the door open and peered inside. His back stiffened and he carefully pushed Phoenix back. Silently he moved through the door and around the edge of the room until he was behind a kitchen girl and looked at what she was doing. Phoenix slowly entered the room and closed the door with an almost imperceptible click. "Some special herbs going into the soup?" Tiger whispered. The girl jumped and ran through a door opposite to the one where Phoenix was standing.

A strong beefy man, built more along the lines of an ox than a human being, entered the kitchen through the door the girl had escaped through. "Why in heaven's name did you have to scare the newest maid?" He looked grumpy and his deep voice matched his expression. He folded his large muscular arms across his chest waiting for Tiger to answer.

"Unless you are now allowing kitchen girls to handle the Master's breakfast, I suggest testing it all for poison. I also suggest finding the girl. We need to know who she is working for. Either someone has found out the secret that many have died to protect or our master's prominent position has created a new enemy since all the ones we know of haven't been actively trying to kill him of late." Tiger was in his element. Putting together a clear picture of what was happening had been drilled into him for years. "I'll take a new meal to him and tell him what has happened. Please try to find the girl. You know what she looks like better than anyone. And lock down the mansion, no one in or out. We need to figure this out."

Mistress Mole brought out the extra food for their mutual employer and sent them away. Tiger led Phoenix to another door at the end of the hallway. At first glance the door looked like any other in the mansion but upon closer inspection, Phoenix could tell that this door was meant to keep even the most persistent of men out. "Now before we enter you must know that the code to enter changes constantly and unless you are alerted to the new code you must have a senior agent present for you to enter." Tiger turned toward the door and whistled an odd tune and knocked twice. The door swung open seemingly of its own accord. Phoenix peered into the room and saw nothing but shadows.

"If you have come with my food please set it down and leave. I am in the middle of something important," a grumpy voice floated to them out of the shadows.

Tiger bowed to signify he heard but made no attempt to leave. "I said go. Even if you are new to this house you should know an order when you hear one."

Tiger pulled his shoulders back so he stood straighter, like a soldier at attention. "Sir, there are matters more important than your orders today. I have grave tidings to report."

"Very well." The Shadow Man sighed, "Report to me, Tiger. But first close the door so that no one with open ears may discover what is being discussed."

Tiger pushed Phoenix into the room before he closed the door. The man lit a lamp so that he could see Tiger better. When he saw Phoenix he smiled. "Not even a full day, not even two hours, and you are standing before me. What has she done that you must interrupt my work to report to me?" He looked at the man standing behind Phoenix. She felt Tiger stiffen behind her but she spared no thought for him. Instead she focused on the man who had hired her the night before. His lean figure was accentuated by well tailored clothing. It was obvious to her the previous night that although he was wearing common looking clothing he was used to better and now she saw that he was used to the best.

"Sir, this is not about young Phoenix. She has been an outstanding help in the time that she has been here," he stared into his leader's eyes. "Sir, this impromptu meeting is in regards to a recent attempt on your life."

The Shadow Man slowly shifted his gaze from Phoenix's face to Tiger. "How recent?" he asked. His expression hid all emotion and without training the average person would not have noticed the slight tremor of worry carefully controlled in his voice.

"Not ten minutes ago, sir. A kitchen girl tried to poison your meal. Wolf is hunting her down as we speak. It shouldn't be long now. He is the best we have for finding people. It is a pity that he only wants to cook now." A slight smile crossed Tiger's face. The three of them turned toward the door as they heard the code to enter. The door swung open to admit Master Wolf dragging the kitchen girl. Wolf had scratches on his face showing that the girl put up a fight. The girl had a split lip that was gently oozing blood and her once neat hair was in snarls around her head.

Wolf bowed. "Master, I thought you might like the pleasure of interrogating her yourself." He bowed himself out of the room and shut the door with a soft click.

The Shadow Man grabbed the girl and thrust her into a chair. "What is your name, girl?" He waited but the girl wasn't going to say anything. Phoenix saw in her eyes that she knew she wouldn't survive the day. *Death can be a strong motivator unless you have already accepted it in your heart.* "You will not survive long in your position unless you answer my questions." The venom in his voice made Phoenix struggle to cover a flinch. Tiger shifted around Phoenix to get closer to the girl.

He pulled out a dagger and pressed it to the poor girl's throat. "I believe he asked you a question and I suggest you answer." His voice was considerably gentler than their master's tone. After the silence continued for several more minutes, Tiger made the move to strike the girl down.

"Wait," Phoenix hissed. Tiger looked at her startled that she spoke but he took a small step back. She knelt down to the girl's level and looked her straight in the eyes. "There should be no unnecessary bloodshed today so please answer me. What is your name?"

"My life to live, my life to give. Wound me all you like and I will still tell you nothing." She spat at Phoenix. Phoenix didn't like being spit at but knew that if she didn't stay in control of her emotions she wouldn't get any information from this girl. Tiger, however, moved in again. Phoenix looked up at him and he stopped. He nodded at her to continue.

Phoenix placed her hand on the girl's shoulder. Almost imperceptibly, she pressed on the soft hollow of the collarbone with her thumb. The girl made no sound but began to shake violently, beads of sweat were breaking out on her forehead. "I can make your life full of pain and I don't have to kill you to do it. All I have asked of you is your name."

"As you wish. My name is Marie and I am just a humble serving maid. The maid that almost killed your master." The girl smiled wickedly. Phoenix stood up and stepped back so the men could ask anything of their prisoner. Before either man could speak, Marie sprang out of her chair and ran at Tiger. Instinctively, he brought his dagger up to protect himself. Marie crumpled to the floor. As the light left her eyes, she looked extremely satisfied with herself.

Phoenix tore her eyes from the scene in front of her and studied the men. Tiger looked dissatisfied but he had already shrugged off what the girl had done to herself. The Shadow Man seemed to be thinking about his next move.

"Get someone to clean up this mess. I will be in the private gardens for the rest of the day and will take my meals there. Please notify Wolf and Mole but tell no one else. I want the girl burned, let her master think she is still in place for now. Take the new girl out of my sight and make yourself useful in discovering how someone got a covert agent in what should be the most secure household in the world." The Shadow Man turned away from them and was shaking with fury. It was not often that he did not get answers.

Phoenix and Tiger left by the door through which they entered. They headed down the hall in unbroken silence. Phoenix had no idea where they were going but she just kept walking with Tiger. Tiger seemed to be deep in thought and did not pay any attention to her.

"We must equip you with weapons that will not be noticed." Phoenix jumped in surprise at the sound of Tiger's voice.

"I'm sorry?" she had also been deep in thought.

"Your weapons. They need to be something that women are often carrying around. Any suggestions?" His voice seemed older than it had only an hour before.

"I think a belt knife would not be noticeable." Phoenix responded. "Tiger are you alright?"

"I think you are right but only one would pass and you might need more than that. You will have to check the stores with Badger." Tiger paused for a moment, "I will be well when we learn who is threatening the boss because someone has found out about our business. That means that we have a leak." Another pause, "Thank you for your concern."

Phoenix held the silence that followed his words. Tiger took her down a long hallway until the light of day was gone. The hallway was lit by lamps and then further down the corridor it was lit by torches in brackets. Finally, they reached a door. Tiger produced an iron key and fit it into the lock above the handle. The door opened to a room so dark that light seemed to be absorbed and nothing could be seen.

"Grab a torch from the wall." Tiger disappeared inside while Phoenix grabbed the torch. Carefully, she stepped back toward the room not knowing what to expect.

"Step back. You are not one whom I know." The soft voice slithered from the darkness. Phoenix jumped away from the doorway. A skinny man suddenly appeared in the doorway, surprising her. He held a dagger that was pointed at her heart. There was no doubt that he knew how to use it.

"Friendly Badger, I would expect better manners of you." Tiger, it seemed, had to defend her once more. Phoenix turned to look at Tiger with a cold gaze showing clearly that she was mad at him. Tiger seemed to get pleasure from not warning her about what to expect from her new colleagues though he had worked with them for so long that he didn't even think of their quirks now. Badger lowered the dagger but it was still in a ready position in his hand.

"Master Badger, I had come here with the hope that you might provide me with a weapon." Phoenix stepped forward once more. Badger reluctantly allowed her into the room.

"You are only welcome to the weapons I show you, not one other piece. I'll know if you take anything else." Phoenix heard Badger moving behind her but he had moved out of the circle of light provided by her torch. She found herself standing beside Tiger once more and made to hit him again but Tiger had been ready and dodged it like before with a smirk. When he was out of her reach he bowed to her and raised his hands in surrender.

"I apologize, Phoenix. I should tell you more about what we are to do but you must get used to thinking quickly." Phoenix suddenly felt bad because he was right, she needed to think on her feet in this line of work. Tiger turned back to the darkness. "Badger, I was thinking of a belt knife but we also need weapons that are inconspicuous. It is harder to hide a knife in a dress than loose shirt sleeves, if you get my meaning."

Badger thought for a moment. "Maybe a shukusen, a bladed lady's fan will do. Fans are fashionable again so carrying one or two will not cause suspicion." Phoenix heard him moving around as he spoke. There was a pause in the movement as though Badger was suddenly uncertain. Then he entered the circle of light right in front of her. In his hands, were what appeared to be two delicate folded fans. The fans might appear to be fragile but when Badger handed them to Phoenix she felt their strength and their weight. They were only slightly heavier than what she imagined the proper fans to be. She flipped one open and found it was the deep colour of twilight except for thirteen golden stars standing guard over the coming night. She ran her finger over the design but when her finger ventured close to the top edge Badger stopped her.

"Do not be fooled, child. The edge is sharper than any sword carried by the thugs on the street." Phoenix carefully closed the night fan and opened the other. This one was fashioned after the leaves on the trees in the autumn season with seven bronze leaves falling through a brown background. Badger also gave her oil and cloths and proceeded to show her how to keep her new accessories in good condition.

"I will have more made to match various outfits depending on where you are stationed. Tiger will get them to you." With a polite, if cold, nod of dismissal to Phoenix and a friendly goodbye to Tiger, he sent them out the door and closed it behind them. The travel up to sunlight was one of silence, Phoenix admiring the fans and Tiger using the silence to think.

"Tiger how am I to learn the use of these shukusen? I mean to say, does Mistress Hawk teach weapons as well as hand to hand combat? Without training with all my weapons they are worse than useless because then they become a hindrance." Phoenix realized she was starting to babble and fell silent taking a deep breath.

Tiger paused and looked down at her with a smile. His response was simple, "You are wise for your age."

"You have not answered my question." Phoenix was not going to let him avoid answering. He had already caused her enough trouble today to last a lifetime the least he could do was answer a simple straightforward question. It wasn't like a "yes" or "no" would be betraying any secrets.

"Hawk does teach weapons along with the hand to hand combat. If she feels another teacher is appropriate she will arrange it." Tiger turned and resumed his walk.

"Tiger did I say something wrong?" Phoenix ran to catch up with him.

"No." He stopped walking for a moment. "Do you know what you were hired to do, young Phoenix?" he seemed to put particular stress on young.

"I was hired to act on the whims of your boss. What is wrong? Really I want to know." Phoenix heard the worry in her voice but did not care.

"I do not know how to tell you this but you have entered a world that can never be escaped. Have you heard people say, 'It chews you up and spits you out' about anything?" Phoenix nodded and Tiger continued, "This business is something like that. It will chew you up but nothing so welcome as being spit out will ever happen to you. If you are complete rubbish in this line of work you will be killed at a young age. You could survive about a year at most with no training. A worse fate awaits those who live past that year. The man or woman who survives that long now has to deal with the paranoia. When you make it your business to force other people to look over their shoulders eventually you do the same. That is the worst part of the watching business." There was a hint of resentment in his voice. He must have been recruited without any knowledge of the repercussions of leading such a life.

"I know about the affects of this profession on our lives already. The information game killed my grandfather when I was young. I have to learn to deal with it because I do not plan on letting the paranoia consume me." Phoenix's voice became the merest of whispers and only Tiger's training in hearing the smallest of sounds allowed him to hear every word and inflection.

"I know it does not matter much but I think you are talented in this area of work just by what I have seen today." He winked at her and started walking again. "You mentioned that your grandfather had some connection to this trade. Did he manage to impart any knowledge before he left this life?"

"He taught me how to read lips, force the other kids to leave me alone, and break codes. He hid little messages for me and I had to prove that I was worthy of them by breaking the code." She smiled at the memory. Her grandfather had been a hard man but they had found ways to get along.

"Is that where you learned to extract information like you tried to do with the maid?" Tiger apparently didn't notice Phoenix had stopped walking with him as he asked the question.

"No," she whispered. "I learned that...elsewhere."

Tiger turned to look at his young charge. She suddenly didn't look like the strong woman he was getting to know. She seemed to have folded in on herself and she was shaking slightly. "Phoenix?" he asked.

"I'm all right," she responded. "My family lived in this world. I was raised learning many of these lessons as a babe. But my parents died and I ended up living...a very different life than they intended." She cleared her throat and her voice became stronger. "There are a lot of people out there who enjoy inflicting pain. I happened to fall into the clutches of one and got quite the education." She shook herself and began walking down the hall again. As she leveled with him, Tiger resumed his pace.

"Why don't we get that food that we missed out on and over the meal you can demonstrate your understanding of codes." With a nod Tiger led her back to the kitchens. Phoenix regained some of her natural coloring as they moved.

The sun was high in the sky by the time they were done with their discussion. Tiger led Phoenix back to the front door where she saw the rude maid from that morning cleaning once more. As the maid went about her chores, Phoenix noticed the dagger at her hip and the grace with which she moved was indicative of martial training.

"Now it is time for you to return to your home. Make sure you are back at dawn for your training. Oh..." he turned and tossed a few gold coins to her, which she managed to catch before they fell to the floor. "Buy some new clothes. We cannot have you coming here looking out of place but remember do not get anything too extravagant. You must blend in." He turned to leave but Phoenix put out a hand to stop him.

"Tiger wait," she paused trying to decide how to pose the question that had nagged her for the better part of the day. "Have you been testing me since I arrived this morning?"

Tiger looked her straight in the eyes. "I am always watching and testing new blood. I am even testing the older more experienced people. Complacency is a killer in this profession. While you are shopping, I want you to listen. Take in everything you hear but also take in specifics. Like when you eat a meal. You want to taste the dish as a whole but you also want to taste the individual pieces." Tiger walked away before Phoenix could do or say anything else.

She decided to make the journey to the marketplace while it was still open. She needed to find a place for the new clothing. After some thought Phoenix decided that a working woman's dress with a form fitting bodice for freer movement and a skirt that is not quite as full as a lady's skirt in order to be able to move faster was the best option. Just to be safe she bought two, one to match each fan.

When she finally made it back to her flat in the city slums, her landlord was nowhere in sight. Breathing a sigh of relief, Phoenix took her new weapons and purchases up to her room and laid everything out neatly in preparation for the next day.

Phoenix woke up two hours before sunrise. The first hour she spent hiding her new clothes so the landlord or any thief who might think to take them would not find them. Then she dressed and placed her fans through her belt, feeling much more secure with the protection. Once she was ready she left her flat.

As she stepped out she almost ran over her landlord. He was the last person Phoenix wanted to see. "Sir, it is indeed a pleasure to see you on such a nice morning but I must get to work. If you would kindly move aside to let me leave, I would hate to be late on my second day." Phoenix tried to manoeuvre her way around him.

"Not so fast, my dear. It appears you have bought some new clothes. Maybe you've forgotten but you owe me last month's rent. If I don't have the money by the end of the day you are no longer going to be able to call this home." Phoenix tried to move but her landlord still blocked her way looking at her new dress hungrily. Maybe the tight bodice had not been such a good idea after all. "Unless you plan to pay me in some other manner, I would not argue." He stroked her arm and brushed his fingers against her breast. Phoenix's skin crawled where he touched her with his revolting fingers. Even though she had recently bathed, she had never felt more filthy in her life. Definitely not the best choice of clothing. Looking down demurely, Phoenix casually checked the placement of her new weapons in case she needed to defend herself.

Finally, when he realized she was not going to respond in the fashion he wanted, the landlord stepped aside and gave her a greasy bow. His hungry eyes promised they would continue the discussion later. Phoenix looked at the sky and realized that her plans for a leisurely walk were now no longer viable. She had to rush through the early morning foot traffic to Wood Lane. Luckily, the farther she travelled the lighter the traffic became. The tenants of the more wealthy sections of the city had the leisure to stay abed until the sun was well over the horizon.

As she hurried through the house to the courtyard, the sun began to show itself. Hawk was standing in the center with her back to the door but when Phoenix entered she turned and let her gaze fall on her student. Phoenix carefully put all thoughts of her landlord aside and focused on her teacher.

"Mistress Hawk, I have come as you ordered. I do not know where to begin for the lesson though." Phoenix gave Hawk the politest bow she knew how to do.

"First of all, don't bow to me," Hawk growled. "Second of all, did you receive weapons yesterday?" Hawk's gaze flicked to Phoenix's belt.

"Yes ma'am, I have two fans. I believe they were called shukusens." Phoenix held them out for inspection.

Hawk gently picked up the bronze fan and slid it open like a woman opening a love letter. "Badger must like you to give you these two beauties." As though she had made a mistake and showed too much humanity, Hawk snapped the fan shut and said, "Then again, he probably does not think that you will see any fighting." She handed the fan back to Phoenix and watched her gently replace the fan in her belt. "Still, you will need some real training for those."

Hawk looked around the courtyard and then at the sun, which was truly rising at that point, and a nasty sort of grin crossed her face. "The others are late which means it's only you and me for lessons today. First, you are to learn how to fall." Very much like one of Phoenix's old school teachers giving a lesson, she asked, "Why?"

Phoenix had been drilled in this since the day she could start picking up the family trade. "I need to know how to fall properly because escape usually means fighting or a jump off a roof and if I trip or hurt myself from the jump I can no longer escape. Learning to fall allows me to make those jumps safely and get away from anyone who might want to know what I have learned in the pursuit of information."

Hawk did not look at all surprised that Phoenix knew the proper applications of falling but in this profession hiding emotions and thoughts is second nature. *Or Tiger has been speaking freely about the new recruit,* thought Phoenix. "Very good, so today that is what we are doing. We are falling until we are so bruised we can't get back up. Now watch as I do this." Hawk launched herself into the air as gracefully as if she were the bird for which she was named. When she hit the ground she rolled off her arms and came back up to her feet. Calmly she walked back to Phoenix and offered her hand.

Knowing what to expect, Phoenix took the hand and found that she was flying through the air. One instant the ground was beneath her feet and the next it was quickly approaching her head. Phoenix used her arms to break her fall and her forward momentum to bring herself to her feet. At the last second, she lost her footing and landed on her back. All the air was forced from her lungs and she laid there for a good fifteen seconds before Hawk came over to make sure that she was okay.

"Not too bad for a first time. In fact, it was better than most do by their tenth time. Have you caught your breath yet?" Hawk reached down to help her student to her feet.

Phoenix's head was still spinning a little but with a deep breath and a shake of the head she reached her hand out to Hawk. Before she could think she was flying again. This time she did not let her mind process what she was about to do. As a child, her father had drilled falling into her muscles and although she had not practiced in years she knew instinctively what to do. This time she hit the ground rolled and came back up on solid footing.

Hawk stood watching her but the look in her eyes told Phoenix that she would not like what would come next. Hawk extended her hand and Phoenix took it slowly. Once again she found herself flying. As she rolled to her feet, a leg came out of nowhere and Phoenix was once again on the ground. Hawk stood over her smiling down at her. She extended her hand again to help Phoenix up. Phoenix felt that now familiar feeling of vertigo as she was sent flying once more.

This time as Phoenix rolled to her feet she jumped to avoid having her feet swept under her. She didn't see any kick. Instead she felt a push from behind and was once again sent sprawling.

Phoenix felt heat rising to her cheeks. She slowly got to her feet and turned to look at her teacher. As she turned, her feet were once again swept out from under her. Instead of falling flat on her face like she did before Phoenix tucked and rolled. She remained in a defensive crouched position with her centre of gravity low to the ground. When Hawk kicked, Phoenix jumped and when Hawk made to push her over, Phoenix dodged. Hawk smiled and seemed satisfied but suddenly she kicked and pushed at the same time. Instead of trying to dodge both at the same time and getting into trouble, Phoenix batted the kick away and ducked the push.

"The block was weak but it is nice to see you finally thinking on your feet. Life rarely gives us what we expect. We must learn to roll with the punches." Hawk crossed her arms over her chest. "Tomorrow we will work on your blocking. I will not teach you how to strike until you can block. What use is it to be able to hit an enemy hard if you can be hurt right back?"

It seemed like hours later when she had rolled so much, Phoenix was starting to feel a bit dizzy that Hawk announced, "We are done for today." Phoenix relaxed her stance though was still wary of any strikes coming her way. She had learned to expect the unexpected from her new teacher. Hawk smiled, "As soon as you run four circuits of the inner wall. The stairs are to your left."

Phoenix looked to the left wondering why she hadn't noticed the stairs before and saw that they were covered with moss, before she was once more lying on the ground.

"Pay attention, girl! How often can I say it? Now get going!" Her bellow shocked Phoenix into motion.

She jumped to her feet and ran up the stairs to begin the first circuit. The sun was well above the horizon, warming the stones beneath her feet. There was a slight breeze carrying sounds and smells from the nearby market. Phoenix's mind was brought back to the present as her legs began to protest. She had made one complete circuit and was just starting her second. Her thoughts wandered back to her youth when she could run for hours just for the fun of it and now her legs protested after a very short period of work. Remembering lessons from her father and grandfather, she began focusing on her breathing. The strain eased but was still present as her legs moved in ways they were not used to. By the end of the second circuit, Phoenix fell into a rhythm and although she began to feel tired she knew she could keep going.

As she was beginning her final circuit, Phoenix felt a change in her surroundings. All her senses told her she was in danger. Then she heard the footsteps. Without showing any concern, she bent her knees more and lengthened her stride to prevent anyone catching her and to provide any leverage needed should she be attacked. Phoenix risked a glance behind her and saw Hawk charging at her like a bull. Phoenix had learned that Hawk was unpredictable. There was no telling what she would do or how she would do it. The best option in

Phoenix's mind was to stay out of the way, so she started to run faster.

Hawk just moved faster and faster, quickly closing the gap. It was not long before she was shoulder to shoulder with Phoenix. The path around the wall was wide enough for three people and Phoenix had enough room to run, even with Hawk beside her. Hawk, however, had different ideas. She started pushing to the side, giving Phoenix no room to run. Rather than be pushed off the wall, Phoenix slowed slightly allowing Hawk to get ahead and continued her running while watching her instructor for her next move.

When she was knocked from behind and had to roll out of a fall, Phoenix knew that she was dealing with more than one opponent. The end of the circuit was in sight, but who knocked her down? She continued her run hoping to finish before anyone else attacked her. All of her senses were on overload. Phoenix did not want to fall again. This time she heard the rustle of cloth behind her and dodged to the side. Because the wall was so narrow it was hard to dodge the oncoming blow but Phoenix managed it by turning slightly. Now she saw her attacker. Behind her was Tiger, the man who likes to keep people on their toes.

The end was in sight. In another hundred meters, Phoenix would be done with the run. Waiting for her at the finish line was Hawk, another wicked smile playing on her lips. Phoenix dodged another attempt to knock her down by Tiger and sprinted the last few meters, coming to a stop in front of her instructor. Both Hawk and Tiger were smiling and seemed to have enjoyed themselves.

Phoenix was not fooled. *What are they going to try next?* She thought. Rather than wait and find out, Phoenix launched herself off the wall toward the courtyard two stories below. Rolling out of the fall, she came up to her feet without a scratch and looked at her two attackers.

"Very good, Phoenix. That'll be all for today. Be here at the same time tomorrow to work on those weak blocks. Do not be late." Hawk turned and walked down the other side of the wall.

Tiger came down the stairs and just nodded to Phoenix. Judging by his expression, Tiger was still preoccupied with the events from the day before and Phoenix knew that was all she would get from him. He motioned for her to follow him and began down the hall toward a study that was available to all of the agents.

Tiger knocked politely, then held open the door. When Phoenix entered the room, Tiger shut the door leaving her alone in total darkness. She stood there silently as her eyes slowly adjusted to the gloom.

"Hello, my dear." The voice drifted over her from one of the dark corners of the room. This was not very surprising to Phoenix. She was beginning to understand how the household functioned. There is a purpose to everything, including scaring the new agents constantly.

"Good morning." Phoenix answered with a slight nod in the direction of the voice.

"Etiquette, very good. We have something of a base. That is what you have come to me to learn. During these hours of the day you will learn how to address superiors, inferiors, royalty, law enforcement, and masters from every perspective. I hope you can act because in here you will play the layman and the noble, the slave and the mistress. In this line of work, you play many roles and one small slip-up leads to your death and to more difficulties for us. It is very hard to get a new agent in place when their predecessor was caught." Finally, an elegant hand lit the flames to a branch of candles and Phoenix could see the woman speaking.

The woman was neither old nor young and looked to stand at approximately five feet three inches tall, although currently she was sitting. Her lovely auburn hair was in a cascade of ringlets and braids going very nicely with her high quality dress of powder blue with sunset orange needlework. On one finger was an understated white gold band adorned with a sapphire. The woman's face was round, but not plump, and looked like one of the dolls in the shop windows Phoenix passed on the way to the house. Her eyes were a lovely green color and full of intelligence and deception. Phoenix knew this was not a woman to cross or to trust.

"Let us see what we have to work with. Slowly turn in a full circle." The woman raised one elegant finger and made a circle motion.

Rather than getting this obviously powerful woman mad at her, Phoenix followed the order. Slowly she turned with her chin up and standing straighter than straight. "You have good posture when you think about it. Obviously someone taught you something when you were younger. At least I do not have to teach a total barbarian to be civilized." The woman was looking down at a sheet of paper and did not seem to notice Phoenix glare at her.

"Your hair needs to be combed and you need to take care of it every morning. I will teach you different ways to dress your hair that is appropriate for common work as a maid or house servant. If you have an assignment that needs further instruction you will receive it but for now this will do." The woman raised her eyes to take in Phoenix's face, which was now under control and showed no emotion. "You chose very flattering clothing. I think I can trust your judgement in that department unless you need a different costume than a serving girl."

The woman motioned for Phoenix to sit in a chair before a table with a mirror set on it. Phoenix was very wary. After the morning training, she was ready for anything. The woman lifted a comb and started tugging and pulling it through the knots in Phoenix's hair.

Very slowly the knots gave way to the woman's ministrations and Phoenix no longer felt as if her hair was being pulled from the roots.

Phoenix watched her hair transform in the mirror. "I assume you know how to braid." It was not a question but a statement. Phoenix did not know how to braid and the arrogance of this woman was astounding. She must have sensed Phoenix's lack of knowledge because she immediately started showing her how to twist the hair together in a braid.

"The braid is the simplest way to keep your hair under control and looking fashionable. It is also a quick and easy look that any woman can pull off."

Does this woman realize that I could easily kill her for her demeaning words? Phoenix closed her eyes and slowed her breathing, pushing the air to every corner of her lungs forcing her muscles to relax. *This is essential to work for this man.* She opened her eyes and gazed in the mirror taking in the patterns the woman was creating in her hair.

For the next two hours, Phoenix learned how to stand, sit, do up her own hair and do the hair of another woman. The latter was practiced on a bust with a wig. Her teacher would never let her touch those auburn locks. After the lesson, Phoenix was able to braid hair almost flawlessly and do many other hairstyles as well. Her fingers were numb with this foreign usage but she knew that eventually she would get used to it.

"Now, I am going give you this ointment for your hands. After you wash up for the night and in the morning, apply this to both hands and rub it in everywhere. It would not do to have your hands callous up during your martial training and give you away in the future." The woman handed her a jar of a viscous white liquid. "You should also apply some to your face after you wash up. You only need to do your face at night. You're done for today."

When Phoenix left the room her guide was nowhere to be found but the aromas wafting through the halls guided her to the kitchen. She found that this was her favourite part of the house she had visited thus far. Carefully, she opened the door to find Tiger nursing a bowl of soup. He waved her in and passed her a bowl of her own.

"I am glad you found me. I was not quite finished with my lunch yet. I was going to wait but I got hungry." His impish smile crept across his face.

Phoenix chose not to answer. Instead she asked, "Have you found out anything about the maid?"

Tiger stopped eating for a fraction of a second. "You don't need to worry about that, girly. What you need to worry about is codes." He smiled at her and she almost couldn't see the worry the smile masked. He pushed a sheaf of papers at her and they got started decoding as she indulged in the warm, delicious soup.

The afternoon had been spent on learning new codes and practicing her techniques of code breaking. She felt very good about all she had accomplished and walked home with her mind reviewing all that she had learned. She was so absorbed in her thoughts she did not notice that her landlord was home.

"There she is," he called to her back. "Do you have rent for me girl?"His voice was heavy with the tell-tale slurring of alcohol.

"I have only a portion of it on me and I will have more tomorrow, I promise." She turned reaching for the gold coins Tiger had given her for her supper.

"Not good enough," he spat, "I guess I will have to take the rest of rent some other way." His smile was hideous as he weaved his way toward her. He grabbed her arms and threw her against the wall. "This won't hurt a bit, girly. Well, it won't hurt me anyway." He laughed. He pressed into her and pushed a knee between her legs. One hand pulled out a knife and the other dragged at her skirt.

Phoenix gasped, realizing what was happening and struggled against his strength. Her muscles, sore from that morning's lesson with Hawk, protested the movement. Her fingernails raked across his face. He yelled out and slapped her as his hand came away from his cheek streaked with blood.

The landlord opened her door, throwing her onto the bed. "Be good, little girl, and this won't take long." He started unbuttoning his trousers and threw himself on top of her. Phoenix had been twisting off the bed so his weight landed on her right hip and her chest was pressed against the hard frame of the cot. The landlord grabbed her shoulders and wrenched her around so that she was facing him. He pushed her legs apart and thrust himself between them. It seemed nothing would stop him.

Phoenix heard herself screaming and continued to struggle. The landlord was at least seventy pounds heavier than her and she couldn't budge his bulk. His knife was cutting into her arms as she pushed back on him. *This cannot be happening* she kept thinking. All she could see was the pleasure he was getting at her struggles. He was taking his time, enjoying every second of her powerlessness. His breathing quickened as he became more and more aroused. His manhood swelled and stood erect. He heaved himself up and thrust his hand between her legs. "Get wet for me, girl," he spat at her. "Do what I tell you and it will all be over quickly."

His breath stank of alcohol and rotten food as he pressed his lips against her mouth. His tongue forced her teeth apart and as it thrust deep toward her throat. A look of pure pleasure dawned on his face as he shifted his weight. "I won't let you have me yet," he hissed. "First, you will beg me for forgiveness." He place his hands either side of her head and slammed it into the wall. Phoenix's vision dimmed momentarily and her body felt like it was moving through molasses. She mentally shook off the feeling and began twisting under him again. She didn't dare stop moving or fighting. The landlord slammed her head against the wall again. By the time Phoenix's vision cleared for a second time, her bodice had been ripped apart and her breasts were exposed. His hands moved to her throat and he squeezed ever so slowly. Every second felt like an eternity as Phoenix gasped for air.

His body shook with anticipation and excitement and tears streamed down her face as he removed his hands from her throat. She had to think of a way out of this situation. Her throat was raw from the abuse and screaming. He held his knife at her neck as she struggled and once more probed between her legs with his fingers. Phoenix felt trickles of blood running down her skin as she collected cuts. His eye was turning purple and puffy from a momentary blow that she didn't remember landing but that just made him all the more excited. She felt his fingers outlining her privates and she continued to twist her hips, trying to get a knee between their bodies or use his own weight to push him off her. He pressed her back into the bed and wrapped his hand in her hair, dragging her head back. Thankfully he hadn't penetrated her yet but she knew it was coming as he began positioning himself for the thrust that would truly bring them together. He once again grasped the sides of her head and slammed her against the wall. In her daze, he hiked up her skirts to her waist.

Phoenix was gasping from her struggles and the throbbing headache but could see no way of escape. She squeezed her eyes tight and imagined herself anywhere but that room at that moment. Tiger's face swam before her closed eyelids and, though she knew she had no right, Phoenix wished that he was able to come and save her. She felt her landlord lean over her. "Open your eyes, bitch. I want you to watch." He smacked her on the side of her head and she opened her eyes. His saliva ran down her cheek as he smiled menacingly at her. She felt him shift between her thighs and his knees pressed her legs further apart.

Out of nowhere a primal roar erupted. The landlord was ripped off of her and thrown against the wall. The man who had burst into the room stood over him as he spat out blood and glared at his attacker. "She owes me rent and this is how she chose to repay me. The bitch knows she wants to spread her legs for me." He started to rise and the man pushed him back down.

Phoenix sat up slowly, trying to arrange her tattered skirt and hold her bodice together so that she was completely covered and looked at her savior. She could finally breathe without the landlord's weight pressing into her though each breath continued to hurt and her body was wracked with coughing. Tears streamed down her face and soaked her torn bodice. She was shaking with rage, fear, and humiliation. It took her several precious seconds to recognize the man who had come to her rescue.

Tiger turned to her with fury written all over his face. "I decided to make sure you were able to eat and I heard what was going on."

"She hasn't paid her rent! There was nothing going on that shouldn't have been except for her not giving me what was due!" The landlord once again struggled to stand up. His trousers, which were tangled around his ankles, were fouling him up. This time Tiger turned and punched him in the face. When he went down, Tiger added a ferocious kick to his stomach.

"Stay down," he growled at the now unconscious man.

Phoenix just stood up and gathered her few belongings into a small bundle while trying to keep herself covered. Tears continued to flow as she looked down at her former landlord and kicked him in the stomach for good measure. She then left her room and went down the hall to his. She picked the lock and strode inside. The room stank of drink and bile. She almost gagged but quickly regained control of her revulsion.

"What are you doing, Phoenix?" Tiger asked from the doorway.

"That pile of shit in there has been stealing from me since I came here. I am leaving and I am taking everything that is mine," she replied scathingly rifling through his chest of drawers. She grabbed all of her possessions and all of his gold for good measure then strode out of the building with Tiger jogging to catch up.

"Where will you go?" he asked.

"Anywhere would be preferable to here," she replied still crying quietly. Phoenix couldn't stem the tide off tears which upset her even more. She couldn't stand losing control of her emotions like that. The other people on the street were starting to stare at her tattered clothing and tear streaked face and whisper behind their hands. She was so humiliated and felt heat rising to her cheeks. She raised her chin high and radiated her rage. The people ducked their heads and fell silent.

"Okay then, come with me." He grabbed her arm to stop her. She winced and he dropped his hand, immediately regretting making the contact. "What I meant is that I know of a place you can stay where you will be safe," he said dropping her arm.

"Where?" she asked warily.

"Please come with me," he said looking around. "I cannot stay on the street too long or somebody will recognize me and I will not be able to help you."

"What do you mean?" she demanded planting her feet.

"I am more than just a spy," he whispered, "I am from a family that is very well known to the guards and they really don't like it when I am on the streets. That is all I will tell you. Now, if you want to keep working for our mutual friend, you will listen to me and move." He walked to a side alley. She was still wound tight and her head felt like it would explode but she turned and followed him.

Tiger led her through the alleys until he reached a dead end. Phoenix, fearing a trap similar to the one she had walked into earlier in the evening pulled out one of her fans and snapped it open while balancing her bundle of possessions in her other hand. Her balance was off and if he rushed her she would have to drop everything to defend herself.

Tiger looked back with a thin smile. "You won't be needing that, little bird. We are going to climb this wall to the roof of that building." Phoenix looked to where he was pointing and saw a flat roof. "We are getting off the streets. It will be safer for both of us that way. Your landlord will be looking for you by now. He didn't seem the type to let anyone get away with beating the snot out of him."

Phoenix nodded and put her fan back in her belt. Tiger handed Phoenix a satchel for her belongings from a pile in the shadows and began climbing and Phoenix stuffed everything in the bag, slung the strap over her shoulder, and followed suit. Once they reached the roof, they rested. Tiger pulled two loaves of bread from his pack and handed one to his companion as they watched the sunset.

"It wasn't your fault you know," he said gently, breaking the silence.

"Oh, I am well aware of that fact," she snapped bitterly. After a moment, she said, "It's not the first time a man has tried…" She took a deep breath. "It was the first time I felt helpless though. I was distracted by everything that happened today and I allowed myself to get complacent because I was in my own home." She tore at her loaf in anger.

"It wasn't the right place for you. That man should be killed. He got off too lightly." The venom in Tiger's voice surprised Phoenix but she did not comment. "You should be safe in your own home and from now on you will be." He stood up and dusted off his hands on his trousers. "My lady, it would be my honor if you would accompany me to a safer place to lay your head." He bowed to her and held out his freshly cleaned hand.

Phoenix allowed him to help her up and followed him along the rooftop highway. She was unsurprised two hours later when they stopped at a building across the street from the Wood Lane mansion.

"They know we are here and they have a room ready for you," he said simply. Phoenix felt a little surprise at the second half of his statement but she knew that the household was aware of their presence because she had seen the sentry run off in the darkness.

Tiger led her to a small bedchamber in one of the lesser used hallways. Off to one side was a private washroom and she also had a small closet. When she opened the closet doors, she almost wept with gratitude. Inside was a collection of dresses that were fit for a housemaid in a manor such as this as well as a new nightgown. The simple bed in the corner was clean and solid with at least 2 inches of padding and a warm thick blanket on top. Phoenix couldn't remember ever having lived is such luxury.

Once again, she felt herself starting to cry. This time her tears were of joy and relief rather than anger and humiliation. She turned back to the door to thank Tiger and apologize for her rudeness, but he was gone. The only indication that he had been there at all was a key hanging from a leather cord around the door handle.

Phoenix opened her door to find steaming basins of water for washing. She took them into her washroom and ripped off her rags so she could wash the filth from that evil man off of her skin. Once she had scrubbed herself raw, she pulled on the new nightgown over her stinging skin and wept herself to sleep. She barely noticed when one of the actual maids came in and grabbed what was left of the dress she had worn that day.

Phoenix was happy to be away from her old residence. Her ledger with her employer was increasingly in the red with his providing a new home to her. She was determined to repay him with her diligence to her studies and her commitment to hard work. What she wouldn't admit to herself, or anyone else for that matter, was that all of that work kept her focus away from what had transpired. She threw all of herself into her duties.

She woke up early and worked through exercises and patterns Hawk had taught her at least an hour before sunrise and she worked on learning new codes or practiced her etiquette long past sunset. If her boss knew what she was doing, he hadn't given any indication. However, Hawk had moved her own morning workouts to the courtyard where she gave lessons so that she could correct Phoenix's technique or teach her new things. She had also started using Phoenix to demonstrate moves and countermoves to her other students. Tiger had taken to joining Phoenix for her late night decoding sessions when he wasn't busy with his own work, which he was still extremely secretive about.

Her skills and knowledge increased at a prodigious rate and for the first time since her family had been taken from her, Phoenix was happy. She was confident that she was here to stay; that she had found her real home. It didn't matter that it was a dangerous line of work. All that mattered was she had a family again.

The Shadow Man watched the change in her. She had yet to face her demons but she was getting stronger. He knew what had brought her to live at his house. He also knew that what had happened to her would have destroyed a lesser woman. Her greatest weakness lay in the fact that she had not faced what had happened. He was afraid of how fragile she might be but he did not know how to approach her.

As he stood in his study staring at the candlelight coming through his window there came a knock at his door. He continued to gaze out the window without turning to acknowledge his visitor.

"I am worried about her, too," said the knocker. Most of her pupils would say Hawk had no heart but he knew better. If he turned to face her right now, he would not see his arms mistress, he would see a mother mourning over the pain of her child.

"How do I fix this?" he asked. His voice was gruff, full of emotion he normally would hide. "How do I bring myself to open those wounds?"

"They are already open, old friend. She is just simply ignoring them. We need to force her to feel them. We need to suck out the poison." There was a sadness in her voice that the Shadow Man couldn't quite place.

"How?" he asked again.

"I have no idea," she responded, moving to stand beside him, "I just know we must."

They stood in silence thinking of their options. They still hadn't come up with an answer by the time Phoenix extinguished her candle for the night.

They had just said their farewells when Prince Lirith, in all is court finery, materialized out of the shadows. Hawk continued on her way, she needed sleep before teaching the next day, as the Shadow Man turned to his protégé.

"What brings you here so late?" he asked.

"I saw you were still awake and thought we might talk," Lirith replied.

"Concerning?"

"Next week is my twenty-fourth birthday." The Shadow Man raised an eyebrow.

"So it is," he replied.

Lirith took a deep breath and continued, "My uncle is making a huge deal out of my choosing a wife. I know who he wants me to pick but that would give him more control, exactly what we want to avoid." His friend nodded for him to continue. "Well, I guess what I am asking is, how do we hold him off?"

"Take a seat, dear boy," said the Shadow Man, gesturing to a chair. "I knew this was coming. Your uncle wants more power. By pushing you to make a rushed decision he has the chance to get it. The fact that he is your father's half-brother, not full brother, limits his options." Lirith nodded his understanding.

The Shadow Man crossed the room and pulled an old tome off of the shelf. "This is a copy of every law in the kingdom dating back to the first decree," he said. "In here is a law, or really a tradition, that has long been ignored." He opened the volume to one of its first pages and read, " 'In accordance with the belief that a Prince of the Realm should be a person in his own right, with his own feelings and beliefs, it is hereby decreed that such a prince shall have a bride of his own choosing, so long as she consents, to wed. such a declaration should not take place before the twenty-fifth birthday of the prince so that he may understand his duty to the kingdom before he is further responsible for his family.' " He looked up from his reading and smiled at Lirith. "You see? Technically you cannot publicly choose a wife for another year. No matter what your uncle or recent tradition would have you believe."

Lirith grinned but his grin quickly turns into a grimace. "How do I hold him off next year?" he asked.

"We will get to that then. Who knows? Our plan may be ready long before you have to choose a wife," the Shadow Man said.

Lirith nodded and stood. "I should get back," he said. He gazed longingly for a moment out the window before moving toward the door. The Shadow Man knew that he wanted nothing more than to ask about Phoenix at that moment but Lirith couldn't bring himself to do it.

"Have a good night, Your Highness." Laughter danced in the Shadow Man's eyes as he thought about the Regent's reaction to what his nephew had just found out. It was the first spark of amusement he had felt in weeks.

He turned back to his window. His plans were coming together like puzzle pieces, fitting perfectly and forming a beautiful picture. If he could help Phoenix to heal, things would become much easier. He turned away from the window with a sigh. He didn't know what to do. Lirith may have distracted him for a few minutes but he felt helpless once more.

***

"She is hiding in plain sight. I cannot understand her and, as you know, I can usually see past the face. She hasn't opened up about anything; her previous landlord attacking her, her past and family, or even what she would like to do in this organization." Tiger looked at his employer, a question in his gaze.

"Everyone has secrets, her's are just more dangerous than others. If I had not hired her she would have put us out of business, and in hiring her I have put my whole operation in jeopardy." The Shadow

Man let that thought sink in. He would not normally speak so frankly but he trusted Tiger with his life and needed him to fully understand.

"I know the job runs in her blood. That is all I have managed to glean of her past. And she has been trained by one of the best. I have never seen the like. She absorbs information likes it is her life's breath."

"We need to challenge her." The boss's eyes looked past what he was seeing into the possibilities.

Where did this girl come from? And why did he hire her if she is so dangerous to our operation? This work is sensitive and I know he does not make decisions lightly. I need to discover more about this girl. She could not have just appeared out of nowhere. Tiger was turning to leave as the Shadow Man turned to look at him.

"I know you want to know all about her. Suffice it to say she will be important to us one day. I just need you to take her as far as you can. Test her, train her, and help her to not get herself killed. She may be the key to our whole operation but she is still fragile after the incident." Tiger held his gaze.

"Sir, how can someone who puts not only our plans but our lives in jeopardy help us? I can see her aptitude but she is a closed book and you are no more helpful than she and you know something of what is going on." Tiger took a deep breath. "I shall do as you ask. You have not led me astray thus far and I trust you. We cannot fail. You know the consequences of failure, Master Spy."

The Shadow Man did not even flinch. "I know very well the price of failure. It may hit me harder than you. You have a slim chance of surviving if we do not succeed. Try not to get caught up on whether or not we will survive."

"What part is she to take in this? She is too good at this game to be wasted as a low level spy. We need to find something she can do. She does crave to be kept busy after what happened." Now it was Tiger's turn to ponder the possibilities.

"She could make the difference for us. I think we need to find a way to get her into the court. We need a spy there that we can trust and if she proves that we can trust her, she would be perfect."

"So the test then. That is your plan to challenge her. You want her to prove her trustworthiness so you want to use the one plan that we have never put in place or even tried out. It is just a dream. We will never know for a fact who is trustworthy and who is not. There are just too many variables. Who would she betray us to anyway? You say she has a deadly secret, I have had glimpses of what it may be, so I believe you. That means she cannot go to the provost and as far as I can tell this is her first professional job so she has no contacts that could get us in trouble." Tiger took another deep breath. The spy in him took hold of his emotions. *Why am I getting riled up over this? There is no reason to lose my temper or treat my only friend in this manner. Why will he not tell me what is going on?*

"She has connections trust me. I do not take meetings with prospective employees without first checking them out. I know more about this girl than she probably knows about herself. You are right that she has been trained before, though she may not know it, and that this work is in her blood. There are those of us who have kept our eyes on this child and her family for many years. For a while, I thought all was lost. That is all I can tell you, my friend. I know you seek more information. If I were in your place I would feel let down by me but I cannot tell you anything else for all of our safety." Tiger knew he meant what he said and sighed.

"So what information should we let her find?" Tiger knew what the Shadow Man was going to say. There was no other way to truly test their new recruit.

"We need to bring her into the fold, but she needs to discover the plot on her own. Why, I believe we should leave a hint of our doings lying around; nothing that would arouse suspicion, but something that would make her curious."

"Where should the information come from? Obviously, it cannot come from me." After a moment's thought, Tiger said, "Perhaps a 'new recruit' should let something slip in morning training about wanting to know more about our setup. Then she has information and a contact to send it through. A contact we control so the information cannot get to an outside source."

"In your work, have you ever had a spy for another just fall in your lap like that? That would be too suspicious. We will have to find a way to discreetly trail her and see if she talks to anyone we know who could use the information. Do not make this more complicated than it needs to be." Tiger felt heat rising to his cheeks and squashed the blush of embarrassment before it betrayed him. He should have realized that.

"How about door duty?" He asked quietly, trying to redeem his earlier error.

"What do you mean?"

"We could put her on door duty. Those without a position spend a week or two on door duty. We have avoided assigning her there to let her heal, but there is no reason she couldn't do it. The recruits practice decoding the lesser messages and pass on those marked as more important to the higher level operatives. Perhaps when Phoenix takes a turn on door duty a high level message comes in for our eyes only. We know the lesser spies read the messages they pass on but it is our way to keep them honest and flush out those who are not completely loyal to us. Truly important messages rarely come that way but we can make sure one does. This way, she has the information and we are able to see what she does with it." Tiger waited as his friend and boss thought about it.

Finally, the Shadow Man said, "That is a good plan. See to it please."

The two men smiled at one another and left through separate doors, looking to anyone passing them on the street like two men who had just said hello to old acquaintances and not like two men who had just been discussing matters that could drastically change their lives in the near future.

Phoenix rose early and set to washing her face and arms of the night sweats. She did not usually dream but that night she had had a nightmare. It was vague, but she remembered it had something to do with a group of men. Phoenix could not quite remember what had happened. Phoenix could not quite put her finger on what it was but she was certain it was violent. Tiger had been present in the nightmare, too, but she was unsure of the role he had to play.

No use worrying about it now. If it chose, the nightmare would come back and she would figure out what happened in it then. For now, she needed to get a start on her day. The first thing was cleaning her hair and teeth and then she laid out her cosmetics for after the physical lessons. After morning training, she was required to clean up and present a cultured face for etiquette.

Phoenix was not exactly sure how she felt about this aspect of her training. She understood the need for knowing the proper manners for every station and job but she did not understand the need for so many differences. The way a merchant was expected to treat nobility was vastly different than a common craftsman and the different types of curtseys for higher nobility versus the royal family and recognition of respect from a lower class were so vastly different. It was like learning a whole new language for every class. Phoenix knew she was up for the challenge and would never slip up, but the sheer volume of etiquette to be observed explained why nothing ever got done.

At least code breaking and interrogation techniques did not confuse her. Confusion led her mind in an entirely different direction. *What are the Shadow Man and Tiger up to? I know they are plotting something major. I want to help. They saved my life twice over.*

While I hold down this job it is not likely the guards will look into my life and I finally have a home I feel safe in. Phoenix sighed. *I know they are up to something but those two are the definition of 'tight-lipped.'*

Phoenix had noticed that they had been paying her more interest than in the past couple of weeks. Her trial was almost over with. *I hope they allow me to stay.* That was her one true concern. Without the protection and financial security of the job, she would be out on the street trying to survive in a world that was dead set against her. Leaving the house on Wood Lane would prove to be fatal in the end. Phoenix did not plan on doing anything in the near future that would force them to get rid of her.

She stretched the kinks of sleep from her muscles while she contemplated her future with Tiger and the Shadow Man. She wasn't sure what their motivation was but she really felt compelled to help them. She closed her eyes and a picture of Tiger smiling appeared in her mind. She shook her head dispelling the image and returned to her morning preparations.

She quickly dressed and traveled to the kitchen to get breakfast. Mole was working in the kitchen kneading bread. She didn't even look up as Phoenix entered the room. "Trouble sleeping?" she asked finally.

"Yes," responded Phoenix simply.

"Cup of tea?" Mole put a steaming mug of the hot liquid in front of Phoenix.

"Thanks."

"Would you like to talk about it?"

"Not particularly," said Phoenix as she took a sip of tea.

"Well then, here is some bread and bacon." Mole slid a plate of sizzling bacon across the table. "You need to keep your strength up for Hawk's lessons." She laughed and resumed kneading the bread. "You know you can always talk to me if anything is troubling you, dear," stated Mole matter-of-factly as she shaped the loaves.

Phoenix sighed and started eating deliberately. She had no appetite but Mole was right. The first thing on her schedule for the day was her lesson with Hawk and without a decent breakfast she wouldn't last five minutes.

"Are you ok, Phoenix?"

She looked up to see Tiger standing in the doorway. He looked concerned.

"I'm fine, Tiger," she replied.

"Sure you are," he retorted. "Now, what is going on?"

"I just didn't sleep well."

Tiger sat next to her and pulled over a plate of bacon and freshly baked bread. Silence settled over the pair as he studied Phoenix's face. She shifted uncomfortably in her chair.

"I had a nightmare," she explained finally.

"So you really aren't fine then," he whispered. "What happened to you was not your fault. Your former landlord is an idiotic, nefarious, shady thug."

"I am well aware of that fact," she murmured.

"You will get through this and I will help you." He reached out to pat her hand but she winced away. "I am so sorry."

"It's not you, Tiger. I will be fine…eventually. I promise."

An arm gripped her from behind and squeezed. She grabbed the arm, slid herself out of the grip, and pulled whoever it was to fly over her head. Wolf slammed into the table which shook with his weight and Phoenix gasped.

"I think she's doing just fine, Tiger," he wheezed clutching her stomach.

"I am so sorry, Wolf. I didn't mean to hurt you."

"I'm not hurt," he replied with a wince. "Well my pride is." He rolled off the table to stand up once more. "You are healing, child." This time when he reached out to comfort her he didn't get thrown across the room.

"I didn't think anything would ever get you off your ass, Wolf," said Mole with a laugh. Phoenix and Tiger joined in and soon so did Wolf. Phoenix was almost surprised that they didn't wake up the rest of the house with the noise they were making.

Letting out a high pitched squeal of delight, the eight year old girl ran down the aisle to the stretched out arms of her father. Laughing, he caught her up and spun her around. The two entwined in the enveloping hug unique to children and parents. A bystander looking on may, for a moment, have thought the embrace would never end. The pair reluctantly released each other and looked into the other's smiling face instead.

"Well, my child, what have you been up to today?" asked the father.

"Grandfather gave me new books to read. He thought I wouldn't be able to do it but I did!" her chest puffed out in pride.

"Oh did you?" her father asked smiling. "Well Arlaya, I think this means you should get a sweet don't you?" She nodded emphatically and he reaching into his pocket to pull one out.

"You spoil her so," said a woman, striding down the aisle to join them. Her smile was almost bigger than her daughter's and the light glinted off of her necklace.

"Hello mother," said the child, reaching over to give her a hug.

"I missed you, sweetling," she replied

"Why did we have to come here?" asked the child. "Did the bad men find us again?"

"Yes, child, they did, but we will be safe here for a while. The Order of Dirige has been kind to allow us to be here." His head shot up when he heard the large heavy door behind him slam shut.

A man in robes ran to them. Gasping he said, "We couldn't hide your presence here. Somehow they found you." He shook his head and said nothing more as he tried to catch his breath.

There was a clash of steel on steel as the guards of the Order did their duty to protect the brothers and their charges. There was yelling outside and what smelled like smoke. The building's outer walls were stone but the roof and inner walls were made of wood making fire a true hazard and, as soon as he smelled the smoke, the father started running with his daughter still in his arms. His wife was barely a step behind him.

"We have to find a way out," he said in a gruff voice. "They can't kill her. We can't fail."

"Father, what's happening?" shrieked the girl in confusion.

"Everything will be all right, Arlaya," her mother replied almost absent mindedly.

An older man sprinted down the hall to them. "There is fire in the walls," he said. "How did they find us again? The Order of Dirige has always been able to shelter our family for short periods of time. Those bastards could never have discovered who was protecting us. It's not possible." He looked at the child and stopped his rambling. "What is she still doing here?"

"We weren't expecting them. We had no warning, father," said the child's father.

Her grandfather looked upon the child with dismay. "Our family has waited for generations for a girl child who could survive to adulthood and resurrect the family name and now the line is going to end."

The mother stepped up and slapped him. "We are not going to lose little Arlaya. We will protect her and get her out of this."

"All right, Animai. We won't give up. How do we get her out?"

Animai paused for a moment. They couldn't afford to take the time to formulate a plan but doing something stupid would be just as deadly. "We can try the windows but they will undoubtedly be guarded by bowman. Tutela, check the first window but please be careful." She touched her husband's arm in concern.

"She comes first, Animai. Don't worry about me." He kissed her and carefully walked to the window. The glass shattered as an arrow whistled through it. Tutela quickly ducked and rolled away from the broken glass and out of sight. "Well, the windows are out."

Now there wasn't just smoke. The extra air coming through the broken window was feeding the flames which were licking greedily at the ceiling. Little Arlaya closed her eyes against the sight and felt tears roll down her cheeks.

"What next?" asked her grandfather.

"The escape tunnel is the next logical place to check," said Animai.

"Unfortunately we just finished blocking it off," said a new voice and Arlaya opened her eyes to see the leader of the Order. "There is only one option left to us and we are not all going to survive it." He couldn't bring himself to look at Arlaya. "Follow me."

The fire was spreading quickly as the group traveled through the halls. Finally, they turned down a hallway that seemed to go nowhere. The man stopped by the back wall and searched in the stone for a moment. He smiled for an instant as he found whatever it was he was looking for.

Arlaya wiggled in her father's arms to see what was going on. The man pushed a stone aside to reveal a handle to a door. Carefully he pulled on the handle and the door swung outward.

"We can get her out through here," he said and hesitated. "We can't all go with her," he finally said.

Arlaya's parents looked at one another. "What do you mean 'we can't all go with her'?" Tutela finally asked.

"They will be expecting something like this. This is not an emergency exit or bolt-hole, this is a known secret passage. They may not know where it originates but it is well known that there is a way from this building to somewhere in the palace. How do you think your family escaped in the first place?" The man seemed desperate. "They know your faces but they don't know her's. They just know you have a daughter."

"We have to protect her," Animai finally said.

Tutela placed his daughter on the floor. "Listen to me, Arlaya. We cannot come with you. You have to go down that hallway and escape. We are all counting on you." His eyes were full of tears. He looked at their savior and asked, "Is there no way her mother or I could join her? I can't send her through alone." The man shook his head.

Her grandfather stepped forward and grabbed Arlaya's hand. "I will go with her and keep her safe. They have never seen my face and they think I am dead anyway," he said with a shrug. "I will take care of our girl."

Animai, openly weeping, hugged him then bent down to hug her only child. She took her necklace off and lowered it over Arlaya's head. "This is our family's oldest heirloom and now it is yours," she said. She hugged her again and turned and ran to the end of the hall, now obscured by smoke. Arlaya could have sworn that she saw the glint of steel in her mother's hands.

Tutela hugged his father and his daughter and seemed unable to speak. Instead, he kissed Arlaya's forehead, squeezed her tight, and ran to join his wife.

"You must go," the man said and Arlaya felt her grandfather scoop her up and take her out of the smoke into the secret passage. She couldn't see anything past her tears and she didn't care to anyway. Even at such a young age, she understood that she would never see her parents again.

***

Phoenix woke up in a sweat soaked bed with the blankets twisted around her. She still heard the echoing cries of her younger self. The memory was as vivid as the day she lived had it. She remained in her bed listening to the wind whip through the trees and reached up to touch the necklace her mother had given her.

She closed her eyes again and willed herself to go back to sleep. Her mind kept traveling back to that day. She and her grandfather had made it into the palace without running into any guardsmen. They even managed to convince the palace workers that they were simply an old servant and his recently orphaned granddaughter so they could leave undetected. Phoenix never knew why she was being chased, it was just a part of her life.

Her grandfather had raised her for six more years before the men found them again. In those six years, he had put an escape route in place for her because they were apparently not aware of her existence. While he hoped they would never need to employ such tactics again, he was perpetually prepared. He also spent time preparing and training her but never really told her why.

When she had told Tiger that the cloak and dagger line of work had killed him, she was very aware of how true it was. The only way for the pair to have the money to live was for him to reenter that life.

That was what alerted the enemies of her family to his presence in the city.

Phoenix never really understood what happened to her grandfather. She had returned to their modest home after a day spent at the newly instated free public schooling system. The king had decided an educated populace would be more productive and Phoenix's grandfather had agreed. She was forced to endure endless days of men droning on in monotones about what she thought at the time was meaningless stuff. As an adult, she knew differently but, because the mind of a child could not wrap around the concept, she never liked school. It was early afternoon in the autumn and she was distracted when she got home that day.

She entered their home and dropped her books in the front room just like every day before that. The copper smell of blood was in the air but she did not notice it until she was already walking toward her grandfather's study. As soon as she got closer to the study and the scent filled her nose, she was running through the door.

His body was slumped over the desk. His throat had been cut and his blood spilled over the papers and onto the floor. Phoenix froze the instant the death of her grandfather registered. She didn't believe what she saw at first. His body seemed like a large child's doll, just not quite real, and the blood was thick and such a dark red it was almost black.

Her grandfather's life revolved around two things, Arlaya and his spy work. His office was always completely organized and he never had papers on the desk. He never wanted Arlaya to see what he was working on. She could translate all of the codes since he had been teaching her practically from birth. All of which is why her eyes were drawn to his right arm. Under his hand was a letter in code addressed to her.

Dearest,

I am sorry to have left you so soon. You need to move on from this home. I do not want them to come back for you. Go to the Brotherhood of the Order of Dirige. They can protect you there. You are going to be an amazing woman and I am sad that I will not get to see it.

Follow these instructions exactly. We must ensure you are not followed.

He went on to write directions to a secret exit in their home. Phoenix was very careful to do exactly what he had written. She went down the passage then allowed herself to get lost meandering in the crowded streets of the city. There was the possibility that the house was watched and she had to ensure she wasn't followed.

The Order of Dirige assigned many watchers to keep an eye on her education and well-being after that day and each one of them died as her existence became known. The general population had no idea that a war was being fought in the city over the life of one child and she had no idea why. Eventually, she decided enough people had died for her sake, so she struck out on her own.

Phoenix realized that she would be unable to fall asleep again. Instead, she untangled herself from her blankets and changed out of her sleeping clothes. Nothing could cure brooding memories or bad dreams like some time spent in the cool night air.

She donned on her house shoes and slipped out of her room into the quiet halls of the mansion. She did not hear anybody though she knew that the house was not empty. There were at least two trainees on door duty at two locations known only to operatives and guards posted discreetly to cover the entire neighborhood. Nothing ever happened near the house without the occupants and especially the Shadow Man knowing instantly.

She carefully walked out into the courtyard. She took her time walking up the stairs that she had run up on her first day in training with Hawk. The air was crisp and cool as only night air can be. She reached the top of the wall, found a little alcove, and sat down. Taking a deep breath, she gazed out over the city to the stars on the horizon and emptied her mind of all thoughts as her mother had taught her to do when she was young and had nightmares. She focused on one star and counted to one hundred. Her focus and inward reflection became complete as she reached forty-four.

The state that she was in when Tiger found her was like that of being deep asleep while she was in fact completely awake. He cleared his throat to let her know he was there but she didn't respond. He sat down next to her but there was no sign she noticed that either. Finally, he placed a hand gently on her shoulder.

Phoenix jumped so violently she almost fell off of the wall.

"Hello, Phoenix," he said with an apologetic smile.

"Tiger, what are you doing here so late?"

"I never actually left. There was a lot to do today."

"Like what?"

"Nice try, little bird. You'll never get these lips to pass a secret on," he replied with a wink.

"Just trying to pass the time," she joked right back.

"It's nice to see you relaxing around here." He paused then said, "Speaking of you being around here. We like the progress you've made in your time among us." Phoenix held her breath waiting to see what he said next. "The Boss and I feel it's time to expand your responsibility with us. You are living here for free after all," he added with a wink and a chuckle.

Phoenix didn't say anything. She just waited with a look of expectation. When Tiger didn't continue, she poked him.

"Ok, ok. We need you to man the door for a few days this week. We are a bit short staffed at the moment."

"Of course I will man the door. I can use the practice dealing with operatives. One day I will be out there too." The bottom had fallen out of her stomach when she realized that Tiger was not telling her she was here to stay. She did feel a bit better once she came to the conclusion that the added responsibility of door duty was a step in the right direction. Maybe she could discover more about this operation. She knew that she would never betray these men but, ever the curious one, she wanted to know more about their ultimate goal. Tiger nodded at her and left her to her own devices.

Phoenix gazed around the sleepy city, clothed in morning mist. She heard the market starting to wake in the distance as the shopkeepers opened their shops and breakfast began in the public houses. The first rays of the sun were kissing the horizon lightening up the sky from a deep blue to a soft lavender. Phoenix rose from her alcove, dusted off her trousers, and made her way down off the wall to begin her class with Hawk.

Door duty is a particularly boring job. The middle of the night is the easiest time for the lesser operatives to get away and report to their handlers who then took the information and passed it on to the trainees on door duty. The person on the door was to remain on watch all night so that whenever the compiled reports arrived they would be handled by someone in the fold. The trainee on the door typically had only partial training on the codes used by field operatives so there was little chance that the reports would be read by anyone not high enough up on the food chain.

Phoenix fought another yawn as she waited for the reports to start rolling in. The bench and desk provided for the trainee's use were not comfortable in the least but the pull of dream's caress was hard to resist. It was especially difficult after the long day she had had. Hawk had exhausted her during the morning exercises. She had moved on from falling properly to using common weapons and her feet and fists to protect herself. Hawk and Tiger had added a tendency to attack without any warning so that she had to use anything available to defend herself.

She yawned again as there was a soft knock at the door. Rather than open it fully, Phoenix slid back the cover to the slit at the base. Most people would never notice the modification to the door but it was useful and important to maintain anonymity. There was a rustle and a package of parchment was slid through the opening. The reports were tied together with a blue ribbon signifying nothing dire to report and act on immediately. It was a ribbon meaning all was normal and no important information had been received.

She sighed and put the reports in the proper basket for later review. If only the ribbon had been red or black, then she would have something to do. She knew that she should decode the letters but that was barely exercising her brain at this point. She stood up and stretched. She decided to run through a few exercises to wake up then she would decode the blue reports. The size of the room was just right for performing some acrobatics and tumbling passes.

Her muscles felt stretched and she had a very slight sheen of sweat when she sat back down to work on the codes. It was not even an hour later and she had gone through the entire stack of reports and decoded them. As she went along, she flagged the reports that needed to go to the boss and filed away the ones that could go to his chiefs.

There was another knock at the door a few minutes after she finished. It was another stack of blue reports and she repeated the process. Phoenix decided it was going to be one really long night.

She stretched her neck side to side and felt the pops. She rolled her shoulders and stood to stretch again. Turning toward the door, she saw that somebody had come in and left a steaming mug of tea. The warm and spicy tea went a long way to waking her up again.

There was another knock at the door and Phoenix once again opened the little slit at the base. A single envelope was pushed through with a black ribbon tied around it. Phoenix was immediately interested. She was under the impression that the operatives who used this method of communication never came into the truly important information. The purpose of those operatives was to monitor the day to day mundane activities of their marks. Sometimes the most important information seems the most trivial.

Carefully, she picked up the report. Curiously she examined the paper and the ribbon. It was tied simply and the paper was completely normal. For a moment, Phoenix felt the itch in her fingers to untie the bow and open the report. Reading the contents would tell her what is going on, what Tiger and the Shadow Man were fighting for. She decided instead that their trust was worth more than that information. Besides, she would learn what was going on soon enough. She had a plan.

Phoenix pulled the black cord by the inner door to the main house. Somewhere, in one of the many rooms, a bell rang, alerting a senior operative to the presence of the report. She turned back to the desk and placed the report in the proper basket which she then placed on a table next to the door and settled in to wait.

In less than five minutes, Tiger arrived. Somehow, Phoenix knew that he would be the one to respond. She quietly sat at the desk as he entered the room and watched as he gently lifted the report out of the basket. He carefully examined the ribbon and the paper to see if it was tampered with then shifted his gaze to Phoenix. His expression was unreadable as he turned to leave.

Phoenix made a quick decision to follow him. Even though she refused to read the report, she wanted to know the information that was in it. It is extremely difficult to follow someone inside a crowded building, let alone in the middle of the night with nobody around. She listened for his footsteps and followed at a discrete distance. He paused to speak with the guard at the Shadow Man's study door and Phoenix swore silently. There was no way she would get in there without being detected.

It wasn't until Tiger had already passed through the door to the study that Phoenix decided what she would do. She climbed into the rafters and carefully moved down the hall to the wall that housed the door to her boss's study.

Phoenix had studied every inch of these walls over the last two weeks since the assassination attempt. She knew Tiger had done his own work to protect their employer but there was no harm in having a second pair of eyes look over everything. Because of that study, she knew that there was a loose stone in the wall. She carefully moved across the rafters to the stone and silently pried it out of the wall.

"…trustworthy and she just proved it. We don't have to have her followed. We can simply trust that she will not give us away," the Shadow Man was saying. Phoenix was very glad she had chosen not to read the report after hearing that.

"How do we tell her what is going on then?" asked Tiger.

"We don't, not yet at least."

"Let's at least figure out what we are going to do over the next few months since we are already here."

It was a moment before the Shadow Man's voice floated through the hole in the wall. "Your uncle has enacted new laws that the people of the kingdom are not going to be comfortable with. Taxes are increasing and criminals are being released into the streets in the guise of city guards in a 'rehabilitation' program. The council is afraid that they are soon to be disbanded. The Regent wants more money and power and the only way he has left is through them," there was a pause, "and through you."

If Tiger is in the way of the regent gaining more power, thought Phoenix, *that means that he has more power than the regent does. The only one with that power is the crown prince. Could Tiger really be the crown prince?* It took a major amount of self-control to not gasp at the thought. The prince was rarely seen in public so Phoenix didn't know what he was supposed to look like.

"Once we have you on the throne things will get better for the kingdom. First, we need you to attend more diplomatic meetings with Xanthoria. As our closest neighbor, they are our greatest threat and possibly our greatest ally. We will need them on our side when we are ready to move. I have a few pieces in play and I'd hoped

Phoenix would be the last but it seems she is still an unknown. Everything is in motion and as long as we monitor key areas and let events unfold, we should be ready come your birthday next year."

"Is there any other way to bring her into the fold?" asked Tiger.

"Having her on door duty was your plan to prevent her from becoming suspicious. If you can think of any new plan I will certainly listen to it." Phoenix heard a rustle of cloth. "She could be important but she is not the end all be all in our plan. You are."

"I will get back to her and thank her for this information then. I guess I need to act as she would expect. Then I will bid you goodnight and be on my way to my nice luxurious bed with all of my pillows. Being the crown prince has its benefits." Tiger sighed with frustration and Phoenix heard a creak of furniture as, presumably, he stood up.

Phoenix carefully replaced the brick in the wall and lightly climbed through the rafters to a hallway where there was no other soul. She dropped to the floor and quickly slipped back into the door duty study. She opened the slit at the base of the door to see if any other packages had been dropped off. Upon seeing nothing, she settled back into the chair and waited for Tiger to return.

While she waited, Phoenix started reevaluating her plans. She couldn't be sure that the conversation hadn't been meant to be heard. Her personal mantra was to verify everything and trust nothing at face value. She needed to determine if Tiger really was the prince. She was already aware of the hardships faced by the citizens and was a supporter of removing the regent from power as long as the prince would make things better.

Tiger knocked on the door and entered without waiting for an answer. He found Phoenix still sitting in that chair and watched her for a moment. "We needed that information. Thank you for ensuring we didn't have to wait for it," he finally said.

"Just doing my duty, sir," Phoenix replied absentmindedly.

Tiger noted that this was the first time she called him sir but chose not to say anything. He knew that she hadn't read the report because there had not been enough time between his operative handing her the package and her ringing of the bell. Somehow, though, he just had the nagging feeling that Phoenix had discovered the main mission of their little band of revolutionaries. He patted her on the shoulder and left her for the night.

The probationary period was finally up and Phoenix found herself standing at attention outside the office in which she knew Tiger and her boss were waiting. They were keeping her outside until they were ready to deliver their final decision. Phoenix knew of no reason that they would ask her to leave and she knew of at least one major reason for them to keep her around. She knew their secret, but she also knew that the information had been planted. No seasoned spy would let this bomb fall into a trainee's hands without a purpose and here it was. Although she never read the report she vetted as much of the information she had overheard as she could. She followed Tiger as often as she was able and collected rumors and was fairly certain it was the truth. So the question on her mind was, *what are they going to do with me?*

The Shadow Man paced the length of his study. Tiger sat there silently watching him, the picture of serenity. *Am I making the right decision?* thought the Shadow Man. *I need her.* He continued to pace until he seemed to realize he was giving Tiger serious cause for concern. Instead, he sat behind his desk and ran through all his mental exercises for regaining control.

"Doubts?" Tiger questioned carefully.

"She could destroy us but she is undoubtedly the best," the Shadow Man sighed.

"You have told me many times that she could save us. Is this secret of her's so extreme?"

"It could send us all permanently to sleep." The Shadow Man closed his eyes wondering if he would end up regretting his decision. *For goodness sakes, she doesn't even know her secret,* he found himself thinking.

"So could our secret. If her secret is so deadly, why did you approve bringing her in the fold?" Tiger hated to admit it but his friend's concern was worrying him. Phoenix was proving to be a fantastic agent. She absorbed training like a sponge. What took most people a year and more had taken Phoenix a mere few weeks.

"Knowing our secret could not save her from hers. Furthermore, I believe she could fill a necessary role in our enterprise that we cannot leave to chance."

"Then tell her that. Before we bring her in, get control of yourself. Where do you want to place her?" Tiger wanted to know his friend's plans. It was rare that they did not inform each other of their activities. At the same time, though, he knew an overt question would not be answered. Maybe hidden in the conversation he would find out. He was curious about the Shadow Man's extreme interest in one girl. *Even a girl as captivating as Phoenix,* he thought.

He put that thought aside as the Shadow Man said "I am going to play that one close to the chest. You may give it away," he looked Tiger in the eye, "even unintentionally." Tiger opened his mouth to protest but decided against it.

Tiger stepped to the door and pulled it open. He beckoned Phoenix inside. She wasn't sure what to expect so she warily stepped over the threshold. The Shadow Man's back was to her so she stood at attention and waited.

"You have impressed your instructors in your time here," her employer started. A long pause followed the statement and Phoenix had begun to wonder if she was supposed to say something when he continued. "I wouldn't have thought it possible, but you have completed your training in less time than any recruit in our history." He turned to face her.

Phoenix felt her heart skip a beat. *He is going to let me stay. Even after not being able to defend myself, he is going to let me stay.* She took pains to control her features. There was still a chance that he would change his mind or decide she was too much of a risk.

"You will continue to have a position in this household should you choose," he said finally. "However, if you ever feel that you no longer want to be a part of this world, this is your only opportunity to leave. After today, you cannot dissolve this relationship with your life intact." His voice took on a menacing tone and Phoenix knew he would not hesitate to remove her from the equation.

She swallowed a couple of times to moisten her suddenly dry mouth before saying, "I understand, sir. I will endeavour to do right by the trust you place in me."

"Very well, little bird." He smiled as he used Tiger's nickname for her. "You are dismissed. Return to your studies and await your orders." He turned to face the window rather than watch her leave.

Phoenix took a deep breath and opened the study door to leave. She felt as though a great burden had been removed from her shoulders. She practically floated to her etiquette lesson.

The next week, after their morning meeting, the Shadow Man pulled Tiger aside. "There is one more assignment I couldn't mention to our captains. I need you to send in Phoenix."

"She should just be finishing with Hawk so that should not be a problem. What is the assignment?"

"This is one of those special cases when you must know nothing. Act as the public sees you once she enters. Go to the studies your uncle believes you take part in here."

Tiger left the room, his mind working at light speed. What could he be plotting? Why must I play all proper? Too many questions can ruin us. He knows what he is doing. With a shake of his head, Tiger set about his business.

He found Phoenix right where he had told his friend he would. She was doing stretches to increase her flexibility. Needless to say, he found her in an awkward position and before he could hide his presence and try to sneak up on her like usual he was laughing. So surprised was he to see her folded like a pretzel, it took him a good minute before he could control himself again. By that time Phoenix had untangled herself and glared at him and Hawk had snuck up behind him.

Tiger dodged the first blow to the back of his head, and got himself tripped up on Hawk's leg. With the grace of a dancer he rolled to his feet and bowed to the arms mistress.

"If you are here for any specific purpose other than getting yourself hurt, you better set about it. Otherwise be prepared for bruises."

Hawk had her usual stern face on but Tiger could see the sparkle of amusement in her eyes.

"Please Mistress Hawk, one session with you would leave me crippled. Phoenix you are summoned. Please wait for me in the hall, I will only be a moment then I will take you to him." Tiger waited until she left the courtyard, then, pitching his voice so low it barely carried to Hawk, he said, "I need a lesson in the noble's fighting arts when I come back. I have no idea what is brewing so do not even ask. It seems, however, that I must play my least favorite role."

"It is the life you were born into. As much as you like being Tiger, you must, one day, return to your duties."

Tiger grimaced. "I will be back in ten minutes."

"I will be waiting." Hawk was very good at hiding what she was thinking but Tiger saw it clearly. For a moment, less than a heartbeat long, there was pity and concern in her eyes.

Tiger turned away pretending he had not seen. Quietly he joined Phoenix and escorted her to the study where the Shadow Man waited.

"Thank you, Tiger. If you would be so kind, return to your tasks. I would very much like to talk to the young lady alone."

Tiger did not even try to hide his disappointment at being excluded. Phoenix could not see his face but his friend could. In the back of his mind, the Shadow Man approved. He is still spirited and his defiance will come in handy when the guests arrive. Calmly he watched Tiger leave then turned his full attention on Phoenix.

"You are to be arrested for crimes against the kingdom. You will be taken to the outskirts of the city as a thief and whore." Phoenix, for all her concerns, managed to keep her face blank as he spoke. "Your protections seemed to have failed." Phoenix felt her heart drop and her blood rushed through her ears. It was like someone had dropped her into a pond full of ice. "Before you ask it was not I but another in the house who turned you in. It appears that rumors have started to fly that you stole from your previous landlord and that you have been stealing from this house. Your previous landlord is also saying that you tried to pay your rent by spreading your legs and of course he was too virtuous to take you up on the offer. You know that we cannot have people of that nature corrupting the purity of our civilization."

At that moment there was a knock at the door. "Come," called the Shadow Man. A squad of six guards entered and two stepped forward to take Phoenix's arms.

"My lord, we will take her off your hands now," said the young officer.

Phoenix felt herself start to shake. "Sir! I've done nothing wrong, sir! Please believe me, sir! I am innocent!" She would have fallen to her knees if she had not been supported by the two guards. One of the guards backhanded her to get her to stop her frantic pleas.

"I will not have the girl touched. For all her faults and her possible crimes, she is a good worker." The Shadow Man looked into the eyes of every guard. "I will be sending my friend with you to ensure she remains unmolested until she is no longer within the city walls. If I get any word that any of you men have touched her you will regret it and be unable to become fathers." The eyes of the guards narrowed to little slits.

"We understand, my lord," said the officer.

The Shadow Man rang a bell and one of the nondescript maids came to the door. "How can I serve you, my lord?" she asked with a curtsy

"Fetch Lirith, please"

She turned and left. They did not have long to wait for Lirith to arrive.

Tiger entered the room without knocking. "You wanted to see me, sir?" The guards instantly snapped to attention and saluted him.

"I saw you sparring in the courtyard, Your Highness. You're very skilled," said the officer.

"Perhaps, if you have the time around your duties we could spar together," Tiger responded.

"Lirith, this young maid is being escorted to the outskirts of the city. Can I trust you to make sure she makes it there unmolested?" asked the Shadow Man.

"Of course, sir," he replied looking in askance at his old friend. "Are you ready, gentlemen?"

The two guards practically lifted Phoenix off the ground and turned to exit. She was still quietly pleading and protesting her innocence. One of the guards shook her to silence her babbling.

"Wait, bring her back here." The guards turned back and released her. Phoenix fell to her knees in front of her former boss. He knelt beside her and helped her to her feet. "If you prove that you can be an asset to the city again and want to work for me, I would welcome you back."

The guards took their positions again. Phoenix felt like an overcooked noodle and the guards had to support almost her whole weight. She couldn't believe this was happening. Did those men who had hunted her family finally find her? Why would the Shadow Man do this to her?

Lirith walked beside them brooding on his friend's plan. It took him many moments to realize the guard was talking to him again. "I'm sorry, I was preoccupied. What were you saying?"

"Highness, I was merely pointing out that you needn't accompany us all the way to the city gates. We have handled many criminals, what is one more?" The other guards smiled wickedly.

"As much as I appreciate the offer, my good gentlemen, this woman has done nothing but good work for me and it feels improper to abandon her completely. She has my full support and I believe she is innocent of whatever crimes she is accused. Though I may trust you, there are too many who would see harm befall this woman for their own benefit or pleasure." Lirith carefully kept his face bland. He didn't want the guard to feel he insulted him on purpose, though that is exactly what he did. Lirith didn't like this plan of the Shadow Man. He especially didn't like that he didn't know the intended results.

The traffic on the street parted like butter when the people saw the guards dragging the girl. They truly became curious when they saw who walked beside those very same guards.

Lirith allowed his voice to carry to the crowd, "Here in the Kingdom we respect the rights of all people and I will make sure this woman gets to her destination unmolested."

"If you could keep your voice down, Highness, we would really appreciate it. We do not want to attract any more attention than we already have." The guard was looking around nervously.

When they finally reached the gates, all six guards heaved a sigh of relief and pushed the girl out of the city. "The camp is a mile in that direction. If you come to the city again, your life is forfeit," spat the lead guard. They all turned away and started to walk back into the city. Tiger lingered half a beat with a meaningful look at Phoenix.

She was so lost in her misery that she did not notice his gaze. She just slumped in the road.

It felt like hours later when a child grabbed her wrist. "Lady, you have to come with us. They will kill you if you stay here." The young insistent voice broke through the fog and she stood up. The child led her literally by the hand for a mile. By then, Phoenix was walking normally and taking in the sights and sounds. She still felt dull and numb but her acting skills were coming to the fore and she would not let her mask of normalcy slip.

The exiles had built a small city of their own. Smoke rose from crudely built chimneys protruding from crudely built huts. There were children running around laughing as they played. Old men sat together discussing the good old days and old women were sewing and doing needlework in creaky rocking chairs. Men were coming in from farm fields just past the outskirts of town. Women were working at the campfires in the middle of town or in their homes preparing the evening meal.

"It's not much, but it's home," a man's voice said just behind her.

Phoenix jumped then chided herself. *Just because you have been exiled doesn't mean you can let your guard down. You should have known he was there.* "It's beautiful," she whispered back.

"Come let me show you where you will be staying." He beckoned, leading her into the city.

***

Lirith watched Phoenix just sit in the dirt. *Don't you understand, woman?* he wanted to scream at her. The Shadow Man never does anything without reason. There was something he wanted that he felt only Phoenix could get him.

He walked with the guards back through the city. They were morally tasked with ensuring his safe return to his friend's mansion. It would ruin the kingdom to have the crown prince, the only heir to the throne, killed strolling back home.

He was brooding and he knew he was. Luckily, the guards didn't seem to be in particularly loquacious moods either. When they arrived at the mansion on Wood Lane, Lirith said farewell in as gracious a manner as he could.

Upon entering the house, Hawk met him. "He wants to see you," she said. She would never ask what was going on outright but her eyes held the unspoken question. She hoped that whatever was occurring would not cause a rift among the two men that she had served for most of her life.

"Phoenix is on assignment," he said by way of explanation.

"So soon? Well, she is very good at this sort of work." Hawk turned toward the courtyard. She squeezed his shoulder as she passed him. "It will all work out, my friend."

Lirith continued deeper into the house. When he got to the study door, he paused to take a deep breath before giving the signal.

"Come in, Lirith."

Lirith opened the door, entered, and just stood there. He was upset at his friend and was not sure what would be said in this room.

"At least close the door, boy, before you decide if you are going to yell at me," his friend sighed and Lirith shut the door with a decisive click.

"Lord Calden, what have you done?" Lirith felt betrayed.

"We need to know what kind of resistance is in the exile city," he responded simply.

"But why her?" Lirith asked. "You could have put any operative in that place. You said you wanted her in the palace. She is too skilled for this assignment! We need her!" Lirith clamped his jaws shut as he realized how close he was to actually shouting.

"*We* need her?" The Shadow Man's eyes flashed. "I hope that is what you truly meant and that you have not grown attached to a spy. In all likelihood, she will be dead in the next year. In any case, she needed to leave the city and the other arrangements won't be available for months."

Lirith's heart skipped a beat at that. "I don't know where to begin. So instead of asking questions I need you to fill me in completely."

"Arlaya comes from a very prominent and powerful family, historically." Lirith looked at his oldest friend in confusion.

He took a deep breath, "What prominent family? I know all of them. It's in the job description. And since when do you give me an agent's real name?"

"It will all become apparent if you don't interrupt," said Lord Calden patiently, indicating a comfortable chair for his prince to sit in. Lirith sighed and took the proffered chair.

"As I said, Arlaya comes from a very old, powerful, and prominent family, a family that your uncle and his ilk have been working very hard to keep from resurfacing. Two hundred and fifty years ago this land was covered with feuding tribes who were going to wipe each other out. Your ancestor was captured by one of these tribes and kept as a slave. He realized that tribe was no different from his own so, when he was able to, he escaped slavehood and set out to learn of the other tribes. Not of their strengths or weaknesses but of their people.”

“In his quest for knowledge, he came across a man who eventually became his closest friend, Eldwin Rivell. Rivell believed as your ancestor did, that the tribes should be united rather than killing each other. Both returned to their separate tribes to bring them around to the idea of unification. Your ancestor’s tribe had thought him dead and celebrated his return. His tribe elders listened to what he had to say and declared him tribe chief in his pursuit of unification. The tribe did not want to fight others. They were a peaceful group. When the tribe arrived at the meeting place they waited for two weeks before Rivell’s tribe arrived.”

“His tribal chief had not been nearly as open minded as the two men had hoped. He had challenged Rivell to a trial by combat for daring to usurp the leader’s power in his attempt to convince the people of the tribe that unification was the way to win this perpetual war. Rivell accepted the challenge and killed the leader. He was then raised up as the new leader and the tribe decided to follow him on this different path toward peace. The tribe may have been accustomed to battle but too many lives had been lost for nothing.”

“As the friends spread their message of peace through unification, other tribes joined the movement. Many leaders were killed by their people because they would not stop the fighting and the new leaders became the first of today’s nobles. But one thing all of the people agreed on was a single tribal leader was needed. They had lived too long with these traditions to give them up so easily.”

“Many of the tribe leaders began fighting and arguing about who would be the supreme leader. It almost came to war again except that Eldwin Rivell stepped in. He made the astonishing proclamation that your ancestor should be king of all the tribes but the rest of the tribal leaders should still retain their people, their families as he called them. Only direct descendants would inherit the leader's position and in cases where there were no children a child would be chosen and raised as a ward of the leader's household to take over running the family in the event of his death."

"The leaders liked this plan but your ancestor had one rather minor change he demanded. Instead of the people still being divided into tribes, they would become one people. The leaders would have their own personal household and their direct family but their people would be the kingdom's people. The leaders were upset at this proposal but when the people were asked they were delighted at the idea. As the popularity of the king's plan grew, the leaders had no option but to bow to the will of the people and the kingdom was formed."

"I have heard this story before, old friend. What does it have to do with Phoenix?" asked Lirith impatiently.

"As you know, every prince must take a bride in his twenty-fifth year of age. In the first decree of the kingdom, your ancestor determined that his son should marry his friend's daughter, thus cementing the houses further together. Unfortunately, one of the other lords wanted his daughter to be queen. He was never happy that he had been passed over for the crown. He discreetly had Rivell's daughter killed. The assassin took pains to make it look like an accident but I know because of documents I have come across exactly who directed the murder. It was your uncle's ancestor." He paused to let that news sink in.

"Your ancestor, suspecting what had really happened, chose the daughter of another lord to marry his son and the kingdom kept moving forward. That first decree was amended to create the tradition of each prince asking for a bride from the House of Rivell to come forth and be made queen. That way the houses could still be brought together through marriage."

"As the generations came and went, every daughter of the House of Rivell somehow managed to *accidentally* die. It became quite the scandal but no matter how they tried to protect them, the Rivells could not know when exactly their baby girls would be killed. To protect themselves, they started to play the information game. Artem Rivell became the first crown spymaster and his techniques for information gathering have never been matched."

"Eventually, the family discovered who was behind the bloodshed in their family. They started to put together plans for vengeance but your uncle's ancestors discovered the plot. How? I do not know for certain but I know they did. And they attacked the Rivell family in the night. In their determination to exterminate the family, they overlooked the obvious."

"The Rivells had secretly sent their third eldest son with his wife and son into hiding. He was the best trained spy the family had turned out in two generations and he had the best chance of surviving and hiding his family. He was branded with the mark of a phoenix on his right shoulder to signify his family roots and the plan for the family to one day rise from the ashes and begin anew. As was his son."

"He sent a letter to the prince and his cousin, my ancestor, detailing what had happened. In his letter, he told them that his family had survived and was now in hiding. He also told them that his family would be forever branded with the phoenix on the right shoulder. The brand has been passed down over the generations. Your uncle's family somehow learned of this secret and has done their best to eradicate the few surviving Rivells. The last ones I knew of were killed over a decade ago in a fire."

"The name Rivell has been almost lost in the century since the family was killed. It is only brought out at the twenty-fifth birthday of the crown prince and even that is being phased out."

"If they are all dead then, again, what does this have to do with Phoenix?" Lirith demanded. He paused. "Phoenix?" he whispered. "She is a Rivell isn't she?" he asked quietly. "Somehow she survived the fire that killed her family." Lirith though back to that day that Phoenix had move to the manor. Her tattered clothing barely covering her. He mentally turned his attention to her shoulder and remembered her birthmark in the shape of some form of a bird.

"It's why she is so talented at this work," replied Lord Calden. "Her father and grandfather trained her with games and riddles. They were killed in the fire along with her mother and she was forced to make a life for herself at an extremely young age. It almost makes you pity her, doesn't it?"

Lirith took a deep breath. "Now I know who she is and I can see why she is so important to our plan but why did she need to leave the city?"

"Some time ago, you brought her to my house just after sunset. Her landlord had attacked her and you swooped in and saved her. Phoenix's dress was all in tatters when you two left her residence and went down an alleyway together. The dress had fallen off her shoulder. I don't know if you noticed." Lirith nodded his head with a steely look in his eyes as he saw where this conversation was going. "One of the spies following you noticed. He even noticed a curious mark that he drew out for his master." He slid a small scrap of paper across to the prince. On it was an image of a phoenix. "It is her brand. Your uncle knows of her presence and that you know her. Lucky for us, he hadn't discovered yet where you took her."

Tiger pounded his fist on the arm of his chair. "How did I not notice we were being followed?"

"You had your mind on other things; potentially critical things," replied his friend.

Tiger hung his head. "I failed to recognize that we were being followed. I was so preoccupied with getting her away from danger that I put her life at even greater risk." He stood up suddenly and violently and began pacing around the room. "How could I let that happen?!" he roared.

With the icy steel of a drawn blade coloring every word, Calden very calmly said, "Sit down, Tiger." It was a command that could not be ignored. Tiger took a deep breath and sat down once more. "She will be safe and you will see her again one day," Calden continued. "Never doubt that. Now, you need to turn your attention to your other duties. The Lord Regent is attempting to move his agenda forward. Never forget, your first duty is to your kingdom and your second is to your heart." Tiger started to protest but his friend held up his hand to stop him. "Your passion is commendable but for now you need to move past emotions and do your work." Calden squeezed his shoulder and left his workroom. Tiger had never been left in the workroom alone. He took advantage of the solitude and allowed himself to indulge in his emotions for a moment before leaving as well.

She woke up with heavy eyes; a testament to a night of crying. Her muscles ached from tossing and turning in her bed and she had bruises on her arms from where the guards had carried her. *Why has he forsaken me? I know what he plans and I was prepared to help him accomplish his goal!*

She sat up and rubbed her eyes. As her hand dropped and she gazed around the sorry excuse for a home, she noticed a white corner peeking out of one of her pockets in her light jacket that she had been wearing. "That cheat!" She whispered. *This is only a mission.* She picked up the envelope and broke the seal. The letter that was in the envelope contained a unique code; something she and Tiger had put together only a week earlier. Nobody had thought of a code like that before so she knew the contents were secure.

Once the letter was decoded she read. "I'm sure that was a good show for the guards. You are now on assignment, Phoenix. Find whatever resistance movement is present in the camp and infiltrate it. If there isn't a group fighting their treatment then make one. We will be in contact."

He asks the world, that one. Well she'd wanted field work and now she had it. *How to start though? I can't tip these people off so I have to be extra careful.*

There was a knock at her door. "Are you awake, lady?" a child's voice called, "it's breakfast time."

She forced herself to smile, staying in her character of the wronged woman who had just been exiled, and crossed to the door. When she opened it, she saw the same child who had been her guide to the city. "Thank you. What is your name? I seem to have forgotten."

"I am Kitty. I don't have a grownup name yet," she answered as only a child would.

Phoenix knelt down. "Grownup names are not as much fun anyway." She winked and followed the child to the breakfast fires.

The man she had met the night before was waiting for her with porridge and sausage. "How did you sleep, child?" he asked.

"Yesterday was such a shock. I don't think I will be able to sleep for a while yet," she said bitterly.

"I understand, child. None of us deserve to be out here. The government has no idea what it is doing." His voice was just as bitter as hers.

"What can I do to repay your kindness? I do not have anything in the way of possessions but I am a hard worker and you have done more for me in the last day than anyone ever did for me in the city." *Don't lay it on too thick, Phoenix* she told herself.

"For now, just get yourself settled in. As you get used to life out here, you can start pitching in for the chores. We will see how your skills fit in with our group out here another day." He smiled and guided her to a log near the fire to eat. "What can we call you, child? Newcomer just doesn't seem to fit."

"I am known as Phoenix because of a birthmark I have. I grew up an orphan and didn't care for the name I was labeled with so it stuck." She shrugged and began eating.

"Do you mind my asking what got you sent out here?" he queried delicately.

A lie grounded in truth was more believable and the liar was less likely to be caught. With this in mind, Phoenix began to tell her story, "A short time ago, I was attacked by my landlord. I was behind in my rent and had only just found new employment. I gave him what money I had but he was drunk and a pig and felt if I couldn't pay him what I owed him, he would collect payment in a different manner." She allowed her voice to sound dead. She was letting this man see her true emotions which would only help her as long as she controlled what she said. She started crying quietly as she remembered that night. "He threw me against the wall as he reached for my door. Once it was open, he threw me on the bed. I was fighting as hard as I could and he pulled a knife. He undid his trousers and pressed himself on top of me." She stopped to take a deep breath. "He pressed up my skirts and I fought harder, screaming for help. Nobody came to help me. He finished…his business," she choked out, "and left me there." She took another deep breath. *It makes it more powerful if I don't mention Him*, she told herself as a reason for not mentioning Tiger. It hurt too much to think about him. "The next day when he left to terrorize the streets, I packed all of my belongings and went into his room to get everything he had stolen from me in my time there. I also took every last gold coin he had." She chuckled evilly and it sounded harsh to even her ears. "I never went back to that place. I slept on the streets until my new employer gave me a room at his house. I have been so ashamed of myself ever since but I was also thankful to my employer until he let the guards take me away."

"It wasn't your fault, Phoenix, it wasn't your fault," the man whispered as his eyes shimmered with unshed tears.

"I know that but the government doesn't see it that way." She grimaced and hatred lit her eyes. "I was arrested and exiled on charges of theft and sexual crimes. As I sit with you, it takes all of my will to even be near a man, even you, because of what that man did to me. They call me the criminal and throw me out of my home while that spineless scum gets to do this to more women! I want to destroy him! I want to destroy them all!" Her vehemence shocked her companion. To his credit, he did not attempt to touch her, even in comfort.

Instead, he beckoned over another woman. "This is Adrienne. She has a similar story to tell but it was many years ago and she is healing. Maybe you two should talk. It would help you. Remember, young Phoenix, you were not at fault and soon enough, you will have your vengeance. But before that can happen, you must learn to forgive yourself for what happened and begin the long process of healing." He stood up leaving the two women together.

Adrienne was a tall woman with blonde hair and blue eyes. She looked like a stiff breeze would blow her over. "It is a pleasure to meet you, Phoenix," she said with complete sincerity. "I hope you don't mind but I overheard you talking to Jethro. He may seem hard but his wife was taken from him by men like the one who attacked you. They raped her in front of him, over and over again until she went mad and threw herself on a knife. Then they dragged him out here for murdering her. Ever since then, he has taken care of us." She stood up and took Phoenix's dishes. "Come let us go for a walk. I think you have been through enough for a while. I will show you around."

As they wandered around the community, Phoenix didn't say a word. She felt the impulse to confide in this woman but continued to hold her tongue. After a while, Adrienne started quietly telling her story. Jethro had been right, their stories were very similar. The biggest difference was that Adrienne hadn't had a savior and continued to be exploited until she was exiled. Phoenix felt tears rolling down her cheeks as she listened.

"It took me a while, Phoenix, but I am starting to find happiness again. I can finally smile again and laugh. I can see a future for myself. Most importantly, I know to my soul that I was not to blame." Adrienne smiled at Phoenix.

"If I'd been current on my rent…" Phoenix began and stared at her feet.

"Nonsense," Adrienne interrupted. "That man would have found any excuse to do what he did, even manufacturing a lie to make it ok to do that to you. He is the only one at fault and you cannot give him the power over your life anymore." Her stern voice seemed to echo in Phoenix's skull and her gentle fingers tilted Phoenix's chin up so that she was looking straight into Adrienne's eyes. "You have spent enough time on this world to know that you are the only one who can dictate your destiny. Don't let that scumbag take away your life." Adrienne released Phoenix's chin and smiled delicately. "The best medicine for you is to draw out the poison. Tell me what happened from the very beginning."

Phoenix very carefully recounted the events of the night she was attacked, making sure to leave the part about Tiger out. Because she had already told Jethro, this time she was better able to control her emotions. Little details that she didn't even think about at the time littered her story. She detailed absolutely everything that happened leading up to that day and leading up to that moment, leaving out only the parts that she needed to to maintain her cover. She truly did feel better. It was as though she was relieving herself of a heavy burden that she hadn't realized she was carrying.

Adrienne just let her talk and would quietly react to certain parts of her tale but would not interrupt. Phoenix had to be very careful about what she revealed as she quickly fabricated a story about living on the streets in fear until her new employer gave her a room. *The more complicated the lie, the easier it is to get caught*, her grandfather's voice whispered through her memory. She based her story on her life on the streets after his death so that she would be able to keep it straight. Phoenix almost felt bad for lying to Adrienne but it was her job.

Lirith had followed the man clear across the city. Very few people looked up when they didn't want to be followed. *The fools believe they will only be followed in the streets; that the only cover is in a crowd of people.* He slowly crept down the wall to crouch on a window sill as he listened.

"It took some time, but we have another operative in place." The man had a nervous, nasally voice.

"It's about time, ingrate," growled a man in the shadows. He had a hood obscuring his face. "Calden should have been dead months ago. You said your woman would do the job." The ferocity of his statement had the puling man cringing in fear.

"Somehow they discovered her. I have no idea how that could have happened. But I assure you she did not give up any information. She was a professional." He seemed to shrink with every word he spoke.

"She better not have or we will not be seeing each other again." The hooded man turned away. Tiger stayed very still. He did not want to give away his position. "Keep closer tabs on this one. If anything goes wrong this time, I want to be certain we are not discovered. They have certainly tightened security if it took you two months to replace the bitch." He rifled through his pockets and came out with a sheaf of papers. "We have another target in the household. Do not let your operative compromise his or herself to take out this target. It's a secondary one. My orders are to emphasize the need for discretion with this one. She has red hair and a phoenix birthmark on her shoulder. She must be killed but not immediately. The old man is first."

Tiger felt his breath catch. *They know about Phoenix being at the mansion. Calden was right to send her away.* The two main said their farewells, or rather the first man scraped and sniveled for the other man's benefit and left. The hooded man stood there for a few minutes then turned to exit the other end of the alley.

When he was far enough away that Tiger would not attract his attention, he slid out of his hiding place and began to follow him on the rooftops. He was more wary trailing this man than the other because Tiger could tell he had more skill. He would discretely check the rooftops for pursuit. Tiger made sure to keep plenty of space between them as he followed him clear across the city.

The man ducked and dodged. He even spent two hours sipping ale at a public house. Tiger was patient though, and watched every move he made. *Where are your comrades? Who do you work for?* The man did not make any contact with anyone, however, and Tiger continued trailing him until the horizon began to get lighter.

Dawn is coming, snake. Where is your hidey hole? Tiger was tired but he did not let that get in the way of his work.

Finally, the man left his most recent ale house and made a beeline for the richer part of town. *Now we are getting somewhere,* Tiger thought. He continued to follow the man until he knocked on the back gate of a mansion.

The door opened and the man went inside the courtyard. Tiger carefully climbed to the end of the nearest roof.

"There is a new operative inside," he heard the man say.

"They know about the additional target?" asked a new voice. One Tiger felt he recognized.

"Yes. I made sure he understood the old man was priority but the girl must die too."

"Good. Now leave before anyone notices you here and makes a connection between us."

"Just as soon as I have my money." Lirith heard the jangle of coins change hands and held his breath as the gate opened again.

The hooded man departed without once looking up. His job was done and he had nothing to worry about.

Tiger stayed on that rooftop for another hour to ensure no one knew he was up there. Slowly he moved, taking the rooftop highway around to see the front of the mansion.

As he reached the front, he continued to try and place that familiar voice. Finally it dawned on him, *It was my uncle's steward!* He looked at the mansion and realized it was his uncle's townhome. The one he bought so that when his nephew took the throne he could retire in comfort.

As realization reared its ugly head, he heard a soft grunt and the scrabble of feet on the rooftop. Quickly, he dropped into a chimney to hide.

"There is nothing up here. See? I told you so."

"I swear I saw a shadow and you know how the boss feels about people on the rooftops. Nothing good came of someone skulking about."

"You just wasted time on a wild goose hunt, idiot."

"No, sir, I don't believe I did. There are footprints over there." Tiger swore silently. "Someone was up here. They must have run off when they heard you slip," the second voice said with resentment.

"Fine. But they are not here now so let's go. I hate heights."

Tiger waited until they were both gone for five minutes. Then he carefully climbed out of the chimney and moved quietly and stealthily back to Calden's mansion, making doubly sure to erase all evidence of his passage.

The maid opened the door with a reproving glare at his soot and sweat stained person. She made him take off his boots and socks and dumped two buckets of water on him before she allowed him into her haven of cleanliness. Once he was free of her, he ran in his bare feet to his friend's study. He quickly gave the emergency signal and barged in.

He was met with the point of a sword and he dodged quickly to avoid the killing blow.

"Calden, it's me. Please, put up your blade," he practically yelled with his hands raised.

"Lirith! You know better, child."

"I'm sorry sir but I could not wait. I found the man who hired the maid." Tiger was speaking so rapidly he was surprised his friend could understand him.

"Slow down, Lirith, it will make more sense if you take your time. I told you to leave it alone. We don't need to know who tried to kill me. It doesn't matter. What matters is they did not succeed."

"I know," Tiger breathed. "It still bothered me and I wanted to get as much information as possible before they tried again." He took a deep breath and continued, "I noticed a man that would wait to see the maids coming out of the mansion every day for a week. He seemed disappointed and angry when the old maid didn't come out. So I waited to see him again. There was no way they wouldn't plant another person in the household." He waited and Calden nodded for him to continue. "Last week I saw him again. I did not see who he was meeting but I knew they had planted someone new. So this week, I followed him. He had no idea I was there."

"He met another man in an alley about a mile from here. They were discussing the new operative and...," he paused trying to choose his words carefully.

"And?" Calden prompted.

"The second man added a new target." Tiger sighed. "You were right. They know about Phoenix. She is the new target. He described her as having red hair and a phoenix shaped birthmark."

Calden stood up quickly and began to pace. "This is good, Lirith." He smiled and Lirith just felt confused. "Don't you see?"

Lirith shook his head.

"Oh, Tiger, you still have much to learn. If they have marked her as a target, they don't know she isn't here anymore; which means they have no idea what we are planning." He started laughing and Lirith felt himself smile.

"Now we just have to locate this new operative, sir."

"That's easy enough. The only new person in the household is the new pageboy that your uncle forced on me. He is younger than I would have expected for a spy but your uncle is clever. I cannot, however imagine the child acting as an assassin. We need to keep our eyes on this situation and take extra care to make it look as though Phoenix is still here."

"I didn't tell you that it was my uncle's steward, and most probably my uncle, behind the attack. How did you figure it out?" Lirith asked.

"It wasn't that hard, boy. I am his staunchest political foe and you listen to me more than him. He hates how you look up to me." Calden shrugged. "He probably sees me as a major obstacle in his mission to gain more power."

Lirith thought about it from those terms and realized just how obvious it was. "I really do need to pay more attention to politics, don't I?" Calden chuckled and nodded with approval as Tiger made a face of disgust at him.

Phoenix grunted with effort as she shifted the buckets so they sat more comfortably on her shoulders. It was hard work bringing water to the village from the river a half a mile away but someone had to do it. Jethro had determined her skills lay in areas other than farming and carpentry so she was given tasks that required no skill. She ought to have resented that fact but it helped her credibility with her new people that she did not complain once.

She had noticed that every night the able bodied, both men and women, got together and trained as though preparing for a battle. She had decided that this was the night she was going to join them.

She set down her buckets with a sigh and then dumped them in the central cistern. Standing straight once more, she wiped the sweat from her forehead and shaded her eyes against the glare of the setting sun. Grabbing a cloth, she dipped it in the fresh water and wrung it out carefully so as to not waste a single drop. Then she wiped her face thinking. *If we can dig irrigation trenches to the fields we will be able to grow more. We could dig another one to bring water into the city and take our waste away downstream.* She pondered that for a moment as she heard Jethro come up behind her.

"You know, I was just thinking about irrigation, Jethro," she said by way of greeting.

"I don't know how you do that, Phoenix. Try as I might, I can never sneak up on you." He joked and laughed.

"You are trying too hard," she explained quickly and cringed at the statement quickly returning to her thoughts from a moment before to distract him from her slight slip. "Now for irrigation, we can dig trenches from the stream bring the water through the fields and the city and connect them back with the river further downstream."

He contemplated her idea for a moment. Finally he asked, "Why would the water follow the new track? We certainly can't and don't want to block the river. That would be too much water and it might bring the capitol city's guards down on us."

Phoenix quickly made a mockup of the river in the area and the fields around their makeshift home. "There's enough water that the river flows very quickly here," she said as she pointed to the diagram. "If we dig the trenches here and line them with stone, the water will have a path of little resistance and the river will want to get rid of the pressure. In the fields, we have to leave the stone loose to allow the water to seep through but in our little city we can have our stoneworkers make a seamless canal so the water keeps moving."

"On top of that," he added, "the water would be a convenient way to remove our waste rather than using holes in the ground. And as long as we make sure everything is done downstream, we have clean water." He scratched his chin, "The city folk made a mistake letting you go, child." He smiled and walked off.

"Jethro!" she called. When he turned, she hurried back to his side. "I wanted to know if I could join you tonight." His eyebrows rose. "I know how to defend myself but I fear I may be out of condition if I do not keep my skills up." She waited quietly until he nodded.

"I was actually going to suggest it myself in a few days," he said then resumed walking toward his house. She turned to her own hut. *I know he is planning an attack on the city and he knows I have skills. It's only a matter of time until he comes to me.* She smiled to herself and hummed a merry tune as she cleaned up for supper.

***

Phoenix put on her most comfortable clothing for her first martial arts session with Jethro and his people. She made sure her arms were free and that movement would be easy.

She was very nervous because she didn't want to give herself away but at the same time, if she was to fan the flames of this rebellion, she needed to help their army get better. She had to find a balance between her cover story and the mission. She planted the seed by telling Jethro she could take care of herself but how far could she go with that?

If they ask, I need a reason for my skills that is plausible. A thief would lose their trust. A daughter of a Lord or rich family would go against my cover. Keep it simple. She ran her fingers through her hair as she thought about it. "The simplest answer is that I started studying with a trusted friend after i was attacked. I didn't want to feel helpless again," she whispered to herself.

Taking a deep breath, she stepped out of her little hovel and stride through the square to join her new army.

It had been three months since her first night training with Jethro and his people. It took less than five minutes for his former city guard turned arms master for the exile city to discover she really did know how to defend herself. It took all of ten minutes after that before she was helping him teach the rest of the people. Now her skills were recognized around the small city and she was just waiting to be invited in the inner sanctum. Outwardly, she projected the calm of somebody going about their business unaware of any other activity going on in the city. She intentionally discussed the evening training sessions from the standpoint of self-defense rather than strategies to attack an enemy. Inwardly, she was screaming in frustration. It was taking too long for Jethro to come to her and bring her in the fold.

There was a knock on the doorframe. Phoenix habitually left her door open to allow the women, who had felt it their duty to help her face the fact that she had been raped, full access to her home. They were constantly checking for any instrument of self-harm and discussing what had happened. Phoenix did not feel that it would help her at all, especially since he had not been able to complete the act because of Tiger's timely interruption but surprisingly, even after her talk with Adrienne that first day, the emotional ache had still been there and the women really had been helpful. Phoenix felt profoundly grateful for their presence. However, when she looked up, it wasn't one of those women at her door, it was Jethro and Adrienne.

"Who are you?" he asked calmly. Adrienne stood at his back with a dagger in her hand.

"I am exactly who I have said I am, Jethro," replied Phoenix coolly, standing up.

"I believed your story about being raped, child. You played the victim to perfection but there is no way you, the answer to our prayers, are exactly what you have told us." He shrugged his shoulders. "Our conclusions are that you must be a spy. It's too perfect; you're too perfect." He sighed.

"A spy," Phoenix chuckled, "If I were a spy, I would be reporting to somebody wouldn't I? Other than the work you have given me that takes me out of this city, I have not left. Nor is there anyone here I spend an inordinate amount of time with." She opened her hands and raised the palm outward. "I will do nothing to you. If I were a spy, backed into a corner and discovered, wouldn't I fight my way out?"

He studied her for a moment then turned to Adrienne. "What do you think, Adrienne?"

"I think she has made very good arguments and honestly she could still be a spy but she has already proven useful."

"Well, I happen to agree. Lucky for you, child, I feel the need for you outweighs any risk you might pose."

"What are you talking about, Jethro?" asked Phoenix. She projected nothing but innocence but her mind was celebrating. *Finally they have come around, even if they are suspicious.*

"We are going to fight back and we need you to do it." He watched her face as she allowed understanding to color her expression after a few seconds.

"The city," she whispered. "You are going to attack the city."

"Yes we are. We will be ready soon." There was a dangerous glint in Jethro's eyes. "Would you please accompany us to my hut? Bring anything you cannot leave behind. Until this is done, you are under my watchful eye and my protection. We need to pick your brain on the attack plan and there is no way we are going to give you the option of giving us away."

"Would you allow me a few moments alone to process and pack?" she requested quietly.

Jethro glanced at Adrienne who looked uncertain and nodded. "Be ready in fifteen minutes." Then they both stepped outside and closed the door behind them.

Phoenix worked quickly. She used the code she and Tiger had invented to write a letter detailing what she had just learned. Her contact had made herself known weeks ago when she came to discuss Phoenix's past. So Phoenix placed the letter in a secret compartment in her table she knew the woman would find. Once that was done, she packed up her clothes and left all of the other possessions where they were. The only material objects she truly cared about, other than her fans and her mother's necklace, were in the mansion on Wood Lane.

She took a deep breath and joined her cohorts outside. Adrienne went back inside and did a thorough search of the hut for any message Phoenix may have left. She came back outside having found nothing and shook her head at Jethro.

"Smart girl," he remarked as he led the way to his hut.

Phoenix's contact was across the way tending the central fire and watched as she walked between Adrienne and Jethro. Phoenix caught her eye, held it for a heartbeat and looked away. The woman nodded as if to her companion who was gossiping away in her ear and turned back to the conversation. *Good,* she thought, *he will get the message in the next few hours.*

A hand shook her vigorously awake. "I don't know how they found out, child, but the city army is on its way." The panic seemed out of place in Jethro's voice but Phoenix understood it. He was concerned for his people. Truly, he had the biggest heart in the world. When he was acting in his capacity as general for the city militia, he seemed to be so cold and distant but Jethro could not stand the thought of his people being killed for no reason.

"I'm awake, Jethro. Tell me what is going on." Phoenix sat up slowly.

"Somehow the city has learned of our plan. I know it wasn't you and I apologize for our suspicion but now you have to get out of here." He pulled her to her feet forgetting, or not caring, that she didn't like men touching her. "You are too good to die here. Please just go."

He dragged her to the door and physically pushed her out.

Her contact was in the shadows a hundred feet away and Phoenix flicked a hand in her direction but to Jethro it looked like she was just trying to regain her balance. "I'm sorry, Phoenix." He was almost crying as he spoke. "Please take our story with you and get out of here." He grabbed his sword and ran to the outskirts of the city where the defenders were lining up in their regiments to defend their homes. They had prepared to defend their homes using tactics employed by street toughs. They started overturning tables to block streets and set strategic fires to hide their movements from the oncoming enemy. Those not joining the defenders were gathering the children and moving to a safe location. Phoenix had helped Jethro develop the evacuation plan weeks ago after discussing the strategic disadvantages of the village's location. The resistance would continue after the village fell. The children had been learning defense with the adults and their guards were chosen specifically for their ability to fight and their strategic minds.

"They are going to die," Phoenix whispered looking at the phalanx of village defenders.

"You have a job to do, ma'am. Please, we have to get you to safety." Her contact had moved to stand next to her. "This way, please."

Phoenix followed the woman into the darkness. They walked for about an hour before the screams came floating across the plains. Phoenix was tempted to look back but she knew she couldn't. Her companion was right, she had a job to do.

After another half hour of walking in the night, Phoenix heard a horse ahead of them. She stopped and crouched behind a bush. The other woman must not have noticed her actions or the noise because she kept plowing ahead.

Suddenly she let out a piercing whistle. A moment later her whistle was answered and the horseman dissolved out of the darkness in front of her.

"Where is she?" asked a familiar voice.

"I am right here, sir," Phoenix called coming out of her hiding place but not venturing any nearer.

"It wasn't me child. There must have been another spy in the camp," he said simply to her unspoken question. Both of them snapped around to look to the west as they both heard the horses.

"There *was* another spy at the camp," the woman said as she began running toward the horses, "and you put her there, you idiots." She began laughing as she ran.

Phoenix sprinted to the horse her master rode and grabbed hold as he spurred the horse into a gallop after the woman. He grabbed her around the waist to hold her to the horse. She snapped one of her fans open and removed the woman's head from her shoulders as she ran. Then the Shadow Man heaved and swung his operative in front of him in the saddle.

Phoenix found herself hugging her employer for dear life as he directed the horse away from their pursuers.

Phoenix could not hear anything but the pounding of the horse's hooves and the heavy breathing as it strained to hold the pace. When it started to stumble, the Shadow Man calmly slowed it down to a walk. When they had traveled far enough, he stopped the horse and they dismounted.

"I truly hate when things do not go according to plan," he sighed. "It seems I was wrong about the identity of the spy he placed in my house."

Phoenix thought for a moment. "What did she think would happen? How was she turned against us?" she asked. "What's do we do now, sir?"

"It's not very difficult to turn a common agent to your cause. I can only assume that I was meant to die in this attack as well. Otherwise, why pass on your message instead of just informing her true masters? Unless she couldn't break your code." He paused in thought. "We are almost at the rendezvous point for my caravan. We will walk the rest of the way and camp out until they reach us." He chuckled at her moonlit expression of confusion. "You didn't think I came out here without a pretense did you? Court season is over and I must visit my estate to check on the affairs there."

"My Lord Calden, you are a surprising man," he stiffened at her use of his given name.

"I suppose I should have guessed that you figured a few things out."

She smiled. "It's especially easy when you tell me what is going on," she replied.

"So you figured that out as well."

"Yes, sir. What I could not figure out was why you made it so easy and why you would tell me."

"It's quite simple actually." It was his turn to smile. "You are essential to our plans."

"Essential? I was nobody before I came to you; just a beggar child, an orphan with no future and few skills." She shook her head as they started their walk to the rendezvous point.

He didn't respond right away. Instead, he dug into one of his saddlebags. He pulled out a necklace with a pendant in the shape of a phoenix dangling on the chain. "I believe you recognize this rather remarkable piece of jewelry," he said.

"It's the same as my necklace," she said. She resisted the temptation to snatch it out of his hand. Gently he helped her put the necklace on and removed the other one.

"That particular pendant has quite the history. The one that you were wearing is a replica. This is the original. It is good to see it around the neck of the true owner," he said and Phoenix's eyes opened wide. Nobody outside her family was supposed to know the meaning of the pendant. "It confirms who you are almost as much as the 'birthmark' you bear." He coughed awkwardly when he mentioned her phoenix brand.

"Your family was once one of the most powerful in the kingdom. So powerful in fact that some of the other lords feared them and had them purged. They were obviously successful but not completely, considering the fact that you are walking here beside me." He smiled at her again.

"There is something you may not be aware of though." His tone became contemplative and there was something about it that Phoenix could not quite pick out. "The first king decreed that his son would marry his best friend's daughter. She was killed before their nuptials. As a result, the king, determined to cement their two families together, amended the decree to state that a son of the royal household would be presented with a daughter of his friend's household for marriage whenever the crown prince reached twenty-five years of age. There was one family that despised the decree and set out to kill every female child of the family for generations. They were surprisingly effective. Eventually, the family put together the information they needed to guard their daughters and went after the murderous family. Before they were able to put an end to the murders, they were attacked and killed. There were thought to be no survivors."

Phoenix looked on her employer with confusion.

"You still don't understand, little bird?" Phoenix shook her head. "Well, what if I told you that the first king's best friend was named Eldwin Rivell?"

Phoenix gasped and her eyes widened at a name she had only heard in her childhood bedtime stories; the name of her ancestor. "You mean?" she couldn't even finish the question.

"You are essential to our plans, Arlaya." It was the first time he had used her name. "Without you, we may end up with a queen who is manipulated by malevolent people. The lord that killed your family still has descendants alive and they are just as determined as he was that they will get the crown. They have come further than any generation before them and we must stop them from taking the full power of the crown. The prince is under pressure to marry an easily manipulated woman from their group. As soon as he does, the Lords involved will find a way to remove the prince from their path. We need to prevent that from happening."

"It's a lot to demand of one person but I will do my best. What would you have me do?" Phoenix asked.

"You are going to do what I can't have your future husband do. You are going to learn the art of the assassins to protect yourself, Lirith, and your future family from these regicidal maniacs." His eyes filled with regret. "I only wish I'd been able to do the same for Lirith. He is sorely in need of the extra education to protect himself. You will have to learn everything they can teach and return to the city within the next six months." He shook his head and looked around.

"Here is our stopping point for the night." He tied his horse to a tree with enough slack in the line to eat grass and quickly unsaddled the beast. From his packs he pulled grooming tools, a tent, and two bedrolls. Phoenix set up the tent and laid out the bedrolls as he groomed his horse. She listened to his deep voice tell his horse how good he had done to carry the two of them away from the threat.

"Tomorrow, you will travel to a secret citadel on the coast." Phoenix jumped as he addressed her for the first time in almost an hour. "I have a horse for you coming with the caravan. You will also have a guide and more than enough food to get you there. They are expecting you so do not stray from the path." He laid down on the bedroll next to hers.

"Thank you for coming to get me, sir. I really appreciate it," said Phoenix.

"It suited my needs," he replied. "Besides, I have grown to like you, little bird."

***

The birds greeting the sun woke her. *I am to be an assassin. That was never in the cards was it, Grandfather?* She rose, stretched, and started straightening up her camp, all the while trying to not wake up Lord Calden. She finished cleaning and started grooming the horse again.

It was not long before she heard her companion stir. She waited until after he had come back from relieving himself to address him. "Good morning, sir," she said.

"That it is, little bird, that it is," he responded with a smile. He carefully shook out the bedrolls and folded the two together with the tent. "They should be arriving soon."

"Sir?" Phoenix hesitated. Calden looked up and nodded for her to ask her question. "What will it be like at the citadel?" She had lived in the city all of her life and did not know what to expect.

He paused for a long moment contemplating how to explain. "You will do more work than ever before in your life. They will teach you about everything from code languages to horsemanship, don't think I didn't miss the way you held onto me in the gallop," she blushed, "and how to blend into different backgrounds so completely it will be as though you disappeared." He paused again. After a deep breath, he continued, "Your knowledge of the martial arts is nothing compared to what it will be a month from now and those cute little fans you have in your belt will be more than just ornaments. I know Hawk wasn't ready to teach you how to wield those yet but you will certainly learn at the citadel. You will become an expert in every weapon you could ever imagine and a few you couldn't. The assassins that come out of that 'school' are the finest in the world. Any nobleman who has need of their services will pay exorbitant fees to get them."

As she listened with rapt attention to his description, Phoenix was filled with anticipation. She couldn't wait to get started.

"Before you are fully inducted, you must first be assessed." The anticipation was washed away as fear swamped her stomach like a bucket of ice water. "I have already sent reports on what you learned in your time with me," he continued, seemingly oblivious to what Phoenix was feeling.

They sat in silence together; he watching the sunrise and she trying to control the butterflies that had invaded her belly. It wasn't that she was afraid to go and be tested, she was afraid that she would fail. She didn't want to fail the man sitting next to her. She wanted to help end the reign of the regent and put Lirith on the throne. Whether or not she survived the venture, Lirith must save the kingdom. The people needed him.

"You will be fine, child," said Lord Calden without looking at her. "You are well trained and you are very teachable. I would not send you on this mission if I did not believe it would help us and if I did not believe you were perfect for the job. They will be able to teach you more than I ever could."

"Thank you, sir. I just don't want to fail you. Too much is at stake." Phoenix stared off into the distance.

"Yes it is, but the sooner you start the better you will be when we need you." He stood up and put the gear back on the horse. "Time to go."

Grabbing the horse, he led Phoenix down the hill. Not even two hundred meters away, hidden in a copse of trees was a camp that was just waking up.

Phoenix stopped at the edge of the camp and looked at him. "If they were here the whole time, why didn't we camp with them last night?"

"Well, first off, you and I needed to talk. We had a very good conversation, I thought." He winked at her and walked the horse over to a picket full of his fellows. "And secondly, our friends are distracting Tiger." She smiled at the thought of seeing him again. She hadn't realized how much she missed him.

The Shadow Man shook his head sadly. "You will not be able to see him before you leave, Phoenix." Phoenix just stared at him open mouthed, not knowing what to say. "I'm very sorry, little bird, but it has to be this way. He has a few lessons to learn." He shook his head again. "I hope you will understand in time."

He pulled another horse from the picket. "This is the young man who will take you to the citadel." He smiled again as she went completely gooey eyed at the beautiful beast. "Ah, and here is your guide."

"Well, girl, you have missed every lesson for the past few weeks. How am I supposed to feel about that," came a voice from behind her.

"Hawk, how good to see you too, you senile old fart," Phoenix replied as she turned around with the biggest of smiles.

In a rare demonstration of love and friendship, Hawk gathered up the younger woman in a hug. "We have missed you, Phoenix," she said simply.

"Ok you two. Get going before Tiger comes back," said their boss.

"I still don't understand why you have chosen to create this added difficulty, sir," responded Hawk with a meaningful look. The Shadow Man returned the look and jerked his head to the southeast. "Come, girl. We have a distance to travel."

Phoenix mounted her horse clumsily as Hawk swung herself gracefully in the saddle. "Squeeze your legs as soon as you get settled and he will move," Hawk told her quietly. Phoenix obeyed and the two women started out at a steady pace.

The Shadow Man watched them ride off then slowly turned to face the camp. He carefully schooled his features into a mask of calm as though he had just received bad news and wanted to keep it from his friends.

Carefully, he picked his way through the camp toward the rendezvous with Tiger. He was having a knife throwing competition with Wolf. He heard the whooping and impact as Tiger sank a knife into whatever target they were using.

He walked slowly up to the pair and cleared his throat. Tiger looked up smiling. His face fell as he saw his friend's expression. "What happened?" he asked.

"Somebody discovered the plans of this Jethro character." Tiger nodded, they had already known that which was why they had chosen to extract Phoenix. "Neither of our operatives made it out. The army got there too quickly." The fact that Phoenix's name was not mentioned drilled the reality home to Tiger.

She didn't make it out, his heart felt like it would never beat again. There was a ringing in his ears. He didn't even feel himself start crying or his friends each put arms around his shoulders. It took a while, but eventually Tiger regained some control of his emotions and walked away into the trees so he could be alone for a bit.

Wolf made to follow him but the Shadow Man held him back. "Give him some time, old friend. He will come back." *I wish it didn't have to be this way but while he knew she was alive he believed the plan couldn't fail. Now he will take fewer chances.* He knew he was just trying to reason away his guilt but he let himself do so. *Besides, now his reaction will be genuine surprise when she shows up again.*

He turned to the men and women in the camp and started organizing the dismantling of the tents and the loading of the pack animals. It was another half an hour before the group was ready to leave for Lord Calden's estate.

Wolf was still holding vigil on the most likely point of Tiger's return. "We are ready to move on, Wolf."

Calden started toward the trees and Lirith but Wolf grabbed his sleeve. "Perhaps I should find him, sir," he said with a look as cold as ice. He was clearly not happy with his master's plan.

Calden opened his mouth to respond but Wolf cut him off with a shake of his head and walked toward the trees.

***

Lirith had stalked off without thinking about where he was going. After a few minutes he found that all he wanted to do was sit. He made himself comfortable in the roots of a massive tree and just stared into nothingness. His mind whirled as he sat in the silence broken only by the twittering of birds.

She's gone. How can she be gone? I never got to tell her how much she meant to me. Over the last few months we worked well together. How could she do this to me?

He knew his brain was working around in circles. He just could not believe she was dead. Lord Calden must be wrong. He had promised that Phoenix would be alive and they would see each other again.. And he had never known his friend to be wrong.

He did not know how long he sat there sifting through his feelings but the woods were waking up around him as he brought his emotions fully under control. His thoughts kept coming back to one disturbing reality for him. Lirith never realized how he truly felt about Arlaya until that moment. She had always just been there in the back of his mind and he knew their futures were intertwined so he never really paid attention to how he felt.

She will never again be Phoenix to me. I don't care how I met her. Arlaya is a beautiful name and it fits the beautiful woman I came to admire. I just wish I had a few more seconds with her to tell her how much I love her.

Footsteps interrupted his grief. He snapped back to the present and looked around. His eyes were sore from the crying and his nose was runny. He wiped his face on his sleeve before quietly standing. He turned to face whoever was coming. Friend or foe, he didn't care.

Wolf materialized out of the branches and trucks. "It's time to leave, Tiger," he said sadly. All he wanted to do was reach out and show his friend that he was here and felt for him but the look on Tiger's face said that his efforts would go unnoticed. Instead, he stood at a distance silently waiting for Tiger to join him on the walk back to camp.

It was a few moments before Tiger moved. Finally, he straightened his shoulders and strode forth toward the camp.

When the two were close enough to smell the smoke of the campfires, Tiger's instincts went on full alert. The rustle of cloth nearby told him there were other men in the area. Wolf kept walking seemingly not noticing.

Four hooded figures appeared out of the wood. One tackled Wolf and knocked him in the forehead with the hilt of a sword. He went down unconscious.

Tiger dodged a similar attack and dropped into a defensive stance. He had walked out of the camp without any blades for protection but he hadn't worked with Hawk for years for nothing. *Come and get it.*

He snarled at his attackers. They had chosen the wrong day to confront him.

The three who hadn't attacked Wolf circled around him. They had obviously trained together as a team. Two feinted in trying to push him toward the third but Tiger didn't play by the rules. He stood his ground, blocking one advance and kicking out at the other watching the third to make sure he didn't have to fend off an attack from that direction. *They won't get me that easily.*

Then the fourth joined the fray. He came at Tiger from behind, pinning his arms to his side. The other three advanced on their struggling quarry.

Tiger let out a growl and struggled harder, using his legs to keep the three at bay. One got a foot into his gut though and he had the wind knocked out of him. While he was recovering from the blow, a second one, he didn't know which, hit him in the side of the head with a hilt.

As he realized how helpless he was, his struggles got weaker. *I just want it to end. Then I can be with her again,* he thought. But as he closed his eyes, it wasn't Arlaya he saw. The face that came to mind was his old friend, Lord Calden, his second father.

If Lirith gave up and died, Calden's plans for the improvement of the kingdom would have failed. But Lirith would not only have failed his friend, he would fail himself, his people, his ancestors, and, yes, Arlaya if he gave up without fighting harder. He would never let his uncle win.

He snapped his head up just as a blade was swinging toward him. He surged to his feet, dragging his captor off balance and dodged the blow. Once he had thrown off the fourth man, he turned to face his other three attackers with renewed strength and sense of purpose.

"Halt!" called Wolf. "He gets the point, I think." The attackers bowed and melted back into the surrounding greenery. "I am sorry for such a drastic lesson, my friend, but you were going to kill yourself. I saw it in your eyes when you walked away." He walked over and placed a hand on Tiger's shoulder. "You didn't feel you had anything left to live for did you?"

Tiger shook his head. He was working to control his breathing and calm his heart now that he knew he was not fighting for his life. Such an effort did not leave much energy for speaking.

"I didn't think so but, judging by how you fought in the end, you found something more important than your grief." Tiger nodded. "Hold on to it. You will still mourn but it won't be the end of the world." Wolf walked away allowing Tiger to ponder what he said.

Five minutes later, Tiger was standing next to him saddling his horse in abject silence but fully aware of what was going on around him with a sword strapped to his hip and several daggers hidden about his person.. He would never be caught without weapons again.

Hawk was a very good travel companion. Every morning was spent on exercises. Phoenix's martial skills increased exponentially in the month it took to reach the citadel. They had even begun work on using the fans as both a defensive and offensive weapon. She wasn't particularly loquacious but would carry on a conversation with Phoenix when the silence became oppressive.

Exactly one month into their travels, they crested a hill at sunset and the citadel was on the other side. Phoenix shaded her eyes to take in the sight.

She had thought it would be a grand castle; the best construction money could buy. There would be an enormous stable and an army of servants tending to the greatest assassins in history. Instead, what she saw was a mansion not unlike Lord Calden's with a small stable attached. What she did notice right away were the large sand arenas where people were fighting each other oblivious to their observers.

A man appeared out of the ground next to her causing her to jump but she hid it rather well.

"State your business," he demanded.

Hawk pressed her mount forward and looked down at the small man. "This is Phoenix. I have brought her to learn from you," she replied coolly.

"Hawk?" came another voice.

"Yes?" she responded.

"It is all right, brother," the second voice said. Phoenix could not locate the speaker. "I know this woman. We have been expecting her," he paused, "and her protégé."

The man in front of them nodded. "If you would be so kind as to dismount and follow me this way," he gestured down the path toward the mansion.

The trip to the house was quick and silent. Hawk and Phoenix untacked their horses and left them in the stable while their guide directed them to the guest quarters so they could freshen up from their journey.

Their rooms were a suite and as Phoenix came out of her bedroom she saw someone standing in the center of the lounge. She quietly prepared herself for a fight. The Shadow Man had told her that she would be assessed so she was prepared for the testing to begin at any time.

"Relax, child," said someone behind her. "You will have plenty of time to be suspicious of us and we will have plenty of time to see what you can do."

Slowly, she turned to face the speaker and saw Hawk smirking from her doorway. "I told you she was good, Syril," she said.

"I trust your teaching, Hawk. Tonight, I will not be testing her. Tonight, I extend the hand of friendship. Will the pair of you join us for the evening meal?" he asked.

"We would be honored, sir," Phoenix replied.

***

Phoenix was allowed a week to settle in and learn the layout of the building. Hawk left her two days after her arrival. It had been a tearful farewell but they knew she had to return.

"I must get back before anyone starts to speculate about why I am gone," she had said. "They will test you, Phoenix, and you will pass only if you use their strength against them. Let them exhaust themselves against you, then you strike." After a single hug she was gone.

As Phoenix woke up on the first day of training, she was very nervous. *What are they going to throw at me today?* she asked herself. She got out of bed and dressed in tighter trousers than were strictly acceptable even for men and put on a skirt over it. Her blouse was also tight and it was sleeveless to allow for full range motion. She was fairly certain that she would be tested on her physicality first. It wouldn't do to waste the sunlight after all. Once properly garbed, she ate a light breakfast and began her morning warm-up exercises, taking care to stretch every muscle.

Just as she was finishing there was a knock at her door. She strode over and opened it to find Syril, the man she had met on the first day.

"Follow me, young Phoenix. It is time we began your training." He turned and walked away without looking to see if she would follow.

She hurried after him, focusing her breathing to keep her heart rate down. Once she was a step behind her guide, she stilled her body and only allowed for the necessary movements. Hawk said to conserve her energy and she had every intention of doing so. No energy would be wasted, no effort would be needless.

Syril stopped her outside one of the sand arenas Phoenix had seen on the first day. She had watched the other students practice their fighting skills here every day since. She looked around. There were two tables set up on opposite sides of the circle from one another. On the tables were various weapons and sitting next to the table opposite Phoenix were the students she had seen practicing every day.

"We begin with the martial arts," Syril explained needlessly. Phoenix could easily deduce what was about to happen. He continued to speak, however, and she paid close attention to his words. "You will fight one opponent at a time. The fight ends when one of you dies or is incapacitated." He turned to look at her as her heart tried to pound faster and harder but she put more focus into her breathing to maintain control. "You can use any weapon available and there are no rules to the fighting. If you survive we will teach you; if you don't then..." He let his words hang menacingly in the air, stood aside, and gestured for her to enter the ring.

Let them exhaust themselves against you, then you strike. Hawk's words rang ominously through her mind as she stepped into the sand. She walked to the middle of the arena and just stood there. She felt a calm settle over her as she accepted what was about to happen.

Phoenix's first opponent stepped up. She watched him walk into the arena with a cocky swagger. He made a show of perusing the available weapons and shook his head, coming in empty handed.

Throughout this entire performance, Phoenix did not move a muscle. She simply watched his movements, assessing his speed and strength as he walked to meet her. What she saw was a young puppy with an elevated self-worth. She could already see the battle unfolding.

"Begin," came the call.

The boy, Phoenix could not think of him as a man, started moving on the outskirts of the circle. She chose not to follow his path. His shuffling steps allowed her to hear his every movement. He continued circling, getting closer and closer, until he decided it was time to strike his immobile opponent. His breath hitched from behind her right ear and she dropped and kicked his feet out from under him. The boy went down hard and she clipped him on the side of the head to knock him out.

While the instructors moved the unconscious boy, she sat calmly and sipped water. Those instructors not dealing with her previous opponent discussed her performance in hushed tones. Finally, Syril waved his fellows to silence and signaled the next student to step up.

This one chose to grab a knife. She stood and strode over for her own knife. *This is going to be fun,* she decided as she settled into her relaxed immobile pose once more.

This opponent came in more cautiously. He wasn't going to let her catch him unprepared like his predecessor. All she did was watch him. He certainly knew how to wield a knife. His blade was held at the perfect angle to both attack and defend.

Her grip was one that was most often used in defense but, for those who knew how to use it properly, could be used offensively with fatal efficiency. Phoenix did not want to kill anyone but she would if she had to.

He shuffled in quickly and struck at her stomach. She calmly deflected it and followed up with the accepted counterstrike. The man smiled as he dodged. He thought she only knew the basics but he was about to learn his mistake. Rather than come in with another basic strike, he tried to weave a complicated pattern and distract her from his goal, her heart. She was not swayed by his movements. Instead, she struck through his pattern and cut the tendon holding his hand closed on his knife. Before the blade hit the ground, she reversed her swing to bring the hilt against his head. Once again, she knocked her opponent unconscious and sat sipping water.

The third man stepped up and grabbed a mace. Phoenix had never learned to use one so did not match his play. Rather she put the knife back on the table and secured her customary fans to her belt. As she turned with seemingly no weapons, she heard a ripple of chuckles roll through the gathered students. She ignored them and stepped back to the center of the arena.

Any man who chose a mace clearly valued brute strength over speed and finesse, as he demonstrated by immediately rushing her. She easily dodged to the side and his momentum carried him clear past her. He turned surprisingly quickly and faced her again. He carefully closed the distance between them and swung his heavy weapon. Maces are clumsy and generally slow. They are also quite large and you can see them coming very easily. Phoenix dodged again and danced away from him on light feet only to stand still once more. With a roar of frustration, he rushed her again. This time she snapped one of her fans open, to the enjoyment and laughter of the other students, and slid it between his arms to slice his biceps as she dropped and slid between his legs to dodge the rush.

Phoenix heard a gasp of surprise from the instructors as she stood once more but that was almost drowned out by the jeers from the students and the cry of agony from her opponent. He rushed her again, this time from the side, blood splattering against the sand. Phoenix dodged once more and kicked out at his stomach. She knew she hit one of his kidneys and she watched him fall to the earth with a whimper of pain. His legs twitched and Phoenix turned to her evaluators. "This man is in no shape to continue. Please, allow him to be removed and seen to for his injuries, I have no intention of killing today," she said and returned to her table to sip more water. They nodded and her third opponent was removed from the arena. Phoenix took a deep breath. So far she had gotten lucky but now the men knew what they were up against.

As if to prove her point, her fourth opponent stepped up with a pike in hand. Phoenix thought about which weapon she could use to counter him. Her fans were too short, as was her knife, and she knew very little about pike-work. She scanned the weapons on the table and her eyes fell on a long curved blade fastened to a pole. When she was younger, her grandfather had given her one of those weapons for her birthday. The blade was eighteen inches long and the pole was seven feet long so it would counter the pike perfectly. But did she remember enough of how to use it to be effective? Her time was running out so she grabbed the glaive and hoped her muscles would remember.

She could feel the surprise around her as she chose that weapon. It was heavy and, if you didn't know how to use it, clumsy. She didn't know if she had chosen properly but she had chosen and now she stood calmly once more in the sand. Her opponent had the advantage in this fight and she knew it. His weapon was longer and he was probably more experienced with it than she was with hers.

He adopted a pose similar to hers, standing rock still with the weapon at the ready. Rather than stand with the blade hanging out in the air in front of her, Phoenix reversed her grip and allowed the blade to point to the ground just like her grandfather had taught her. From this position it would be easy to swing up to meet the pike or injure her opponent without expending the energy needed to hold the blade at waist height.

Neither combatant moved for what felt like half an hour. Phoenix felt sweat dribble down her spine. *I can outwait him* she told herself. *I have more battles to fight and he's allowing me a respite.* No matter what she told herself, holding herself ready for the attack was taxing. Their audience was clearly bored but that didn't matter to her. She just maintained focus as sweats dribbled down her face and back.

She saw the muscles in her opponent's chest tighten and swung her glaive up just in time for his initial attack. The glaive's blade made a clacking sound as it impacted and sliced through the ash shaft. Her block wasn't fast enough though, or it may have fallen too far down the shaft, because she felt the lick of the pike blade on her shoulder.

She ignored the lance of pain as she reversed her shaft like a staff and knocked the feet out from under her opponent. He scrambled back upright and changed his grip on what was left of his pike. The two of them exchanged staff blows while Phoenix got in a better position to use her blade.

She saw the opening and swung hard and fast. Her blade was headed straight for the man's head and he had no way to stop her from killing him. He closed his eyes and waited for death, but it never came.

When he opened his eyes again the blade was a fraction of an inch from his head. Phoenix had stopped the downward swing. "This one is done too," she said simply and took the glaive back to the table. She was very glad to not be holding its weight any longer.

She carefully washed and dressed her shoulder and waited for her next opponent to step up. By her count she had seven more fights ahead of her. Her next opponent stepped up and she took a deep breath before stepping once more into the fray.

***

Her chest heaved and her arms shook as she stood over her final opponent. The fingers of her left hand were full of the pins and needles of numbness and her bandage was soaked through with blood. Unsurprisingly, she had spent much of her time and energy protecting her wound. She had further accumulated a black eye slowly swelling shut, a split lip, a few cracked ribs, and at least one broken finger. The point of the sword she was holding slowly drifted down to the sand.

She caught herself, picked up the point and calmly, albeit slowly, strode to replace it on the table. Determined not to give away any sign of her exhaustion, she spent an extra minute or two cleaning the blade. Once she was satisfied, she replaced the weapon and turned slowly to face Syril and his brothers-at-arms.

"Well done, child," he said with a smile. He looked to the west where the sun kissed the horizon. He shook his head as though dismissing a thought. "Supper is in an hour. Allow me to escort you to the physicians. Let's get your wounds tended to." He walked to her side and put his arm around her shoulders with a wink. Outwardly, it looked like a simple gesture of friendship or mentorship but in reality Syril was supporting her weight. She almost sighed in relief as the pressure was taken away from her muscles. The students who didn't participate in the trial stood and scattered to complete any chores before they ate.

Together, Syril and Phoenix walked back into the mansion and to the physicians. Once inside the medical hall, Syril deposited her on a bed and left to prepare for dinner. Phoenix just sat there and looked around.

Many of the men she had fought were conscious once more and sat in beds of their own while their injuries were tended to or with fresh bandages clearly in evidence. She was concerned that they would hold the fact that she defeated them against her but, as she looked around, the men smiled at her.

Well, most of them did. Her first opponent glowered at her from the corner. Clearly he felt humiliation at being beaten. Whether that humiliation stemmed from the fact that she was a woman, he had been beaten so quickly, or she was as green as grass and should not have been able to fight as she did, Phoenix doubted she would ever know. One thing of which she was certain was that she had just made an enemy.

"Don't worry about him," said the man in the bed next to her. She turned to see the pikeman, the one who had wounded her in the shoulder. He reached over and started undoing her bandage. "When he came here he didn't make it past the first fight. They allowed him to train here because he didn't give up. Even when his arm was broken and his skull was cracked, he got up to fight. We told him it was normal to not make it further than the second or third fight, which is true." Phoenix winced as the bandage came away from the cut. His fingers began gently prodding the injury. "Very few people ever defeat us all. In fact, I haven't heard of it happening in the last few generations." He picked a few loose threads out of her shoulder and smiled. "You may have dressed this properly for a nice relaxing day but not for fighting."

Phoenix contemplated what he'd said as he continued pulling out threads. So not only did she defeat the puppy in the arena, she had proved how weak and inadequate he was by defeating everybody else as well.

She winced with a hiss as her caretaker started cleaning the wound with a cloth dipped in spirits.

"So," he asked conversationally, "where did you learn to use a glaive like that?"

"My grandfather," she replied through gritted teeth.

"It is a very unorthodox style," he stated as he dropped the now bloody cloth into the bowl. He picked up a needle and thread and looked at her curiously. "Can you handle this or do you need some…hmmm assistance?"

"Just stitch it up. I don't need anything."

Instead, he exchanged the needle for clean bandages. "It's not bad enough for that," he said, laughter dancing in his eyes. "I just wanted to see what you would say." He laughed in truth, a full boisterous guffaw that bounced off of the walls.

"Stop hogging the new girl, Quint," the man on the other side of him complained, "we all would like to meet her, you know."

"Yeah," came another voice, "it's not often we are beaten, by someone of the female persuasion."

"That's what we have you for, Cal. So the few times you win we know what it feels like to be beat by a woman."

Laughter raced around the room, even Phoenix was laughing. It felt good to let loose. The man, Quint, tied off her bandage with a flourish, handed her a cloth for her split lip, and bowed.

"Far be it for me to deny the lady a little courtesy and support amongst a group of ragamuffin pinheads such as yourselves. Now that I have cleaned and properly dressed my mark of shame upon her lovely person, allow me to humbly step aside so that you may undo the work I have so carefully put in place." He winked at her. "By being the callous ingrates you are, you prove what a gentleman I am." As he was finishing his grandiose speech, some of the other men tackled him from behind.

Another roar of laughter shook the hall and Phoenix looked up to see Syril return. He had a very serious look on his face but the sparkle of amusement danced in his eyes. "What is this? I am gone for a few moments and what I thought was a room full of disciplined fighters turns out to be a playroom full of little children." All of the men put on masks of shame but Phoenix knew that was all it was. "You have all had a very trying day and you are lucky to be here at all," Phoenix blinked and Quint nodded ever so slightly. "So," Syril continued, "let us show some decorum if you please."

He smiled for the first time in his speech. "Besides," he said, "why would you want to celebrate on empty stomachs?" the men cheered at that and streamed out of the room toward the great hall. Phoenix moved to follow but Syril waved her back.

"We do not often have someone perform as you did today," he said. "I wanted to thank you, Phoenix, for sparing their lives. It is our tradition that, in a trial such as yours today, lives of the defeated are forfeit. It took remarkable strength and control to do what you did and your actions did not go unnoticed. Tonight you rest but tomorrow we need to see how extensive your knowledge of codes is." He linked her arm with his and walked her down to the din of the great hall. "Welcome to the family, Phoenix," he said with a pat.

She had spent the entire next day and much of the night decoding letters and manuscripts. Her nightly work with Tiger all those months ago had paid off. She was not given a code she was unable to decipher. As the time went on, she was given more complicated codes to translate and some of them took her longer than others. Yet, she persevered and translated them all, except one.

It was an old book that Syril dusted off before handing to her with a curious look. She carefully took the text from his grasp and opened to the first page. One look at the gibberish on the page sent her heart sinking. On the page was a jumble of musical notes and nonsensical words. Phoenix knew how to read music but there was no cleft, key, or meter notated. Everything was continuous rather than split into bars. She spent the better part of an hour trying to decipher the code and came up empty.

Syril did not seem at all surprised. Instead, he suggested that Phoenix take the book to study at length. Now, as he stood in his office with his back to his garrulous petulant visitor, he wondered if he had made the right choice and if Phoenix would be able to decipher the text.

"All I am saying, Syril, is that this girl has only been here for a few short days. She did very well during her assessments thus far but we have no idea if we can trust her. But rather than have her study and work up to it, you gave her the book that our order has been studying and trying to decode for the last century."

He finally paused to take a breath and Syril held up a hand. "Brother," he said to halt the speech he had already spent half an hour listening to, "in that hundred years of study, we have yet to break the code. Phoenix has nothing more to learn from us when it comes to codes so she may be the fresh eyes we need to see what is hidden in this text." The other man opened his mouth to speak again but Syril cut him off. "That is my decision."

"She is supposed to be here for only a few short months. How are we supposed to properly train her in our ways in that time. To become one of our experts takes years of training." Syril had been listening to this argument since the day he decided to take her on.

"Phoenix needs very little in the way of new weapons training and no training in codes. She will learn the other more subtle parts of our work; the silent language, disappearing, leaving no trace. That is the final stage for any of our trainees as it is." Syril straightened his shoulders. "She will receive the training meant for her and I will have no other word in argument from anyone."

Syril's guest heaved an exasperated sigh, stood up and left the room. Syril let out a sigh of his own and let himself slump over. He was tired and he didn't know if he was making the right decision but he would stand by it.

Straightening once more, he decided to go for a walk. Secure in the fact that he was safe in his home, Syril did not pay attention to the path his feet chose. It was only because his training as an assassin was so absolute that he knew when the other man joined him on his midnight constitutional.

"She is important, isn't she?"

"Yes, Quint, I believe she is," Syril replied.

"She is very good. How many codes did she crack?"

"All of them." Syril paused before nodding. "She has the Voltera Codex now."

"Hmm. She is very, very good then." Quint seemed lost in thought for a while as they walked.

"Where does she start?" he finally asked.

"Riding, obviously, and the upper level combat classes. She needs to learn more about the *shukusen* and long pole weapons." He continued thoughtfully, "Poison and drug identification and tolerance and dancing as well, I think. Also, sign language, I have no idea where she will end up but I want her prepared for everything."

Quint shrugged. "Then you will want to add stealth to her educational plan," he said and smiled. Raising his voice he called, "Right, Phoenix?" Nothing happened and he turned to his left and glared into the bushes. "Come on out, girl. It's bad form to remain in hiding when you have already been discovered."

Syril tapped Quint's shoulder with a chuckle and pointed to the roof behind and to the right. Sure enough, there was Phoenix dropping lightly to the ground to meet them. Quint grimaced then started laughing. "I guess you're better than I thought," he said between chuckles.

"I've been playing the 'Don't Get Caught' game most of my life. If my grandfather or father were unable to find me I got a sweet." She winked at Quint. "You never stood a chance."

Quint smiled at her. "We were just discussing your skill level," he said.

"I know," she replied. "What I don't know is who are you, another student, to be asking for information about me?" Her suspicion was palpable.

Before Quint could respond, Syril piped in. "He is going to be your mentor," he explained. "Quint has been here for quite some time and knows how we operate."

"So he is asking everything to help me." It was a statement not a question.

"Exactly so," Syril replied. "I will leave the two of you alone to discuss this." He walked off into the night in deep thought once more.

"So, where do we start?" asked Phoenix.

"Well how about with your first name," Quint replied.

"The direct approach, that's different."

"I find it eminently refreshing. Back to the point. Your name?"

"Phoenix."

"Very good, you stick to a character well. Your real name, please." His expression was one of pertinacious efficiency.

She opened her mouth and closed it again. *Should I just give him my name?* she asked herself. Finally she spoke up. "I'm Ari," she said.

"A half-truth but I will take it," he said, "for now." He smiled again. "Tomorrow morning we are going to start building up your tolerance to poisons. Then you will join us for morning combat no matter how ill you feel, then horsemanship, dance, identification of drugs and poisons, stealth, sign language, and you can study your code book after supper."

"That is a full day."

"Yes it is so go and get some rest." Quint left her there and walked back to his rooms still wondering who she was.

***

"Heels down!" A hand grabbed her heel and wrenched it toward the ground. "It feels like your feet will slip out of the stirrups but it's actually the only way to ensure that they don't." Phoenix grimaced. Usually, she did so well in her studies but riding horses required so many small body movements and posture changes she believed she would never understand. Gritting her teeth, she pushed her heels down as far as they could go.

"Better," her teacher said. "Now stand up."

"What?" Phoenix gasped before she could stop herself.

"I said stand up," he said again with a wicked grin.

Taking a deep breath, Phoenix extended her legs. She made it a few inches out of the saddle, let out a whoop, and promptly dropped back into the saddle as she lost her balance. The horse snorted, flicked his ears, and turned his head to look at her with what was unmistakably a glare.

"I said stand up not break your horse's back. Now stand again."

Phoenix lifted herself up more carefully checking her balance as she went. Once she was fully out of the saddle, she locked her muscles to stay there.

"Good, now let go of your reins and raise your hands."

Phoenix looked at her teacher in disbelief but she did as she was instructed. She wobbled and clamped her legs on the horse's sides for support.

Suddenly the horse moved forward. Letting out a yelp, Phoenix dropped into the saddle once more. Her weight suddenly slamming into his back surprised her horse into a canter. Phoenix lost her balance completely and she was bounced out of the saddle. Her training kicked in and she rolled to her feet panting.

"Your heels weren't down," her teacher said. The horse had come to a stop right next to him and had his eyes closed in bliss as the man scratched him between the ears.

"He moved," Phoenix complained.

"You told him to," her instructor responded with infinite patience.

"No I…"

Her instructor cut her off. "Get back on the horse," he said.

With a sigh of resignation, she shuffled her way over to the horse like a sullen child.

That thought brought her back to a halt. She was acting like a frustrated three-year-old standing with arms crossed and cheeks puffed out in stubborn resistance. *Am I that petty?* She stood there a moment longer and decided this was not how she would ride a horse. Rather than resisting because of frustration, she would grow up. Her spine straightened and her shoulders squared and relaxed. As she started walking to the horse once more, her steps were surer. Phoenix swung herself up into the saddle. Her legs relaxed with her heels down and her feet firmly in the stirrups.

"So the legendary Phoenix has finally shown up to learn." The sarcasm dripping from her teacher's words was softened by his smile. "This isn't an easy thing to do. There is a lot to think about at once and oftentimes reflex and instinct are wrong. Let's start again. Stand in your stirrups."

Phoenix stood and tried not to squeeze the horse. She was so focused on balance and holding her position that she almost fell over when she felt her teacher grab her leg. "Put your foot here," he dragged her foot toward the horse's hind leg by about two inches, "and it should become easier." Phoenix felt the explosion of support that leg now had and moved her other foot to mimic the position. "Good. Now relax your leg a little bit and your heel should drop even further." Phoenix allowed herself to relax. "Very good. Now take your hands off again." There was no wobble or falling back into the saddle this time. "How do you feel?" he asked.

Phoenix thought about it for a moment and said, "Like I am not going to fall off again."

"That is exactly what we want. Now sit gently. Do not slam into his back." Carefully she allowed her knees to bend and the only sign the horse gave that he noticed she was there was one ear turning to face her. "We are ready to move now. Remember where your feet need to be, keep your heels down, and grab the reins. Give him a little click of your tongue and a tight squeeze with your ankles."

The horse moved slowly forward. Phoenix let out the breath she hadn't realized she was holding as he did not start running off again. She had ridden this horse every day for a month and she felt like she hadn't learned anything in that time. Suddenly, she was more relaxed and so was the horse. She could appreciate the way his back move and his one ear stayed steadily pointed at her while the other flicked around catching sounds from all the other activity around them.

It seemed like hours later when her teacher said, "That's enough for today. Take him back to his stall, untack him, and groom him really well."

Phoenix carefully dismounted and pulled the reins over his head. He closed his eyes in pleasure as she lightly scratched his forehead as her teacher had done earlier in the day. The she walked him into the stable. First his tack came off and she grabbed some brushes. Hawk had shown Phoenix how to groom a horse during their travels and she lost herself in the task. Her nose was full of the indescribable horse scent, her hands felt his hair go from coarse to silky, and all she heard was his relaxed breathing. Phoenix could take her time with her horse because, although she was supposed to be having lunch, she could eat very quickly or wait until dinner. She heaved a sigh of regret when she had to clean up and prepare for her dance lesson.

Phoenix left the stable, ran to her room, and washed her face and hands free of dry sweat and horse musk. While she donned her gown for the lesson and quickly straightened up her hair, she grabbed an oat cake. *That will hold me over until dinner,* she hoped. She grabbed the heeled shoes that matched her gown and trotted out of the room in her bare feet.

"Ah, there she is," came a hiss.

Phoenix instantly stopped and her skirts swirled around her at the sudden change in momentum. Slowly, she turned to face the speaker and was unsurprised to see the spoiled little puppy.

"You actually look like a lady. You belong in a dress, raising little children, and leaving men's work to men. You don't belong here." His contempt for her felt like a slap in the face.

"That's funny," Phoenix snapped back, "if I am out of place here then what does that make you? You went down so quickly yesterday I thought you might just break from a poke." She saw death in his eyes as she attacked his fighting ability. She shifted her feet for better balance and focused her gaze on his face while really concentrating on his chest to watch for the inevitable attack.

"I will make you pay for that, wench," he spat.

She said nothing, just stood there and waited. He was breathing quickly and looked confused. After twenty heartbeats passed, Phoenix realized why he hadn't moved yet. He was trying to provoke her into striking first because he didn't understand his actions for himself. The young man was all spirit but his confronting her confused even his high strung mind. He couldn't believe he was actually speaking to her like that.

Taking a deep breath, Phoenix decided to head off the battle. "We do not need to fight today," she said. "I know you are upset about what happened the other day but it was the other day. There is no reason for blood to spill over nothing. I did what I had to do to survive but that is no reason for us to not be friends. If you want to hit me, I wouldn't blame you but you won't land the punch." She sighed and shrugged, "If you'd like, after dinner, we can sit down and discuss our sparring match and get to know one another. I am fairly certain that the views of women you just expressed aren't your true feelings so I will let that slide." She turned to start back toward the hall where she would soon be dancing no matter what he chose to do.

"Wait! You can't just walk away from me!" He grabbed her arm and turned her around. "You cannot be allowed to humiliate me like that."

"You already fought me once and I would love to repeat the experience but I don't want to be late. A bit of advice, though, for the next time we meet up for a fight, don't be cocky or let your emotions get the better of you. That will make you a better fighter." She peered deep into his eyes. "Fighting is not about winning, it's about surviving." With that she snatched her arm out of his grip and made her way to her lesson. She glanced behind her once to see him with looking at the floor lost in thought.

"Chess is all about moves and countermoves. You must think twenty moves ahead of your opponent. It is all about cause and effect. If you control the cause, you create the effect. That is what makes a true tactician." The Shadow Man lifted his bishop and moved it three squares to the left along the diagonal.

Tiger still had not forgiven him for allowing Phoenix to die but their mission was too important for it to hinge on the life on one person. Recently, his old friend had taken to teaching him the game of chess. Although Tiger found it fascinating, he acted like he resented the time spent on what a normal person would consider tedium. He studied the board for a long moment and moved one of the rooks three spaces to the right.

The Shadow Man smiled wickedly. "That move only takes two of my possible moves into consideration," he said. "By your reasoning, I should move my pawn here to block your attack on my queen." He pointed at the square on the board. "Your response would logically be to move your knight to this spot and then I need to move my own knight here to protect my king. What you haven't considered is if I move this pawn instead of that one. That way, if you take my queen, I get my revenge on your rook with a lowly pawn. So, instead, you move your bishop to assist the cornering of my queen and my knight is perfectly placed to thwart that attack." He drummed his fingers on the table and studied his pupil's expression of dismay. "That is what I mean by thinking twenty steps ahead. You are getting better at it but it will take time. At least you have the knack for it. Otherwise, this would be a hopeless exercise." He fell silent and moved his knight. Tiger looked up in confusion and settled in to determine his next move.

An hour and three games later, Tiger's brain physically hurt. *How can anyone think about that much at one time?* His mentor had proven time and again that he could envision every possible variation and gambit. It wasn't that Tiger was frustrated with the slow progress at the game of chess or even at the larger game of tactics, the struggle was worth it, in and of itself, simply because it distracted him from his grief and pain. He also enjoyed the challenge.

Many people think a life of privilege and luxury is a dream of perfection. Tiger had lived that dream all of his life and hungered for the struggles of humanity. He watched on in jealousy as his agents were sent to the slums and the darkest, most hard hit corners of the kingdom. Everything had been handed to him on an embroidered pillow all of his life and he wanted to struggle to succeed for himself.

He wanted to go to the slums and infiltrate a group of thugs. He wanted to work as a man who could barely pay for the food on his table let alone the clothes on his back. He wanted to understand his people but they had lived these lives while he had eaten from the most delicate of dishes with the most intricately wrought diningware made of precious metals. He desired nothing more than to escape his cage of privilege to discover these unknown trials and tribulations.

Tiger decided he needed to get some air. He checked that his knives were within easy reach and headed out into the street. He was not concerned about anybody attacking him. He would have honestly welcomed the distraction.

While he mulled over thoughts about his subjects and what it would be like to be one of them, he did not take the time to watch where he was walking. He knew the streets of the city so well at this point that if he ever looked up to get his bearings he would instantly know where he was and how he would get back to the palace. He also was well aware that Hawk ensured he was tailed wherever he went so he was doubly unable to get lost. She had recently doubled his shadows because of the threat on the manor from his uncle.

He walked past a group of beggar children and absently scattered some small coins on the ground for them to find. He was unconsciously cautious of letting the children know where the money came from but it still made him feel better knowing that they would probably be able to buy a morsel to eat before any of the city's criminals could stop them.

A hand tugging on his trouser leg suddenly brought him back to reality. He looked down and saw a woman in her middle years. Her sandy colored hair was knotted so badly that individual strands were not noticeable. It was a mass of clumps. Her face was wizened and stretched like old leather. He was surprised to see a woman of her age living on the streets. The beggar's game was for the children not adults.

"Do you have any money to spare?" she asked. "I cannot work as a laundress anymore and I have no money for food. I would take bread if you have any of that instead."

"I am sorry, ma'am," Tiger replied.

"That's too bad, lad. Times are getting tougher around here what with the regent allowing his guards to use common folk as punching bags and the prince not giving two shits what happens to his people." She laughed manically and turned away. "Best you be getting home before dark, child. That's when the bad ones come out to play," she called over her shoulder.

"Wait," he said reaching out toward her.

"What?" she demanded.

"Turns out I do have a bit of money. Will you allow me to treat you to some supper? I want to talk to you about something." He held out his arm in a gesture of support and respect.

"Supper?" she asked, licking her chops.

"Yes, in one of the finer eateries in this part of the city."

"Very well then, lad, lead on."

He walked her to the best inn in that area of the city and requested a quiet table for dinner. After supplying the silver, the pair was served two meals of goose and steamed vegetables and each had a drink.

"I want to hear your story," said Tiger simply.

"Why would you want to hear about me? Usually when a rich man buys dinner for a poor woman he is expecting something entirely different. I may be getting old, boy, but that just means I have more experience in what makes a man feel good." She grinned and Tiger saw she was missing three teeth and two others were chipped.

"Let's just say I have a vested interest."

"I'll not say a word until you answer my question properly"

Tiger sighed. "I come from a powerful family and am soon to inherit the title. I have come to realize in the past few weeks that I do not have a grasp on the needs of the people. It is hard to figure out what the people who look to you need when you are spoon fed anything you may need or want or not know you want."

"Wise for your years, lad, very wise. Very well, I will accept that argument." She took a large swig of her drink. "I was a maid in the house of a rich merchant as a young girl. Those rich folk love to have child companions for their daughters. They think it is good practice for having children of their own. Let me tell you, those girls are brats from the moment they leave their mother's wombs. They are born to be conceited and mean." She coughed.

"My father could not support all of his children so we had to get employment at young ages. Going to school was not an option no matter what the king said about bettering ourselves making the kingdom a better place to live in. School isn't worth a damn without the jobs to back it up. Merchants don't need school. They are just born into the right families or marry into them and make all of the money. The rest of us just have to find what work we can. Anyway, I was the maid to this little bitch of a merchant girl. Her mother would hit me instead of the child whenever she acted up and I had to endure haircuts that made it look like someone had taken a sword to my hair rather than scissors. I was smacked, whipped, and beaten. When I came of an age to be a young woman, roundabouts thirteen years old, the father of my mistress became interested. His wife was a whore and would not satisfy his manly needs."

"One night, he grabbed my arm and told me if I did not spread my legs for him, I would lose my position in his house. I was impressionable and, even though I knew that I didn't want to have anything to do with the man, losing my position in the household was not an option. Needless to say, he raped me that night and I went home weeping. I couldn't tell my father and when I tried to talk to my mother, she pretended to not hear me."

The old woman took another drink before continuing. "I got pregnant from either that night or one of the nights following that my master pulled me aside. For the first few months, I had no idea what was happening, after all I had only bled once. When my stomach started showing, my mistress got wise to what was going on between her husband and me. Of course, it wasn't his fault, it was mine. I led him on and teased him with my womanly whiles. Not only did I lose my position that day, I lost my baby when the guards she had called into the house beat me in the alley. After beating me, they took turns raping me.”

“This was just after the king had died and his brother had taken up the regency. The regent is a devil, he is. He has decided that if you do not have money, you don’t deserve to live. He thinks that it only takes hard work to make money but he hasn’t had to do the work I have had to do to try and keep my belly full.”

“After I lost that position, I tried other jobs as maids. The problem is that rich ladies are always talking to one another. My first mistress told all of her rich lady friends that I had seduced her husband and had the gall to get pregnant from him. Once I had had the baby, I expected him to take care of the both of us but luckily I had a miscarriage and they had been saved the embarrassment. I never worked as a house maid again.”

“I eventually ended up working in the laundry at the palace. I still cannot believe I worked for the man who is ruining the kingdom.” She took another swig of her drink and fell silent for a few moments. Tiger allowed her to catch her breath. He ate quietly while she thought.

“The regent decided that he only wanted to be surrounded by beauty.” Tiger almost jumped in surprise as she suddenly spoke again. “He said that only the pretty women were welcome in his palace. They were the only worthy companions for his daughter and the only ones who would ever touch her clothing. For the second time in my life, I lost my position, my income, and my livelihood. I was forced onto the streets. I couldn’t pay for my lodging or my food. After some time spent starving, I turned to satisfying the carnal needs of the city guard. You don’t need a pretty face to sleep with a man and they don’t give a damn what the woman looks like. So long as they have somewhere to stick their dick.”

Tiger resisted the urge to reach out and grab her hand. Instead, he took another sip of his drink. How could he not know what his uncle had done to these poor people? He knew the man was power mad didn't want to give up the throne to his nephew but he did not realize he had abused his power to this extent. *How did he get the backing in the government for these policies?*

He placed a few coins on the table. "Thank you for talking to me. Allow me to compensate you for your time." She snatched the coins and left him to his thoughts. He saw the defiance in her eyes and for the first time, truly understood it.

Fang carefully peered at the new student over his morning bowl of porridge. He was well aware that it was rude but he was just so curious. Fang had gotten very good at hiding who he was and thought that hiding his true self would be how he spent the rest of his life. Then this girl comes waltzing in and proves to this testosterone filled group that women can fight and play the game just as well as men.

The persona of Fang had been built so long ago that he almost believed he was who he said he was. The mask was becoming the reality. Now that Phoenix was here, however, he could reveal who he really was, or rather who she really was.

She had been watching Phoenix for days and decided that she would pull her aside and extend the olive branch. She started to stand when a hand pressed her back down. "Hold it, little man," a voice said. Fang looked up to see Druj.

"Druj, what do you want?" Fang asked in her husky man voice.

"I've been watching her, too. I want her gone and I want your help to do it," he replied.

Fang looked him up and down. "Is there any particular reason or is it simply that she is a better fighter than you? I mean she did kick your ass, thoroughly, her first day in training." She knew it was probably the wrong thing to say and would make them enemies but that's the way the game was played. She could not show any weakness to the men in this place.

She moved to stand again and, once more, he placed a hand on her shoulder, this time with a more vice-like grip. "You can't talk to me like that, little man," he said. His voice was dark and she could tell he was trying to be threatening but he just sounded like a toddler throwing a temper tantrum.

"I can talk to you anyway I like. The problem is that if you are trying to threaten someone, you need to have the upper hand and you don't." She yanked away from his grip and left the table.

Druj was not one for letting things go but Fang knew his kind. They were all bluster and bully but when they found somebody that they couldn't overpower with attitude alone or with physical violence that is heavily skewed in their favor, the hot air that filled their heads became insignificant and they don't know what to do in that situation. Druj would be angry at Fang for a long time for daring to defy him and it would become his personal mission to get the power back.

She let the problem wash off of her back as she walked away. Her real problem of the moment was how to introduce herself to Phoenix. She also needed to decide whether to introduce herself as Fang, her male persona, or as Ruadana, her real self.

Ruadana was a runaway from the capital city. She fell in with the wrong crowd as a child. If she didn't earn her keep, she didn't eat and most often she played the role of bed warmer to one of the more powerful crime lords in order to pay off her debts. At a very young age, she discovered that panhandling wouldn't bring in enough money to keep her out of the beds of the nasty old men or the violent young ones. She started out stealing belt purses and moved on from there until she was breaking into houses in the middle of the night for the big money making thefts. She learned to protect herself as she got older. Ruadana always had a blade on her person and, after a few years, fended off unwanted advances.

By the time she was twenty, she had made quite the name for herself. The major crime lords wanted her in their camps to enhance their wealth and low level henchmen, the nobodies of the underworld, started congregating around her. It was as though they thought her skills and the infamous quality of her name would rub off on them. Ruadana didn't like the attention. She didn't want to ally herself with any of the other criminals in the city; she just wanted to survive and eventually hoped to make an honest living for herself. When she turned down every criminal in the city it was a declaration of war in their eyes. They felt that she was trying to rule over them all and they were having none of it. She woke up one day to find that there was a price on her head. That was the day she left and months later found herself at the Citadel of Assassins.

In the year and a half that she had been there, she had played the role of a man the entire time and kept her head down. She was a master fighter and was gaining proficiency in coded languages by the day but she didn't want to be noticed. She had been noticed enough for one lifetime.

Now she had a decision to make. Did she allow herself to be noticed or did she keep her head down and stick to the shadows? Phoenix had come into her life with a bang. Ruadana hadn't thought the instructors or students would accept a woman in their midst then Phoenix came along and proved her wrong.

As she was caught up in her musings, Ruadana wandered in the direction of her room. Her senses went on red alert though as she sensed someone stepping out of the shadows behind her. Ruadana slipped a dagger from her wrist sheath in preparation for an attack.

"You may as well put it away," said a female voice.

"Phoenix," sighed Fang, "you really shouldn't sneak up on the people here. We are trained to attack surprises."

"No, we are trained to respond to surprises. As you just proved, we evaluate the danger before acting." Ruadana turned and saw Phoenix's smile. "Now, can we discuss something pretty pressing?"

Ruadana just stood there waiting to hear what Phoenix would say. As she waited, she got the first good look at the newest student. Phoenix was lithely built, tall for a woman, with red hair and almond shaped eyes that were a deep deep blue or perhaps purple with silver flecks embedded in the color. She was the picture of classic beauty combined with lethality. She had high cheekbones, a small nose, and a rounded chin. Her hair was longer than fashion dictated but she kept it tied back and out of the way.

Phoenix finally spoke again cutting into Ruadana's scrutiny. "What I want to know is why a woman of your caliber and skill would hide in the guise of a man. You are better than most of the students here yet you keep your head down and stick to the middle of the pack. So what are you doing?"

"How?" began Ruadana, then she paused. She was always so careful about what she said. Many of the men thought she was slow but it was a matter of thinking before speaking and making sure to pitch her voice lower to mimic a man's. "How did you know I am a woman?" she finally asked in her normal voice.

"There are a few signs that men generally overlook or attribute to other things. For instance, the way you move is a good indication that you are definitely not what you seem. Your fluidity could simply be because of your training in the martial arts but there is an element of it that is simply feminine. Men have certain movements that do not come as naturally as women because of how they are built and yet they seem second nature to you. Added to that, you don't swim with them in the summer or bathe in the community bath house according to the men I have spoken to. It really isn't all that hard to figure it out, Fang." It seemed so simple when Phoenix said it out loud but Ruadana winced as she realized just how flimsy her character of Fang had really been. "Don't worry. The men haven't put it together. They just think you are eccentric and considering the kinds of people this line of work requires, they have accepted your story at face value. Fang is exactly who he says he is to the men here."

"Ruadana, not Fang."

"Ruadana?" asked Phoenix in surprise.

"You have heard of me." It was a statement not a question.

"You were one of the best criminals in the city, not to mention the most honorable. But then you disappeared. Rumor was you were killed by one of the other criminals because you refused to join him."

"I left when I discovered that my life was in danger. Usually I don't shy away from a battle but I was tired of that life anyway," Ruadana explained.

"So what are you planning on doing with yourself here?" Phoenix asked. "Are you going to keep hiding or will you stand with me against these men? I saw you talking to the idiot that I humiliated during my trials and I know he wants me dead for that. I could use a friend."

"He really does not like you at all. He is trying to enlist help in going after you and, because I haven't come out in support of you yet, he came to me. Druj is just a bully and everybody here knows that. The problem is that there are enough young men who he can overpower that he can become a threat."

Phoenix chuckled. "Does this mean that if he decides to move against me I can count on your help?" she asked.

"I think that is a fair assumption," Ruadana said with a smile.

"I will help you in return or at least give you some advice. You should tell the men who you really are and you should stop holding back. You are one of the most powerful fighters here, embrace that fact."

Together, they walked out of the building toward the trainee's study. They were laughing and sharing stories as they walked. It felt good to finally have somebody to confide in. Ruadana had lived so long in loneliness that, although she didn't trust Phoenix, it was nice to have her there.

***

Quint just looked at them with naked astonishment. *Fang is not a he? He's a she? How did I not know this?*

"Hmm…why…" he couldn't wrap his head around the concept of Fang being a woman. A woman named Ruadana. A woman he had heard of, a criminal, thought to be dead was standing before him in the guise of a man.

"I didn't make it easy for you," said Ruadana with a tentative smile.

"I just thought you were an extremely private man. I mean, we all are but I just figured that your history made you slightly more eccentric than most." He shrugged and continued to study Ruadana.

"She no longer wants to hide," Phoenix said.

"To be honest, after more than a year of playing a man, I am losing who I am. It won't be too long before I am exposed, in more ways than one, and I want to avoid any embarrassment on my part and on the part of the leaders here. It hasn't been easy maintaining the façade but until Phoenix arrived, I thought it was necessary." She looked at Quint imploringly. She wanted ever so much for him to forgive her. She had been so nervous about telling him her secret that her stomach was still tied in knots.

"We need to speak to Syril," he said after a moment.

"Do we?" Ruadana squeaked. She was not ready to tell the leader of a school of assassins that she had deceived him for eighteen months.

"He is right, Ruadana," Phoenix chipped in. "I know you are nervous, Ru, but the establishment is going to discover your, erm, particular disposition at some point." Ruadana sighed heavily and her shoulders sagged. Arlaya poked her and winked. "You will be just fine," she said. "After all, isn't this what we are trained to do? Play a role to such perfection that those around us cannot tell it is a disguise?"

Ruadana squared her shoulders and raised her chin. "I was once the most infamous criminal in the capital city. Men were killing themselves to be in my company. Now, I have been learning to be an assassin for the past year and a half. The entire time, my life has been dictated by an old man who has been nothing but a father and a mentor to me since I arrived. How can I be so afraid to tell him the truth? Fear is not something I am accustomed to." She stood even straighter and started to march toward the door. "What are you wankers waiting for? Syril's office is this way."

Phoenix and Quint smiled at each other and followed Ruadana down the hall. He leaned over and whispered in Phoenix's ear, "Ru?"

"It's easier than saying Ruadana every time. It definitely suits her, don't you think?" Phoenix whispered back.

"Ru, slow down, girl," Quint called to her back with a smile. "Syril isn't going anywhere. He will be watching over the martial arts classes all morning."

"I think she just wants to avoid losing her nerve," mumbled Phoenix.

They suddenly emerged from the gloomy halls to the bright sunlight approximately a hundred yards from the stretching men. Syril and the other instructors were clustered together nearby. Ruadana froze as the sun hit her face. Her determination flooded out of her muscles and she became a statue.

Quint leaned over to whisper on Phoenix's ear, "I think she just lost her nerve." He chuckled and poked Ruadana in the small of her back. She took a hesitant step forward and stopped again.

Quint's eyebrows rose. He was still trying to understand how Fang could be a woman. The man he knew had never been indecisive or intimidated before. He placed his hand on her back and pushed.

Ruadana stumbled and shuffled forward to prevent herself from falling. Syril and the other instructors looked up at the unexpected movement. To say they studied the odd trio with curiosity would have been an understatement.

Syril met Quint's eyes. There was a question hiding in their depths and Quint nodded. They had been together so long that Syril trusted Quint without question, well, without many questions. Syril nodded back and said something quietly to his peers. They all nodded and turned to the stretching trainees while Syril walked over to Ruadana, Quint, and Phoenix.

"To what do I owe this pleasure?" he asked them with humor in his tone.

"Syril," Ruadana gasped. She opened her mouth to say more but couldn't find the words.

"Yes, Syril. Goodness, Fang, you may not speak as much as the others but I have never seen you lost for words." Syril smiled.

"That's the thing, Syril." Ruadana tried to start again. The silence hovered in the air like discomfort incarnate.

Finally, Syril cleared his throat with a touch of impatience. Ruadana took a deep breath and said, "You see, Fang is more of a mystery than you ever thought." She shook her head and forced herself to stand straighter and report to her superior properly. "My name is not Fang," she said.

Syril laughed. "There are not many men here who go by their actual name."

"There is one fewer than anyone here was aware of," Ruadana said quickly before the butterflies in her stomach did anything more to stop her.

"I beg your pardon?" Syril asked in confusion.

"What he is trying to say, sir, is that he is in fact not a he at all," Quint supplied.

Syril coughed delicately. "And your name is, dear?"

"Ruadana," she replied.

"You don't seem surprised," Arlaya said carefully.

"We all have our secrets," replied Syril, "some of them are just easier to suss out." He turned back to Ruadana. "I am very happy that you have finally come clean, child."

"You knew?" Ruadana asked incredulously.

"I knew," he said simply.

"How?"

"Probably the same way Phoenix figured it out." He turned to the newest recruit. "I assume it was you who figured it out. Sorry, Quint. I know you liked Fang and I wasn't going to ruin the friendship for you. Besides, you have been doing this long enough that you should have seen the signs." Quint looked at his feet for a moment and Phoenix could have sworn she saw his cheeks take on a pinkish hue.

Quint looked like he was going to say something but Phoenix stepped on his foot before a single sound came out his mouth. He glared at her but shut his mouth.

"I was so nervous about telling you," Ruadana said. "I thought you might try to kill me."

Syril laughed again. "No, child, we won't kill you. Your fellow students might once you tell them but we will not." He immediately stopped laughing when he saw her face. "Do not worry. There is not a chance we will let anyone kill you over this paltry matter." Syril patted Ruadana's shoulder as she tentatively smiled up at her mentor.

"Now they have two women to beat them up," said Phoenix with a laugh.

Phoenix was so focused on the text that the letters and notes started blurring before her eyes. She leaned back and rubbed her face. "I need to take a break," she said to the empty air. She stood and stretched, relishing every pop in her back as her spine realigned itself. After looking at the calm night outside, Phoenix decided she would go for a walk.

Her candles were burned down to stubs so on her walk she would raid the storage cupboard for new ones. Thus, she had an excuse for wandering the halls. She stepped out into the silent hallway. A hush lay over the house like a thick comfortable blanket.

Phoenix breathed in the quiet, brought it within her soul. She had been working so hard since coming to the citadel and she'd forgotten what it was like to take a moment just for herself. Her feet took her on a meandering journey through the halls, gardens, and courtyards. At one point, Phoenix found herself sitting on top of the outer wall and she spent an hour meditating to relax her mind. After a little more wandering, she decided it was time to grab the candles and return to her rooms. The next day was a day of rest for the trainees so, although it was nearing dawn, she was not concerned about missing out on sleep.

Before she could get to the communal supply closet, the hairs on the back of her neck stood straight up. Her heart started beating faster, pumping adrenalin to her muscles. She may be tired and ready for bed but whoever was attempting to sneak up on her would get a nasty surprise. Her ears pricked at the sounds of the night as she continued her casual stroll toward the cupboard. Her eyes scanned for any sign of movement in the shadows.

There was nothing her eyes or ears could tell her. She knew someone was out there but she could not locate them. Her nostrils flared in frustration and anticipation of the fight that would undoubtedly come. The flaring of the nostrils brought forth the smell of sweat and something she could not quite identify. She tilted her head slightly in the direction of the scent and finally saw a shadow that was almost imperceptibly denser than the rest around it.

Now, she had a target. Not fearing attack, she hadn't brought any of her weapons but she was just as skilled in unarmed combat as she was with weapons. In fact, she had more experience being unarmed and she was ready for her assailant.

Whoever it was kept flitting through the shadows following her. Phoenix did not understand why he didn't just attack. She wasn't doing anything that he could report on. It was almost as though whoever it was following her hadn't thought through what they were doing. Her next footstep had a slight hesitation in it as she realized that was exactly what was happening. Her assailant had seen her wandering around and decided to act without any forward planning. That made the upcoming engagement even more deadly because he would be desperate.

Her nerves stretched to the point of snapping as she waited for him to make his move. When he finally did, she felt a jolt of surprise. She had almost succumbed to the thought that he had lost his nerve. Instead, her assailant bull rushed her. Her only warning was the whisper of his feet on the floor. He made no other sounds.

Using his momentum against him, she swung him over her hip with a quiet grunt of effort. He rolled and jumped to his feet. A blade appeared in his hand and she jumped back as he swung. The steel glinted in the moonlight as he prepared to close the distance again.

She felt the kiss of the blade across her stomach but it was only a momentary annoyance as she focused on his next movements. She quickly recognized who her attacker was. It was Druj. Apparently, he was not going to accept her offer for peace. She had thought that might be the case when he didn't join her for that conversation about her martial trials.

He had been working very hard in the fighting circles over the past few weeks apparently. He had also been watching Phoenix as she worked because he was taking advantage every hole in her defense.

She was starting to tire of this fight. He was dancing just out of reach of her punches and dodged in as she completed her movements to land his own.

Phoenix's hands and forearms were covered in cuts as she jumped back and watched her foe. She had been fighting him with her usual gusto and watchfulness. He was weak on the left side but made every effort to compensate with his right.

Taking a deep breath, Phoenix decided that in order to not be defeated, she would have to change the rules of the game. She rushed Druj, throwing him off balance. He blocked just a fraction of a second too slowly. He raised his knife and she flipped the blade back toward his sternum.

Druj fell backward and Phoenix landed on top of him. He stiffened and his face acquired an odd expression. His hips heaved upward and Phoenix was thrown clear of him. She landed on her knees three feet away as Druj stood up. His knife was sunk deep within his chest.

Phoenix knew that without quick medical attention and quite a bit of luck, Druj would not be able to survive such a ghastly wound. Despite the fatality of his situation, Druj continued to advance on her.

There was a strange light in his eyes; a desperation. If he was going to die then so was she. Slowly he pulled the knife out and held the slick handle in an offensive position. He jabbed at her before she could stand but she simply rolled to avoid the blow.

Before she could recover her feet, he jumped on her. She felt his hot blood seeping onto her back and she twisted until she faced him. Her hands, slick with blood from her wounds and his, found their way to his throat. He may have been bleeding out but he still had his strength and he was taller and heavier than she and he had desperation on his side. He pushed down on her and strived to slam her into the ground to loosen her grip.

It took longer than she'd expected, but after a few moments of their struggle, Druj started trembling. His grip on her weakened and his muscles started going slack. Phoenix kept her eyes on his. She knew from her studies what was supposed to happen. Druj would lose consciousness from lack of air and blood loss and his skin and lips would take on a blue tint. When she saw the light leave his eyes, she held on for at least two more minutes to ensure Druj's death.

She stood up in horror at what she had done. Her hand automatically rose to cover her mouth and she almost gagged as the smell of the blood and the coppery taste filled her senses. Quickly, she dropped her hand and her eyes widened as she looked around. Surely somebody had heard the struggle. After all, they were trained to react to any noise from even the deepest of sleep. Seeing no one, she felt the adrenaline pumping and ran through the halls.

***

Phoenix was back in her rooms. She had run here directly from her fight with Druj. He was lucky he was dead. It was the first time she had killed someone without being in a true battle situation but she would have killed him again, no matter how she felt about the act of taking a life. She could still see the light leave his eyes. His death rattle echoed in her ears. She felt his muscles go slack over and over and over again.

Nobody knew about their fight but they would soon find Druj's body. Once they did, they would either kill her or throw her out. She was dreading the look of disappointment in Quint's face. He had stressed to her the camaraderie that was cultivated by the instructors at the citadel. They emphasized being able to work together as well as successfully conquering solo missions. She felt like a failure. The Shadow Man and Tiger had been counting on her and, in one fell swoop, she ruined everything.

She looked around at her rooms. Everything was neat as a pin. The extravagance she had experienced in her first week had already been whittled down by her conservatism and minimalistic tendencies. She started mentally packing her belongings.

She was just finishing her list of the few things she wanted when there was a knock at the door. Phoenix flinched and her pulse sped up. *Stop being such a child. It's part of the job.* She took a deep breath and opened the door to see Quint standing there with a smile on his face. After chiding herself, she felt calm and looked at her mentor with a natural looking smile of her own.

Quint's smile quickly fell off of his face as he took in her appearance. "What has happened?" he asked in a husky, no nonsense voice.

"What do you mean?" Phoenix replied.

"Ari, look at yourself. Obviously something happened and you will tell me what it was right now. I will brook no lies nor half-truths in this matter."

Phoenix looked at the state of her clothing and body. Her hands were crisscrossed with cuts from Druj's blade and her dress was in tatters.

The wound in her abdomen had stopped bleeding but her clothes were a deep red with the drying blood. She did not doubt that her face was bruised and her hair was a mess.

"I had an altercation," she explained with a sigh.

"That much I could deduce for myself, thank you very much," Quint said satirically.

"I am fine, Quint," Phoenix uttered evasively.

Quint gripped one of her blood soaked hands and rubbed his thumb across her skin. "Child, I mean you no harm. Just tell me what happened. Stop trying to avoid the subject. Nothing is secret here. We will eventually discover what has occurred and if you conceal the truth things will not be pleasant for you." He lifted his other hand to her face and cupped her cheek like a father or uncle might.

Phoenix felt the support he was offering but could not find the words to tell him what had happened between Druj and her in the halls. Her mouth worked but sounds just refused to come out. Quint just watched her as she battled her internal demons and nerves. His patience was almost as scary to her as what she had done to Druj. She counted to one hundred and completed a deep breathing exercise before she was ready to speak.

"I was attacked while I was walking through the grounds. I couldn't sleep and I was getting a headache from studying that text." She swallowed and thought through her next words very carefully. "It was Druj," she whispered finally.

Quint's eyes hardened and he slowly released her hand as he realized where she was going with her story. He grabbed the cut in her shirt and lifted it slowly to reveal her wound. It wasn't bleeding but it was raw and ugly. He lowered her shirt and gripped her hands again. The lacerations were clearly defensive.

"He did not survive the experience," Phoenix breathed with a hard expression. She felt an odd mixture of hatred and regret for what had happened. She knew that Druj would never have been a friend but he needn't have died. His own stupidity and arrogance created that night's events.

"Tell me everything," Quint commanded.

"I was studying the text. I do that when I cannot sleep. It helps me clear my mind and relax but tonight it wasn't working. I got so frustrated at not being able to translate the code. I decided it would be a good idea to take a step back. It's a nice night so I went for a walk. I justified it by saying I needed more candles." She babbled on for a few more minutes about the inconsequential moments before Druj attacked her. She didn't want to have to relive what had happened.

"Phoenix, report," Quint ordered, interrupting her dithering.

She jumped and snapped to attention. "I realized someone was following me as I approached the supply cupboard," she said without emotion. In order to give him the full details of what happened, she forced herself to detach from the emotions. "He rushed me and I managed to throw him off of me. He pulled a knife and you can see the damage he inflicted." She bared her stomach and showed him her arms. "He's been preparing for this fight since the first day when I defeated him. I only managed to defeat him because I did what nobody with my skill or of my size would ever think of doing. I rushed him and turned his own weapon on him. Even with the knife sticking out of his chest, he continued to fight. I was forced to strangle him." She stopped speaking and stood there simply processing.

Quint stood. "You defended yourself, Ari. There is no need to be afraid of us." He crossed the room and wet a cloth. Returning to Phoenix, he started cleaning her hands. "You will not be attacked again. You will not be killed. You will not be exiled. Druj made a mistake and we all know one tiny mistake can end our lives. I will go to Syril now and tell him of what has happened. Stay in your room today and try to clean up. Rest and recuperate. I will return to help dress your wounds. You will have no consequences from us." He stood once more and left.

Phoenix sat there for a few moments longer. Then she rose and heated water for a bath. She felt dirty and there was a feeling of insects crawling over her skin. Once the steamy water filled the tub, she added bath salts that smelled of lavender, her calming scent. The salt made her wounds sting but as long as she moved slowly, she could block out the pain. The real challenge came when she cleaned her stomach. The other smaller cuts caused her no issues but the larger abdominal laceration needed to be cleaned out carefully and she was picking off bits of dried blood to see the pink flesh that meant no infection had set it.

An hour later, she was clean and wearing new clothing. Her exhaustion was catching up with her and she settled herself on her bed. That was where Quint found her some time later. He carefully dressed her cuts without waking her and pulled her blanket over her sleeping form. Once that was done, he settled in to watch over his friend.

***

A handsome face swam in front of her eyes. His brown hair was slightly longer than was fashionable and there was a spark of humor is his deep chocolate colored eyes. His smile was enormous and full of mischief. Phoenix felt her eyes fill with moisture.

The blackness of deep sleep started to surround that handsome face. The darkness was consuming the man. As sleep took hold, Phoenix felt a tear slip down her face. Her last thought was *I will never see him again.*

She jolted upright as she felt something touch her face. She rolled off the bed and landed in a crouch away from the intruder. Her visitor lit the candle by her bedside.

Quint's eyes flickered in the light. "You were crying," he said simply. He didn't move a muscle as though he knew how tightly wound she was.

Phoenix stood up slowly. "What are you doing here?" she asked.

"You shouldn't be alone after what happened. I've been here to make sure you are all right. I dressed your wounds and ordered up some food from the kitchens. If you are still concerned that you will be executed, I ordered enough for two and I will eat half. I promise you it's not poisoned." He shrugged and settled back into his seat.

"You have been watching me?"

"I'm your friend, it's in the job description," he replied jokingly. The smile melted off his face as he saw tears in Phoenix's eyes. "Druj brought about his own death, Ari. Remember that. You did exactly what you have been trained to do, you kept yourself alive. It's ok to laugh."

He handed her a cup of clear, cool water. Phoenix carefully took a small sip. Tasting nothing out of the ordinary, she succumbed to her body's desire and downed the rest of the cup in one gulp. Quint laughed and refilled her drink. He also handed her a cracker which Phoenix ate with gusto.

"Do you feel up to coming to the table for some dinner?" he asked.

"Let me change," Phoenix said. She started pulling off her blanket but stopped and looked at her friend.

"I'll wait outside, shall I?"

"Thank you," she whispered. When the door clicked shut, she pulled off the blanket and quickly changed into a pair of comfortable trousers and a loose fitting shirt. She opened the door to admit Quint into the room once more and he smiled down at her.

"I don't know about you, but I'm starving," he said. She laughed and sat down in front of the food.

Just as they were finishing their meal, there was a knock at the door. Quint opened the door and Syril stepped into the room. Phoenix jumped to her feet and snapped to attention.

"My dear, I came to confirm what I assume Quint has told you. You did your teachers credit and stayed alive when attacked. Druj is the only one responsible for his death." Syril placed a hand on her shoulder. "We have taken care of his remains and cleaned everything. You need not worry about repercussions." Phoenix was very careful not to show the relief she felt at his words and just nodded instead. He sat with her and asked her to recount the events of the previous night again. Every few minutes, he stopped her to ask a question but it was clear he was not blaming her for Druj's death. "Now let's get some supper." Syril said after what felt like an hour. He clapped his hand on her shoulder and the three of them walked to the dining hall. Even though she had eaten recently, Phoenix was once again hungry. Answering questions, telling a story, and healing was hard work.

It had been three months since she had killed Druj. Phoenix was able to look back at the incident with very little emotional attachment. She knew that what she had done was the right thing. She no longer had nightmares and she was able to go through her daily routine without a flashback or even thinking about what had happened.

She had continued in her studies. She was one of the best fighters in the citadel and her riding and dancing had improved by leaps and bounds. For the last month, she had been living without speaking a word. Instead, she used the sign language that was an essential part of assassin communication. Now, she graduated to speaking and using sign language at the same time to carry out two different conversations. It was difficult but she relished the challenge. She even felt she was making headway with the ancient text that Syril had asked her to decode.

The musical notes still confused her. She had absentmindedly started singing the notes and recognized the tune as one her mother had sung to her as a very small child. In a fit of excitement, she turned to a random page and started singing the notes on that page too. It was a song she had heard beggar children sing in the streets, an old ditty about a game played by the ancient tribes. She removed all of the words of the song from the jibberish and found she could read part of a message. It was a code within a code within a code.

She was sitting outside of Syril's office to tell him what she had discovered. She needed an old songbook to complete the translation. Hopefully there was one among the assassins. The first entry was a note which identified who the text was written by, the original ruler of Belevis.

Syril's door opened and he stepped out to greet his guest. "How are you today, Phoenix?" he asked in his gentle, caring voice.

"Syril," she said, "I have discovered the key." She could barely contain her excitement as she stood with the volume enveloped in her arms.

He looked at the eagerness in her face then at the book in her arms. "Are you saying you have translated the code?"

"Yes, part of it at least."

"Come in please." He gestured toward the inside of his office and guided her to a cushioned chair near the fireplace. "Tell me what you have discovered and how you finally broke through the code."

"This text contains music and words. What causes the code to be so effective is the nature of the music. There are no defining markers, no tempo, key, or even bars."

"Ah, you play and read music," Syril said thoughtfully.

"Yes. Thus, I knew what notes I was reading and started humming the tunes. Most of them I did not recognize but when I turned back to the first entry, I recognized the song. It was one my mother taught me when I was little." She started humming the melody and Syril smiled.

"I know that song as well. It's a very old lullaby," he said.

"Look at this first page sir and remove the lyrics to the lullaby," Phoenix replied.

Syril gently took the book and opened to the first page. After a few moments of reading, his face took on an odd look of contemplation, pride, and what seemed like a bit of awe. "This code is intriguing. It is definitely an old text. The first king of Belevis wrote these words."

"Yes and I think it is very important to finish the translation." Phoenix paused. "I need an old song book. I don't know every tune that is used in this code."

"We have no song books here but you will definitely find some on your next mission." Phoenix sat up straighter and looked at her mentor. "I have received a letter from the Shadow Man. He is recalling you to the city. Apparently, events are unfolding and your presence is needed earlier than expected." He held out a letter and she carefully took it from his grasp.

Scanning it, she saw the simplistic code that her employer used. Quickly, she realized that that simple code was not the full decryption of the message.

The first letter said, *Hello Phoenix. It is time for you to come home. Tiger is about to take on the Hyena. Make all due haste to return to the city.* The second letter, hidden within the first, said, *Child, come as you were born to be not as the common girl you thought you were.*

He wants the Lady Arlaya Rivell, Phoenix thought. *I know I can play the part but can I live the part? It is who I was born to be and who I have been prepared to be for the past year and more.* She turned her thought back to the handsome Tiger and all of her fears melted away. Her heart ached with the need to see him again. Tiger would help her figure out her new life. *Lirith,* she thought. *His name is Lirith.*

She looked up as Syril cleared his throat. "I understand you will be needing a rather extravagant wardrobe. Our seamstresses are used to fixing tears and making black skin tight suits but they are having fun with this assignment. You will receive your new clothes this afternoon." He smiled at the expression on her face.

Phoenix was not typically a clothes horse but she had always envied the beautiful gowns made of the finest shimmering silks that the rich girls would wear. The thought of feeling such fabric hug her curves made her as giddy as a young girl. Syril winked at her as he understood what was causing her expression.

"I have decided you will not be traveling alone. Fang, pardon me, Ruadana will be joining you. I do not believe the men will mind no longer having two women besting them at every physical challenge." He laughed. "I also want Quint to join you."

Phoenix looked at Syril thoughtfully. She had believed that Quint was like a son to Syril. Quint had so much respect for the old man that Phoenix doubted he would want to leave the citadel. She would be thankful to have the both of them with her no matter the circumstances. She had never felt like she had real friends. If she ever got close to somebody they would inevitably end up dead. She had stopped allowing herself to trust or build a relationship with anyone else. She didn't want that responsibility.

She had lived a very lonely life and in walked Ruadana and Quint. They had cracked through her armor and she allowed herself to become attached to the two of them. As she contemplated the matter, she realized Hawk and Tiger had also had the same effect on her. She suddenly acknowledged her growing list of friends, or more correctly, family.

"I have spoken to the two of them." Phoenix jumped as Syril's voice cut through her contemplation. "You three should be ready to leave in the morning."

Phoenix nodded at the obvious dismissal and stood. She had only a small amount of packing to do so she decided to visit her horse instead. Her feet carried her slowly through the halls toward the stables as she mulled over what she would have to do in the capital city. *I am Lirith's first line of defense, both politically and physically.*

She entered the stables and stood in the gloom for a few moments to let her eyes adjust. The smell of hay and dust filled her nostrils. There is no way to fully describe the scent of horses.

She heard a noise down the aisle. Her horse was sticking his head out through the stall guard and he was looking at her. The two of them had gotten very close over the past three months. He came to recognize her as his person and she felt a connection to him that was akin to what she thought a mother might feel for a son.

She quickly made her way toward him and stuck her face near his. Phoenix had learned his quirks very quickly. He would tuck his head around her back as she hugged him and run his lips over her cheeks and face in a kiss of sorts when she leaned in close. He loved to be scratched about six inches down his crest from his ears and right over the hip. He would lean in to the scratching or the curry comb to increase the pressure and relieve any itching. One of his greatest pleasures, however, was when she would rub the inside of his ears. He would drop his head to make the reach more comfortable for her and he was in ecstasy.

All she did in this moment was stand with him. He pulled her into a hug and just held her there with his head on her shoulder. It was as though he knew exactly what she needed because she suddenly felt completely at peace. The anticipation and nervousness that had knotted her stomach without her knowledge suddenly disappeared. She found a state of calm that she had only acquired around her steed. He didn't ask anything of her. He was simply there, a solid rock of support. She remained with him, unspeaking until her stomach alerted her to the time. She hugged him and headed to dinner with a much lighter heart.

Quint fell in step beside her as she left the stable. "Watching me again?" she asked.

"You can't tell me that you didn't know I was there," he responded. "I didn't want to interrupt you. You looked so happy for a time." He shrugged and grinned at her.

"I'm going home," she said. "And I hear you are coming with me." She poked him in the ribs with a grin of her own.

"I've put in too much time with you to let you leave unsupervised. What if you fall into a ditch or go north instead of south? Knowing you, you'll get lost somehow," he teased.

"Is this a private party, or can any vagabond join in?" asked Ruadana as she stepped away from the wall she'd been leaning on.

"My night is complete!" exclaimed Quint. "Perhaps the two loveliest ladies will allow me to escort them into the dining hall? After all, we will be spending quite a bit of time together in the near future."

"I'm actually quite excited to be returning home," responded Ruadana as she took Quint's arm. Phoenix giggled and took his other arm and together the three went to the dining hall for their last supper at the Citadel.

***

Arlaya sat astride her powerful steed. She reflected on her first proper riding lesson. It had been almost six months since that day and she had become very adept at working with her four legged partner.

"What is the plan for making it into the city?" asked Ruadana interrupting Arlaya's introspection.

"Yes, we should be at the gate in about an hour," Quint added.

"Disguises usually help." Arlaya looked at her travel companions and smiled. "Ru, you are used to hiding as a man. Think you can do it again?" Ruadana nodded and Arlaya turned to Quint. "Do you have any enemies who would recognize you?" He shook his head. "Good. Now, I am unable to pass as a man so I need to be a woman. What story can we put together for our travels?"

"Well, you are a properly born lady. You could actually take up that role and act as like the haughty bitch we all know true noblewomen are." Ruadana could not keep the laughter out of her voice at the look on Arlaya's face.

"I can't. If I shove the fact that I exist in the face of my family's enemies we will be hunted down the entire time we are in the city."

"Well, that's not necessarily true," said Quint thoughtfully.

Both women stopped their horses and looked at him curiously. He too halted his mount and sat silently in his saddle. His eyes were distant as a plan started forming in his head.

"Well?" Ruadana asked.

"Ari, you are the right age to be a rich merchant's daughter who is returning home from school for the winter months. It's to be expected that the rich commoners, for example the merchant class, to be stuck up, demanding, and, generally, a damn nuisance." He pointed at Ruadana. "You and I are her body guards. We need to change. Ru, you need to wear your fighting gear not your travel gear and, Ari, put on a nice gown, one that a merchant's daughter would own, and spend some time on your hair and makeup."

They spent a few minutes changing clothes. An additional quarter of an hour was spent as Arlaya perfected her hair and makeup. Once every hair was flawlessly in place, she remounted and checked her fans. While traveling, she was able to carry any weapon she chose but the dress did not allow her to hide anything. She felt secure in the fact that she could still protect herself without arousing suspicion.

"How do we play this?" Ruadana asked.

Arlaya looked at her and tilted her head to look down her nose at her best friend. "Did anyone ask your opinion? It is so difficult to find good help these days." She shrugged and nudged her horse forward. "Your job is to keep me alive not to talk." She huffed and squeezed her ankles to prod her horse into a trot. Ruadana and Quint caught up to her leaving a trail of guffaws and laughter behind.

"I think that will definitely work," Quint said between chuckles.

"You may be right," Ruadana said in her Fang voice.

They settled into a companionable silence as they continued on the last leg of the journey. Quint took on the role of brooding guard and Ruadana became the quietly alert guard. Arlaya's spine straightened with every step her horse took. Her face took on a holier than thou expression and her body language became stiff and more seductive. She knew that if any man dared touch her, they would die, not because she could personally kill them but because she was a rich woman.

They reached the city gates after a couple of hours of riding. The first warning they were getting close to the city was the smell. Cities are crowded and have the smells that accompanied that crowd. The smell of sweat mingled with bile and feces and other vile odors with a sweet overtone of perfumes and cooked meat. The smell was enough to turn any stomach, let alone the stomachs of three people who had essentially been country bumpkins for an extended period of time.

Arlaya's nose crinkled and Quint looked slightly queasy. Ruadana, however, had smelled worse in the slums so she didn't have a reaction. She looked at her friends in amusement. "Makes you glad that they kept things so neat at the…school, doesn't it?" she stuck her tongue out at Arlaya.

"I never really liked the city," Quint replied.

"Hush, we are about to get to the gates and they have guards in the walls listening. The regent has gotten fanatical about purging the residents of undesirables." Arlaya checked her fans and her hair then stuck her nose up in the air as primly as she could manage. Quint nudged his horse ahead of his "mistress" and Ruadana took up position as the rear guard.

Three gate guards stepped up to the trio. They were swaggering under the power of a few too many drinks. "Your Ladyship, if you could come this way." One of them beckoned them over to the side out of the traffic of commoners entering the city.

"Is there a problem here?" Quint growled in his most menacing voice.

"No problem, friend," said a new guard. By the markings on his uniform, this was the captain of the watch. "We just want to ensure your charge's safety in her travels." He turned to Arlaya. "May I ask your business in our glorious city?"

"If you must," she replied haughtily. "I am recently returned from school and am traveling to my family's home."

"Where is that exactly?"

"Wood Lane. Now, if you will get out of our way, I would like to see my family." She sniffed and turned her horse.

The guard grabbed his bridle. "I would like to give you an escort," he said.

"An escort? Who would dare do anything to me?" she demanded with sincerity and naiveté.

"The lower city is no place for a woman of such beauty and substance," the captain replied trying to keep this obviously hot blooded, vain, ignorant woman from getting herself killed. "Please, allow some of my men to see you at least to the edge of the marketplace."

She looked at Quint. "My bodyguards can keep me safe," she said finally.

"Ma'am, we could use the extra hands if things are as, hmm, difficult as the captain is suggesting." Arlaya looked around at him. He quickly signed to her *It would be suspicious if Ru and I don't take his warning seriously and if we don't take him up on his offer of men.* Arlaya nodded slightly and sighed audibly like a petulant child.

The captain smiled in satisfaction and contempt of her attitude. He let out an ear splitting whistle and beckoned over a group of six soldiers. Arlaya looked on in disdain as they formed a circle around her distinguished personage. Surreptitiously, she studied how they moved and the weapons they were armed with. While looking at their faces, she had the nagging feeling that she knew a couple of them.

Her eyes became hard and distant as a memory intruded into her thoughts. She had been betrayed and was dragged out of the Shadow Man's office weeping by two of these men. Her instinctive reaction to their presence was to whip out her fans and cut them down, consequences be damned. Her hand actually moved toward her belt where the fans were located.

Ruadana cleared her throat seeing the dangerous edge her friend's expression had just acquired. "We are ready to take you home, ma'am," she said gruffly with a warning in her voice.

Arlaya blinked and shook the violent thoughts out of her head. "Finally," she replied airily with a flick of the hand that had been traveling toward her deadly fans.

The soldiers set out at a sedate pace, making a hole in the crowd for this obviously rich and vain girl. The beggars, vendors, and travelers displaced by their group glared at her but Arlaya pretended not to see them. When one of the soldiers forcibly lifted a man and threw him out of the way, it took all of her mental strength to keep from protesting. Her persona would not have said a word and she could not afford to give herself and her friends away. The mission was too important.

Quint looked sidelong at his riding companions. Unlike them, he had kept abreast of the matters of state in the kingdom. The soldiers were well within their rights to treat the common folk in such a manner. The regent had decided that he did not like the poor and destitute. He argued that it was their own fault they couldn't afford nice clothing and food for their tables. If only the lazy sods would become more civilized, the kingdom would become a better place. He had issued orders to the city guard to "show them the error of their ways." The guards and soldiers in the city were to ensure that the putrid stench of humanity did not reach the noses of the wealthy and powerful. They aggressively suggested that such people stay out of the way of their "betters." This meant that the beggars and poor were beaten on a regular basis in the name of improving society.

That was what Phoenix and her fairytale "Shadow Man" were trying to fix. She had told them what they needed to know to help her but Quint wasn't sure how their insane plan to supplant the current ruler would work. After all, the only heir to the throne, Prince Lirith, had never done anything to countermand his uncle's orders. He should be the true ruler of the kingdom but if rumor was to be believed, he spent all of his time with one of the nobleman his uncle hated and ate and drank heartily every night. He knew nothing of what the common man was forced to endure at the hands of his uncle. No, Quint was not sure letting the prince anywhere near the throne was a good idea. It may be time for a new ruling family or a change of governmental practice he thought as he watched Arlaya force herself to look away from the soldiers manhandling another beggar.

The group finally reached the wealthier part of the city. They found themselves surrounded by modest homes with manicured lawn, when they had a lawn, and very little foot traffic. The sergeant in charge of the guards turned to Quint.

"You should be fine from here on out," he said and he and the others left.

"Where to now, Phoenix?" Ruadana asked quietly as soon as the guards were out of earshot.

"Time to see the Shadow Man," she replied. She turned her horse down a side street and led them through a mile and a half of twists and turns.

Finally, they reached a stable door. Arlaya dismounted and knocked. The door opened revealing a whipcord woman with long hair in a plait down her back. She had an expression that warned off any wavering or hesitation as she took in the sight of the trio.

"Hawk," Arlaya breathed, "it is so good to see you again."

"What do you call this?" Hawk demanded. "We are not an inn, Phoenix." Quint and Ruadana took a step back from the venom in her voice.

"The boss wants to see them," Phoenix replied coolly then smiled. The two of them were hugging in less than a second. "I have missed you."

"Oh, child, I missed you too. I cannot wait until you see the others." Hawk smiled for the first time in their exchange. "Please come inside. Friends and colleagues of Phoenix are always welcome here." She beckoned them inside, looked around the alleyway, and closed the doors behind them.

"Lemur didn't hurt herself telling you we were coming did she?" Lemur was a young girl who the Shadow Man had acquired the services of just before Phoenix had left on her assignment.

"No, she's doing just fine."

"I only ask because I saw her foot slip when she jumped to that fourth roof." Ruadana and Quint looked on curiously at this exchange. Phoenix looked at her travel companions and smiled apologetically. "I'm sorry. Sometimes we forget that there are others around or that they have no idea what we are talking about." She shrugged. "Lemur is the one who followed us all the way from the market and she is the reason Hawk knew when we would be here."

Quint grunted acceptance of the explanation and Ruadana shrugged. "This is your place. I just thought you had gone crazier than usual for a moment," she said. They all started laughing as they relieved the horses of their burden.

"Hawk, why don't we introduce these two to the man behind the plan and perhaps Tiger as well," Phoenix finally said in a very brisk and businesslike tone.

"Well, his lordship is currently home but your reunion with Tiger will have to wait," Hawk replied with an odd expression.

Phoenix chose not to question her about that just then. Instead, she nodded and started walking from the stable to the main house as her heart sank down to her toes. The other three followed suit. As they passed through the courtyard, the men and women exercising stopped to watch.

"You aren't here to stare," Hawk shouted at them, "you are here to learn to fight." A few of them looked shamed and went back to their exercises. The greener recruits continued to watch them. "Phoenix, if you stop by the kitchen, you will be able to grab some food. I have a bit of work to do. We will see his lordship after you are nourished."

Phoenix nodded and led her friends to the side of the courtyard. "This ought to be interesting," she told them with a smile and a wink. They smiled back.

"Apparently some of you think that my word is not law in this courtyard." Hawk had moved to the weapons rack and grabbed a stave and a whip. She then walked to the center of the courtyard and cracked the whip. Every recruit in the area jumped in shock. She started swinging around her staff. "If you think you can defeat me and rule this kingdom, please make my day." The experienced men and women scrambled out of the way. The newcomers, however, did not know not to mess with Hawk, especially when she was in a mood. The first idiot stepped up and caught the staff on his collarbone.

"This may take a while. Fancy something to eat?" Phoenix turned toward the kitchens without waiting for an answer. Her heart suddenly felt lighter as she grinned from ear to ear.

***

"Child, you have returned."

Phoenix looked to the door as her friends scrambled to their feet and grabbed their weapons.

"Hello, sir. I hear you have let standards slip and you need me to get everything back into tip top shape and back on track." She smiled as her employer stepped into the light.

"Insolence?" he smiled back and sat in the single chair in the room.

Quint and Ruadana still stood with their weapons at the ready. They did not know what to expect from this man who had so easily snuck up on them.

Finally Quint asked, "Ari, is this your Shadow Man?"

"Apologies, my friend, yes this is the man who called us from the Citadel." Phoenix waved her friend back to their seats on the beds. "My lord, why are we hiding away in this glorified storage cupboard?"

"I cannot risk anyone knowing you are back in the city. The enemies have been trying to penetrate our organization and they are getting better at it." He sighed quietly. "The scullery maid was the first salvo. More recently, two of my operatives have been turned and two recruits were originally employed by our foe to infiltrate us."

The Shadow Man paused for a reaction. Instead, the three assassins sat silently taking in the information. The silence held for many minutes before Phoenix cleared her throat to speak.

"Any casualties?" she asked.

"You are the only documented casualty." He waved his hand to cut off her protests. "It was necessary. If you hadn't died, our time would have been cut short."

"Chess," she whispered.

"What?" Ruadana blurted out.

"Moves and countermoves, just like chess," Phoenix responded.

"Exactly," said the Shadow Man.

"So, we will not be meeting with any other operatives." It wasn't a question but Phoenix waited for an answer nonetheless.

"No," he whispered. "You cannot stay here either." He took a deep breath and resumed his commanding voice. "I have purchased your ancestral city home. It has been repaired and refurbished and is ready for you to move in. As far as the people of the city are concerned, you are visiting royalty from a different sovereignty. Obviously, while you are royal, you are not in the direct line for ascension."

"The house has been staffed by men and women we trust completely. You will get settled in there and soon there will be an invitation to the Prince's Birthday Ball. Accept that invitation and expect me to visit that evening." He paused. "Everything depends on that night."

"Ok, everything seems in order. When do we leave?" Quint asked.

The Shadow Man turned to face him. "You leave tonight, just after midnight. You must avoid the city guard or you will be jailed for breaking curfew."

Phoenix's head snapped around. "Curfew?" she demanded.

"A concept brought forth by our esteemed Regent. He has decided that too much violence happens after dark. In actuality, he is trying to limit our movements against him." The Shadow Man's eyes flashed in anger.

Phoenix nodded and stood. "If you would excuse us, sir, we would like to rest before our journey tonight."

"Of course," he stood and silently left the room.

Phoenix turned to her companions. "Well?" she asked.

"I don't like it," Ruadana said. "There is something about that man that doesn't feel right." She shook her head and fell silent.

"He has done so much for me. He took me out of the gutter and set my feet upon this path. He made me who I am," Phoenix protested.

Quint cleared his throat and the women looked at him. "I'm sorry, Ari, but that's not entirely true." He silenced her further protests with a look. "He did not set you on this road. He merely gave you the tools to develop further. Your parents and grandfather set you on this path. They are the ones who sacrificed everything for you to fulfill your destiny. The Shadow Man is simply using you to further his plans."

"My family has been waiting for this for generations. The Shadow Man got me here," Phoenix whispered.

"All we are trying to say is that you cannot trust anyone. We are here to help and protect you, even from yourself." Quint sighed. "All we wanted to do was voice our concerns. It is in our nature to be suspicious."

Phoenix nodded. "I understand."

"I see no reason not to rest, then," said Ruadana with a laugh. "We have a lot to do."

Phoenix smiled at her friend. "Soon you will meet Tiger. I don't know how we will make it happen but soon you will meet him."

Arlaya sighed. She felt trapped in her new residence. While they may not trust the man, Ru and Quint both agreed with him that she should not travel around the city or risk herself in any way. Instead, she whiled away the hours deciphering the coded volume or wishing she could see Tiger again.

Thinking of Tiger brought the most nagging question back to the forefront of her mind. *Why hasn't he come? Does he even know I am back in the city?* She wanted nothing more than to see his smile or have him make fun of her. She began to imagine their reunion. It was a very unrealistic fantasy but she felt the longing to be whipped around in his arms and have him kiss her. As time crept by and she didn't see him, she began to lose hope and felt like she was drowning in melancholy.

A knock at the door broke her reverie. "Come in," she called.

Quint stepped into her study with a page close on his heels. "Excuse my, my lady," he said with a slight bow, "this young man has a message for you." The page carefully walked across the room and bowed as he held out an elegant note.

Arlaya knew this must be the invitation that the Shadow Man had mentioned. She took the note and read it carefully.

You are cordially invited to celebrate the anniversary of the birth of Crown Prince Lirith of Belevis tomorrow evening at the palace.

Carefully, Arlaya pulled a piece of stationary out of a drawer and wrote out a note of acceptance. The page, still holding his bow, took the note delicately. "Thank you very much," Arlaya said. As the child rose from his bow, she handed him a piece of hard candy as way of payment for services rendered. With all the decorum a child can muster, he took the candy and rushed out of the room.

Quint leaned against the wall and gazed at his friend. "That's the invitation isn't it?" he asked.

"Yes," she replied. "The gala will be tomorrow night." She turned toward the window with a sigh. "Is everything prepared?"

"Absolutely," he asserted. "We were just waiting on confirmation of the day."

"And so it begins," she muttered as she rose to her feet. "I'm restless, shall we spar?" she asked her friend.

"I was taught to never hit a lady," he teased. She glared at him and jabbed him in the ribs with her elbow. "Very well, let's take this outside," he said with a laugh. They left the room and headed down to the courtyard to relieve themselves of their nerves.

***

"I stand before you today, my birthday, as tradition dictates. This is the day the new queen-to-be of the kingdom will be chosen by the gods." The prince allowed his voice to carry over the court. All the courtiers were absolutely silent; there was not even a rustle of cloth. Then, a beautiful woman stepped forth.

"Your Highness, I most humbly offer myself as a candidate to you as a future mother to the heirs of the throne." She curtseyed very low and held the position without moving her eyes from his face.

Prince Lirith had expected such a proposal from this particular member of the court. She was stunningly beautiful with dark brown hair that absorbed the light and the palest of skin that seemed like satin. Her name was Oliviette and she was the daughter of the Regent and Steward of the Kingdom; his uncle. The match would be an acceptable one without the risks of madness due to incest because his uncle was only the half-brother to his father, the former king. Oliviette had obviously dressed for the occasion in a gown of the deepest green to offset her eyes and bring out the red in her lips. The cut, while modest, showed enough skin and enhanced her curves so that the eyes of all the men in the room were drawn to her without fail.

Lirith felt a smile play at his lips. He knew his cousin was beloved by the people. He also knew that her father was a man after power and could use his daughter to gain more and that she was as ambitious as her father no matter the masks she would hide behind. "Lady Oliviette, your beauty is unsurpassed and I am honored by your sacrifice. Unfortunately, tradition dictates that I am to wed from the House Rivell." There was a sharp intake of breath. It was true that, many centuries ago, a decree was written with the promise of such a marriage but the Rivell family had been wiped out by unfortunate accident. The tradition had been upheld only once in the past four generations.

Lirith helped Oliviette to stand straight and guided her back to her position among the other nobles and resumed his position at the head of the hall once more. "I, Prince Lirith, heir to the throne of Belevis, stand before you today to fulfill a promise laid down more than two hundred years ago as a part of the proud and honorable traditions of this land and ask that, if any Lady of the House Rivell is present, she would step forth and allow me to humbly ask for her hand in holy matrimony."

Once more, the throne room was silent. Lirith felt his heart constrict. He trusted Lord Calden and, more than anything, did not want to marry Oliviette and provide his uncle with an opportunity to continue to rule the kingdom. At the same time, he knew there was no hope because Arlaya was dead.

Suddenly, the doors to the throne room started to creak open and a woman entered, escorted by the Royal Herald. She walked with the grace of an eagle in flight and her movements seemed as effortless. Most of the courtiers would attribute this to the dancing that any woman of noble birth was expected to do, but Tiger knew better. This was the effortless grace of a stalking great cat and she was just as dangerous. There was no doubt that, whoever this veiled woman was, she could take care of herself and, warily, he checked the balance of his hidden weapons not daring to move a muscle in the process lest he spook her into action.

An assassin in the court? Some trick of my uncle's on my birthday perhaps? If she's a professional, like I think she is, then it would never be tied back to him and he'd have the throne in truth, rather than the regency which ends today as I come of age.

He stood a little straighter and risked a glance at his mentor and friend, Lord Calden. Strangely, he seemed supremely relaxed but knowing the level of acting ability he had, Tiger was only surprised for a moment. *He's ready for her to spring into action, too. He must see what kind of woman she is. How could she even get past our men?*

He turned his attention back to the visitor. He spent the next few seconds studying her movements and trying to decide where she might be hiding weapons. She made a slight gesture that caught his attention. Her long elegant fingers moved slightly so as not to catch anyone else's attention.

I'm not here to hurt you, she signed. She signed the message three times which meant she was completely serious. Among assassins giving one's word three times bound them where once or twice could easily be broken as it might just be subterfuge.

Lirith's interest increased a few notches but he also allowed his muscles to relax a little. "Your Highness, may I present Lady Arlaya of the House Rivell whose identity has been corroborated by the most noble Lord Calden." The call rang through the silence and Lirith thought his heart would leap from his chest at any moment. *She is alive!* The kingdom may yet survive. Only years of training kept his ecstasy from showing as the Lady herself began a slow, measured march toward him leaving her entourage behind with the exception of one maid.

Arlaya had hair the color of fire which, unlike Oliviette's hair, reflected the light rather than absorbing it. Her skin, what could be seen of it, was a lovely olive color. Her face was obscured by a veil which was a beautiful lilac color. She carefully reached up and shifted the veil so that her face could be viewed by all.

Eyes the color of amethyst connected with his and Lirith felt a shiver of anticipation. Quickly, he brought himself under control. "My Lady Arlaya, I welcome you to my home and humbly ask that you accept me as a future husband as laid down by our honored ancestors."

Arlaya turned to address the assembled courtiers. "I am honored by your proposal and I accept. Tradition brings us together and I hope that we can find love in our union, not only for each other but for and from our people." To finish her statement she curtseyed deeply and rose with grace.

"Lords and Ladies, please excuse us as we retire to learn about each other. I hope you are all able to attend the ball tonight and the wedding which will soon take place to complete this union which has been planned for centuries," said Lirith. All the courtiers bowed and curtseyed and the royal couple departed for a more comfortable setting to get to know one another.

The couple traveled through the halls of the palace at a sedate pace until they reached Lirith's private study. Servants bowed as they passed then hurried to completely remove themselves from the exalted presence of these two powerful people and return to their duties. They did, however, spare curious glances at the men and woman who accompanied the pair.

Lirith was never without his own personal guardsmen when he was within the palace. The two men in the livery of the King's Own Guard had been handpicked by Lirith and Calden a decade ago and the servants readily recognized them. The two guards in the livery of the resurrected House of Rivell were unknown entities. They were obviously very strong men and were imposing figures. Then there was the same maid who had stepped forward with her mistress. She was blonde with green eyes and moved with the same grace as Arlaya marking her as an assassin to anyone with a trained eye. She was clearly another line of defense for the lady.

Lirith opened his study door and one of his guards and one of Arlaya's peeled off of the group to take up position in the hall. Under normal circumstances it really wasn't necessary, but everyone in the party knew that these weren't normal circumstances. Inside this room, a plan was finally coming together to remove the regent from power of any kind and return the kingdom to the glory that it deserved. They were going to destroy Lirith's uncle. The other two guards took up stations just inside the door and the maid stood beside the fireplace.

"We can speak freely in here. I know where every listening post around this room is and, before I arrive, my people sweep for any spies outside these four walls." He smiled at his little joke.

Arlaya smiled back. He had missed the warmth of her smiles. "It has been a long time, Your Highness. I find I truly missed your trite jokes."

"Since when am I 'Your Highness' to you, Phoenix?" he asked.

"Since Phoenix discovered who she was working for. Besides, it's funny seeing the veins pop out of your head at the mention of your responsibilities."

"There she is," he exclaimed. "There is the woman I remember." Then he started crying, not weeping just crying quietly while smiling. He reached up and touched her face.

"What is it, Tiger?" she asked tenderly.

"Calden had told me you were dead. I didn't realize how I had felt about you until I heard that news. I had come to really enjoy your company and hoped we would have more time together but suddenly you were ripped out of my life." He took a deep shuddering breath. Then he whooped, gathered her in his arms and spun her around. They then sat across from each other.

There was a knock at the study door and Calden himself strode in. He stopped when he saw the prince who was drying his face after crying but, after a moment, he sat with them. "I am sorry, Lirith," he said simply.

Calden sighed, "I did what I had to do. You were getting reckless and I needed to show you that anybody could die at any time. Phoenix was perfectly placed to do the job. I really am sorry to have deceived you. Besides, I needed you to be surprised at her entrance today even if it was for a different reason than anyone else," he smiled sadly and reached out to pat his friend's arm.

Lirith batted his hand away and punched him across the face. He, then, crossed the room at such a speed that it was almost as though he ran. He just stood there breathing heavily. "You have never lied to me before. I was falling in love with her and you tore my heart out of my chest by telling me that she died." He pulled out a handkerchief and wiped his face. "How can I trust you after that?"

Arlaya stood and slowly walked toward the distraught prince. She grabbed his free hand and squeezed. "You *were* getting reckless, Lirith. It was a difficult time with assassination attempts and your uncle trying to discover my location. He was just protecting your best interest." Lirith tried to pull away from her but she wouldn't let him as she continued, "I am not excusing his telling you that I was dead, but I can understand why and if you look past the emotion I am sure you could too. We won't push you but don't blame him or me. We are in a stronger position now than we could have hoped for a year ago, and it is down to his work." She drew him back to his seat and squeezed his hand again.

"I really was trying to do what I thought was best for you, child," Calden said apologetically. "I won't ask you to forgive me. Instead, we should talk about how we are going to proceed with our plan." He crossed his legs and settled deeper into the chair with a sigh.

"Oliviette is not going to be happy," Lirith said with a watery chuckle.

"Oliviette?" asked Arlaya.

"My cousin," explained Lirith. "My uncle wants us to wed so that he can still control what goes on in the country through us. Throughout my childhood, he would devise ways for me to look up to him and turn to him for advice. When that failed, because I found Calden who told me that I could do anything and I had my own voice, he had to try a new tactic. That tactic came in the form of my cousin. Because my uncle is only half brother to my late father, she is an acceptable match. There is no fear of madness due to incest. So, he would make sure we sat together at dinners and I would have to dance with her constantly at parties. It is an unwritten rule that the prince dances with every eligible woman at a gala or ball, but Oliviette was my partner more often than all of the other women combined."

Lirith could not keep the bitterness out of his voice and Arlaya could understand. He did not like people dictating his future any more than she did, which was strange considering Calden had been planning their union for at least a year. She smiled at the thought but quickly hid it so that Lirith would not take it the wrong way.

"So, it seems I am stepping on a few toes just by being here, then," she said sarcastically.

"That's what always happens with you around, little bird," said Calden with a wink.

There was another knock at the door and the three stood and turned to see who it was. The door opened to admit the regent. He stopped just inside the study and sized up the group he found inside.

Arlaya's maid shifted her weight ever so slightly to be able to draw her concealed weapons at a moment's noticed. Lirith strode toward his uncle with his arms flung wide in an affable greeting. Calden remained where he was, radiating unconcealed dislike and distrust. The contention between the regent and Lord Calden was infamous across Belevis. Arlaya slowly moved around the furniture to stand a discreet distance behind Lirith, waiting to be introduced to his uncle.

"Uncle," Lirith cried in delight, "I hadn't expected to see you. I was told you were taken ill this morning. How are you feeling?"

"I am feeling much better thanks to our wonderful physicians here in the palace," the regent replied with a very posh and clipped accent. "I came by because I heard you had chosen a wife." There was a slight bitter edge to his voice that the average person would never have noticed, but there was not a single average person in the room. They were all very well aware that he was unhappy with the turn of events.

"Yes, Uncle, I have. May I introduce Arlaya of the House Rivell. She came to court today to fulfill the oldest of decrees. We will finally be able to cement our two families together as should have happened in the first generation of Belevis." Tiger's smile got wider as he noticed the hardening in his uncle's eyes.

The regent looked past his nephew's shoulder to the woman standing behind him. She was smiling airily and curtseyed in greeting. "It is a pleasure to finally meet you, my lord," she said as she rose.

"The pleasure is all mine, child," he responded automatically. "Please, let us sit and get to know one another."

Lirith, Arlaya, and Calden resumed their original positions while Arlaya's maid started pouring the tea that none of them had noticed she prepared. The regent glanced curiously at Calden, then sat in one of the open chairs. "I must say I am surprised to see you here Calden. I had thought this was a family affair and Lirith and his bride-to-be were getting to know one another."

"I popped by as soon as I heard the good news, just as you did. Lirith is like a son to me and I felt congratulations were in order." Calden placed a hand on Lirith's shoulder much like a father would his son. The regent fidgeted slightly in dislike at the show a paternal affection.

"I see," said the regent. Then he turned to Arlaya and asked, "Where have you been all these years? Everyone had thought your family was lost to history."

She cleared her throat. "In the attack on my family all those generations ago, most of my ancestors were slaughtered. One of the sons managed to survive. With the help of some of the servants and his personal guardsmen, he escaped to a safe haven. There he stayed with his wife and child. He and his wife made new home of their own but he never forgot their roots. He was determined to resurrect his family name as soon as it was safe for his children. That safety never came, not until now. My family has been hunted down like animals for years but precautions were put in place so that the line would continue. As the first woman to reach adulthood at the same time as the prince, it is my responsibility to bring forth my family name once more and see that the first decree is finally fulfilled and can be put to rest." She looked at Lirith before continuing, "Our ancestors were brothers in the truest of senses; in a way that runs deeper than blood. It is time the families were brought together."

"Please do not take this the wrong way, my lady, but how do we know your story is the truth?" Lirith's uncle asked.

Calden spoke before Arlaya could respond. "Her ancestor, the one who escaped, sent a letter to the archivist of the day. He came to the conclusion that it would not be safe for his new family in his lifetime so he devised a way to always be able to distinguish his family from every other citizen in the kingdom. As soon as the children were born, they were branded with the family crest; a phoenix."

Arlaya shifted uncomfortably for a moment. Slowly she reached up to shift her sleeve down her arm. The regent glanced at her as the movement registered. As the other men noticed his glance, every eye in the room turned toward her.

She moved her hair over to her other shoulder and stood. Trusting that she would not be stabbed in the back, she turned around to show the men her phoenix brand. "I always thought it was a simple birthmark," she said. She felt a hand rub the mark and quickly turned back around. "I assure you it isn't paint."

"I can feel that, my lady. Please forgive me for checking," said the regent.

"I am sorry for not telling you sooner, my lord," said Calden. "Arlaya and I met each other a year ago. I wanted to double check who she was before I alerted anybody to her presence in the city. In fact, she hasn't been in the city since that first meeting. Her family has been perpetually hunted down within the city boundaries, after all." He shrugged. "Her parents were killed when she was young and I didn't want her to follow suit."

The regent coughed delicately. "We could have protected her," he contended. "If you had come to me in the first place, you could have saved yourself a lot of trouble."

"I'm sure you could have, my lord. I just wanted to be sure," Calden countered.

The regent stood. "I'm sure the couple wants some time alone to get to know one another better," he said bitterly and walked to the door. He held it open and waited for Calden to join him and leave Arlaya and Lirith to their conversation. They stood and nodded their farewells.

"I believe you are right, my lord. They should get the chance to know one another better without the old men getting in the way." Calden winked at Arlaya and walked out of the study.

"I suppose all we can do at this point is get you settled in," said Lirith after a few moments of silence. "Come, I'll show you to your rooms." He stood and offered her his arm. She stood and took the proffered elbow.

Together they walked through the halls in silence. The weight of the world was on their shoulders but they supported the burden with grace. Lirith felt relief as Arlaya wrapped her fingers around his hand. Now they shared the burden and supported each other. Their movement was fluid and seemingly effortless. Any onlooker might have thought they were carefree and simply a happy young couple.

Eventually, they reached Arlaya's suite. Lirith opened the door and waved her through. She smiled at him and winked as she walked into the sitting room.

As she surveyed her surroundings, her senses suddenly shouted a warning. Her servants were strewn all over the floor and the smell of blood was in the air. She slowly pulled a fan from her belt and snapped it open. Kneeling down, she checked the closest of her servants. She was not breathing and Arlaya sighed in regret.

"A waste of a life," she whispered.

"Arlaya?" Lirith had come into the room and saw what had happened. "We have to get out of here. Whoever did this may still be here."

"Oh, I know they are," growled Arlaya.

The guards fanned out with weapons drawn. They were careful to look in every nook and cranny. Arlaya moved to the center of the room and fanned herself. She closed her eyes and just listened. Sometimes the eyes got in way. To any onlookers, she looked like a noblewoman simply trying to clear the air around her nose as she stood in the middle of the carnage.

It was only because her eyes were closed that she paid attention to the slight rustle of cloth. Before she even thought about moving, she was whipping around with her fan fully extended while simultaneously drawing her second fan. She heard a grunt of pain and opened her eyes to see a man dressed in common clothing on her floor bleeding from a cut in his stomach.

She bent over him as Lirith materialized by her side. "Who do you work for?" she asked her victim.

He squirmed on the floor and tried to drag himself away from the prince and his deadly betrothed. They were supposed to be soft targets, easy money. How wrong that was. Now he was belly-cut and, in all likelihood, going to die.

"Who do you work for?" she asked again, this time grabbing him and slamming him against the settee.

"Didn't ask his name, now did I, cunt?" he replied. Flecks of blood splattered around his mouth as he coughed.

Lirith punched him in the face. "Treat her with respect, ingrate!" he shouted.

"Lirith, you really aren't helping," she chided gently and pulled him away from their captive with a wink. As she turned back, she felt a knife slide into her side. She gasped in pain and looked at the man at her feet. "That was naughty," she said as she pulled the blade from her flesh. "Now I can make you hurt even more."

"You aren't in any position to make threats, bitch," he coughed out.

"I think you will find that the person with the knife has the upper hand," she retorted.

The captive started laughing. More blood flew out of his mouth as Lirith grunted in pain and fell to the floor next to Arlaya. She whipped around quickly as the man who had snuck up behind her swung his fist once more. In the split second before his punch landed, she ducked and rolled. She came up to her knees and quickly stood.

Her foot slipped on her skirts and she fell back to her knees. She raised her fans in a defensive posture and carefully stood again. Her attacker approached slowly.

"That was very clever," she said.

He launched himself at her. Arlaya whipped her leg out and caught him in the stomach. He fell backward and danced forward again. This time he dodged her kick and came in swinging. His fist clipped her cheek and she swung her fan at his neck.

She never knew if she hit him. There must have been another attacker behind her because she felt the impact of a sword or knife hilt on the just above her left ear. The world went black as she fell forward as she lost consciousness.

She had this nagging feeling that nothing was real. A world she had known for years was false. Voices had started to invade her dreams, talking of suffering, secrets, and new ways to obtain information. It was almost as though only in her dreams could she get close to reality. Last night's dream had been particularly vivid. There were no images, just the voices.

"We bring her pain and she just keeps plowing through. Making her hurt has not provided us any information." The whiny voice slid through the darkness like oil.

"I had a thought," a snakelike hiss filled the emptiness. "We change the drugs to make her more comfortable and maybe she will speak freely."

A third voice joined the conversation, a clear peal of a soprano bell with hatred and evil at its core. "You are running short on time. If you have no information in two days, she becomes mine. And I don't use drugs for interrogation. I use whips and knives to cut it out." She heard footsteps then the darkness consumed her once more.

An eternity later, warmth filled her and she heard a tender bass voice. "Oh my darling, what have they done to you? I will return and bring you home."

She finally felt the darkness recede and her day began. She spent the day working and wondering about that dream. A few of the other workers commented that she seemed distracted. She simply could not get that last voice out of her head. It wasn't until she was putting her head down to sleep that she realized how simple her day had been. Much simpler than any day she could recall from the last few years. That thought brought her back to the other voices. *It was just a dream*, she told herself as she fell asleep.

***

There was chaos all around her. Men were shouting and running to and fro. She distinctly heard the sound of steel on steel as blades met in battle. She stayed perfectly still as her mind tried to work through the haze and fog of drugs, slowing everything down to understand what was going on.

Some sort of battle, she thought. And as her heart began to beat ferociously, she realized she was completely exposed. *Move, move, move!* her mind wailed at her. She tried to move her arms ever so slightly and found she couldn't. she tried her legs with the same result. *I have to risk letting them know I'm awake. I have to see what is going on.*

She opened her eyes and crack and peered around. Nobody was watching her so she looked at her arms by her side. There were straps holding her down. *So I cannot move,* her mind's voice sighed in frustration and resignation. *I'm helpless.* Her eyes slid shut as she accepted her fate and she heard a heavy door slam shut with a crash.

"Check her! Make sure she is still asleep." The voice was full of panic. She took a deep breath and prayed they wouldn't realize she was awake. She willed her heart to slow its staccato beat and her body to not react to anything.

She felt someone step up next to her and grab her wrist. "Her pulse is a bit quicker than normal but it is steady, Sir. She is due for more drugs but we keep them in the storage chamber, which we cannot get to." The voice sounded more than a bit irritated at being ordered around by the panicky one.

"Very well, if you notice her waking up tell me. We can hope she has enough in her system to keep her asleep."

Just then the shouting outside the room stopped. "What happened?" The whispered question hung in the air.

The door crashed open and the men behind it were killed before they could even shout a warning. It was all she could do to keep taking deep breaths and pretend she was still asleep.

It wasn't enough. She felt the blade of a knife kiss her throat. "It was a good attempt, pet. You may as well open your eyes, I know you are awake."

She opened her eyes and gazed upon her knife wielding executioner. "That's better, pet. Now you get to watch as I destroy your beloved prince." Her confusion must have showed because her tormentor began to laugh. "You don't remember him? Well, you do still have drugs in you then. Allow me to let you in on the secret. He is your one true love and he is about to die. Just as you are about to die." His smile got bigger as the fighting at the door stopped. The dying men moaned quietly as their lifeblood drained out of them and one man stood alone in the doorway.

"Get away from her," the lone man growled. There was something about that voice that she recognized. *It is him, the fourth man from my last dream.* Her eyes drank in his face, a face that would have been incredibly handsome if not for the fury riddling his features and the panic in his eyes.

"Ah, Your Highness, so glad you could join us." The knife bit into her neck drawing blood. "Your Lady Arlaya certainly missed your company."

She continued to stare at the prince until suddenly the dream world memories melted away and her true memories surged forth as the cage of drugs was burned away. She took her eyes off of the man she loved and studied the bindings on her wrists. She was not some helpless damsel in distress and she would find a way to free herself and return to his arms.

The bindings were slick with the blood of dead men and if she could bend her fingers the right way she might be able to free herself. As she worked her hands slowly, she returned her gaze to the prince. He was watching her and she slowly winked. If he was surprised, he did not show it. Instead, he looked at the man standing over her.

"I said 'get away from her'," he growled again.

"I would certainly like to but unfortunately, I only take orders from the Crown."

"I *am* the Crown and I order you to release her." The prince raised his sword.

"I wouldn't do that if I were you, Lirith. You may hurt yourself playing with a big sharp object like that. Then it would be up to your uncle to shoulder the burden of ruling over the kingdom." As her captor spoke, Arlaya worked her hands through the bindings. The pain in her hands could not overcome her determination to be free.

"Enough of these games, snake. Let us be done with this. After I finish with you, my uncle will follow."

"So impatient to kill your lover? Very well, then." He looked down at his captive as she grabbed his wrist to prevent him from cutting her throat. His eyes lost all of their mirth. "Bitch!" he spat.

In that moment, when all of his attention was focused on her, Lirith stepped up and stabbed him through the heart. As he fell backward with an expression of disbelief, Arlaya wrestled his hand away from her throat, preventing his fall from ending the life Lirith had worked so hard to save. She heard his body hit the floor and breathed a sigh of relief.

Lirith looked down at her and smiled a weary, heartfelt smile. "Let's get you free. What do you say, dear heart?"

"Yes, please." Her voice was hoarse from disuse and the after effects of whatever drugs had been given to her.

Lirith made quick work of the bindings and Arlaya was able to sit up within a minute. Lirith enveloped her in a huge hug. "I have missed you, sweetheart. The last three days have been miserable. Especially last night when I found you but could not bring you home." He scooped her up and carried her out of the chamber.

"Three days," she whispered and fell asleep, rocked by his rolling gate.

***

She woke up slowly in a cocoon of warmth. There was sunlight streaming in through the window caressing her face. Gradually she became aware of voices quietly discussing something. Almost involuntarily, she moved, snuggling deeper under the comforter with a sigh, willing herself to stay asleep as her stomach woke up with a vengeance. It growled so loudly she thought the deafest of men would hear.

She felt pressure on the bed beside her. "I think you're right. She is waking up," a familiar voice said.

"Thank goodness," responded a voice so full of relief she almost smiled. "I almost thought I had imagined it."

"Child open your eyes." That voice was so gentle but some part of her felt that this was the one voice she would never disobey. Her eyelids fluttered as she attempted to obey. "That's it child. You are safe. Take your time, but you need to wake up now. Lirith is worrying himself sick next to you."

Slowly she opened her eyes, blinking rapidly as her vision came into focus. She smiled to see Lirith kneeling next to her bed. Then her eyes turned to the other man.

"It is good to see you, Sir," she said to her former employer and good friend.

He chuckled and smiled, "You look like the job chewed you up and spit you out, little bird."

"I guess I was too tough for it," she joked back and all three of them dissolved into laughter. It was good to see the worry lines erased from their faces. "They were trying to figure out our plans," she stated calmly after she stopped laughing. "They used some sort of drug to try and get me to tell them what we intend to do."

"That is not unexpected," said Calden. "Did you tell them anything?"

"I don't remember saying anything of any value but I can't know for sure," she replied.

"Now my darling, it is time for some food," Lirith declared ending a conversation that would only lead Arlaya to blame herself for something out of her control..

Arlaya's stomach growled again. "Yes, please," she squeaked, blushing, which brought forth more laughter, "but then I want to spend some time in the salle." The men were about to argue but she held up a hand. "I need to do this. Is your uncle in custody?" Lirith shook his head with a grimace. "Then I must be prepared for him to come back."

"Very well, then," sighed Lirith, "but breakfast first."

It had been three weeks since she had woken up drug free and Arlaya had spent every waking moment she could in the salle honing her skills and learning as much as she could of her family history. The rest of her time was monopolized by wedding planning. The date had finally been set for one week from today and she was being fitted for her gown.

Arlaya just knew this would be when Lirith's uncle would strike. It was his best opportunity. As tight as they could make security, it would never be tight enough.

Quietly, she had been bringing in her people from the outskirts of the city to place in strategic locations as guests, guards, and servers. The leaders of the rebels that she had worked with so long ago were very happy to see her. Jethro had died defending his people but Adrienne had taken up his mantle of leadership. Arlaya was surprised so many had come from the Citadel as well. They would be ready for the attack when it came.

It is a very good thing I have unique weapons because this dress would not hide anything, she thought looking at her white clad figure in the mirror. "Is there no way to allow for more movement in the fabric?" she asked her seamstress.

"What kind of flow are you looking for, Highness?" she responded

"I am performing a rather special dance for my husband to be and it would make such a grand effect to have fewer layers than traditional gowns and allow the outer skirt to swirl around my ankles," Arlaya responded with a wink and a smile.

The seamstress acquired a thoughtful expression. "The skirt would have to be slightly shorter than tradition dictates as well."

"I suppose that would be true," Arlaya acceded with a sigh of reluctance, completely feigned of course, "is there any way to overcome that issue?"

"Let me think on it, Your Highness. I am certain we could put something together that would fit your needs and suit tradition."

Arlaya's smile broadened. *Well that is one thing that will work in my favor.* Without the weight of a traditional gown, she would be able to move better and protect herself when the attack came. The day before, her fans for the wedding had arrived in a padded box from her favorite recluse. Badger had gone above and beyond the call of duty in the creation of the fans. They were the exact white of her gown with silver snowflakes worked in. The fans were as gorgeous as they were deadly.

Arlaya sighed as she realized there was not much more she could do to prepare for the wedding and for Lirith's uncle. The seamstress looked up from her work and smiled.

"You will be beautiful, Your Highness, and he loves you. All of your subjects can see that. The wedding will be here in a few days. Just remind yourself that this is the greatest day in your life and you will get through it."

"Oh, it's not that. I'm just so happy that the day is finally here. The kingdom has waited so long," she sighed again, "and so have I to be honest. I love him too and just want everything to be perfect."

The seamstress smiled and bent back to her work.

***

The guests were bubbling with anticipation. Their prince was finally going to be married and to a very beautiful woman. It was the biggest social event in the last decade.

Lirith waited just below the thrones as the doors were flung wide. Every eye turned to look at Arlaya standing there in her beautiful gown. It was snowy white with beautiful needlework snowflakes to match the weather visible through the windows. A sigh of delight rippled through those in attendance.

Arlaya walked sedately toward Lirith and her future. Her heart was full of joy and her feet wanted to fly down the aisle. It was strange to think that she met Lirith a little over a year ago and that they were soon to be bonded for life. She didn't know when she had started loving Tiger but she could no longer imagine being without him.

It was as though there was no other person in the room. Arlaya was completely focused on Lirith. He had the largest of smiles on his face; he was practically glowing. In no time, she was standing next to her soon to be husband.

The Order of Dirige had sent over their council of brotherhood to conduct the ceremony. The history of the Order protecting her family had made them the ideal choice. The councilors produced a red ribbon and wrapped the hands of Lirith and Arlaya together.

"Once separate and now together, the two who stand before the Order of Dirige now become one. Does your highness, Prince Lirith, accept Lady Arlaya into your life as a part of yourself? To love and cherish until the day you die and beyond? Will you protect and honor her through the good times and the bad?"

"I shall," Lirith responded.

"Do you, Lady Arlaya, agree to support your prince in protecting the Kingdom of Belevis? Will you always protect, honor, love, and cherish him until the day you die and beyond? Will you protect and honor him through the good times and the bad?"

"I shall," said Arlaya.

"Then we, of the Order of Dirige, pronounce legally wed under the laws of the Kingdom of Belevis, the Prince Lirith and the Princess Arlaya." The speaker waved the rest of the council forward.

One raised an ornately wrought iron torch and another took hold of the end of the ribbon wrapped around the couple's hands and thrust it into the flame. The guests gasped as the ribbon burned around their prince's wrist. Neither Arlaya nor Lirith even winced as the heat bit into their skin but the ribbon fell apart and the fire went out quickly. There were cheers as the embers hit the floor.

Lirith turned to face the wedding guests. "Thank you for being here, my lords and ladies. We truly appreciate your company on this day of celebration. My wife and I are ready to begin making the lives of our citizens better." He laughed and said, "First, though, it is time for the gala to celebrate the new life we are starting together." There were more cheers as Lirith kissed Arlaya with passion and servants began circulating with food and glasses of wine.

Arlaya stepped out of her husband's arms and down the steps of the dais as a group of musicians started playing from the side of the ballroom. Under Lirith's curious gaze, Arlaya moved to the center of the room and pulled her newest fans from the waist of her dress. She snapped them open and tapped out the beat of the song. The guests made space and turned to watch her.

She started dancing using the fans to enhance her movements. She swirled and swayed. The winter sun streaming through the window kissed Arlaya's body, turning her into a glowing icon of sensuality. Her fans glinted in the light as the tempo increased.

There wasn't a single sound in the room apart from the music playing. The guests were in such awe of her grace and the fluidity of her dance. It was a dance of wonder, of seduction, and, most of all, of love. She tapped her feet to keep time. Her skirts swirled around her ankles. She threw her heart into that dance. Arlaya launched herself into the air and twirled. She landed lightly and held her pose with her arms over her head. There was a collective sigh as she slowly lowered her arms. Her breast swelled with exhilaration and exertion.

Lirith was mesmerized and slowly stepped forward. He stretched his arms out and enveloped her in his embrace. He was lost for words. It was as though there was nobody else in the room and their lips met with passion. Arlaya breathed in his scent and closed her eyes.

"I love you, darling," he said.

They moved out of the center of the room as the musicians started playing again. Ruadana was waiting near the tables heaped with food. She carefully dabbed the sweat from her mistress's face without ruining her makeup. For the rest of the evening, Lirith and Arlaya with Ruadana in attendance mingled and spoke to the guests and danced.

***

The royal couple retired in the early hours of the morning. They were both exhausted but sleep was not in the cards. There had been no incident during the wedding or the gala that followed. Both Lirith and Arlaya felt emotionally drained. They had been on high alert waiting for any indication of an attack that never came. Lirith went into the dressing room and changed into sleep clothes and collapsed on the bed.

Arlaya felt numb. She knew there were expectations for a wedding night but neither of them were up to it. "He didn't attack," she whispered. "Why didn't he? When is it coming?"

Lirith propped himself up on his elbows. "Maybe he has realized that he can't win."

"We can't let our guard down," Arlaya said.

"Of course not, but for now we need sleep."

Ruadana had an arrow protruding from her chest. She coughed and grasped the shaft. If there was an honorable way to die then this was it.

Arlaya knelt by her side blood splattered over her dress. Tears were streaming down her face. "You saved my life, you twit," she teased gently with a watery smile. "I thought you said that we would be friends but I would have to protect myself."

"That was before you proved incapable of doing so." Ruadana laughed and a fleck of blood landed on the corner of her mouth. Arlaya carefully wiped the blood away with a clean corner of her handkerchief as Lirith dropped to his knees beside them.

He had incapacitated or killed every last bowman in the great hall once he saw that his wife and their friends had the close combat troops well in hand. Ruadana had been by Arlaya's side the whole time. A stray arrow was the unfortunate result of her labor. It had come from a bowman who released just as he was cut down. The arrow had been close to hitting Arlaya in the back but Ruadana pushed her out of the way. Even with the arrow in her chest, Ruadana kept on fighting. She fought until her body gave out.

A tear dropped onto Ruadana's face and Arlaya hurriedly wiped it away. She looked into her best friend's eyes and saw the acceptance of fate. She turned to scan the crowd of her allies and fellow fighters who were cleaning up the debris, checking the dead and wounded, and guarding the entrances.

"Quint!" Arlaya yelled as soon as she located him across the room. Quint looked up from his position guarding the main door. His eyes widened and he hurried over.

"Ruadana, girl, what have you gone and done to yourself? The arrows are supposed to go in the other guys," he chuckled wetly. "I bet Fang would not have gotten into this mess."

Ruadana smiled weakly and reached up to touch his cheek. Her hand slipped but he caught it and held it against his face. Arlaya moved to give them some privacy in her last moments but Quint shook his head.

"I love her with all my heart, Phoenix," he said, "but you are all the family we have. Let her be surrounded by her loving family. She deserves that."

"She deserves that and so much more," Lirith responded before Arlaya could. "She is the sister neither of us ever had. We are proud to be the true family she never had." He looked down at Ruadana. "Hey, kitten, you know we love you."

"I know you do. I love you too." She coughed again. A dribble of blood created a track down her cheek. "Finish what we started. Don't let the deaths here go to waste. If you do, I will come back and haunt you." She smiled and suddenly went completely slack. Quint leaned over and hugged his love. He was shaking with sobs as he grieved for the loss.

It seemed like an hour passed before he finally raised his head. There was fire in his swollen red eyes. "She will be avenged," he growled.

Lirith put his hand on Quint's shoulder. "We will find my uncle and we will have our vengeance."

They stood together and turned to face Arlaya. She nodded and waved over a group of their fighters. They came over silently and gently lifted Ruadana's limp body. They carried her to the royal vault. They laid her gently on a catafalque.

Quint knelt by his lady love as Arlaya absentmindedly arranged Ruadana's hair so that it lay nicely. Lirith stood behind Quint. He was a silent pillar of strength and support. He may not have known Ruadana for as long as Arlaya and Quint but he really had like her. He would act as that pillar of support until his wife and his new friend had their revenge on the killer.

A guard stepped up to the prince with a pail of water and a clean cloth. He accepted them gratefully and washed the blood from his hands and face. His court clothes were ruined but at least most people had survived. They had been unprepared for the strike to take place on a random night. They had been too relaxed since the wedding had gone off without a hitch a week earlier.

"What was that?" he asked when he realized the guard had said something.

"Your highness, is there anything we may do for you?" the guard asked again.

"Find my uncle and bring him here for justice," growled Lirith. The regent had much to answer for and it was time to end the bloodshed, once and for all.

***

Arlaya sat back silently. Her emotions were waging war with her rational self. The regent had been captured which made her heart soar in triumph. She wanted to know that his cruelty was at an end and that the murderer was properly punished. However, Calden's council made sense. If the regent were to be executed immediately, it would satisfy the thirst for revenge, at least initially. Calden was calling for Lirith to allow his uncle to defend himself against the accusations.

"I cannot!" declared Lirith for what seemed like the hundredth time.

"Of course you can't," agreed Quint. "That man has murdered too many people." His voice, while soft, betrayed his rage at Calden's suggestion and frustration that the conversation was continuing. "Summary execution is the only answer. We cannot allow this snake to get inside the head of the people."

Arlaya took a deep breath and, after the briefest of hesitations, said, "Thank you, gentlemen. Would you allow Lirith and I to speak alone?"

Both Calden and Quint opened their mouths to object. They weren't used to be being dismissed from these conversations. Arlaya however held their gaze and her expression would give no quarter. Both snapped their mouths shut, stood, and left the room.

As soon as the door closed, Lirith turned to scowl at Arlaya. "Don't tell me you agree with Calden," he growled. "My uncle doesn't deserve this chance. He is responsible for so many deaths. How can we allow him to wiggle out of -"

His rant was cut off quickly when the flat of Arlaya's palm impacted with his face. He immediately blushed and raised his hand to his face. "You slapped me," He whispered. "How dare you - " Arlaya smacked him a second time. "That hurt!" he cried then started laughing.

"Good. Now stop talking, sit down, and listen," ordered Arlaya. She waited until he was fully ensconced in a chair. "You are whining and, dare I say, acting like a child. Calden is right. Furthermore, you know he is right. If you can put aside your anger and your feelings of betrayal you will see it."

Tiger started protesting, "I don't feel betrayed…" Arlaya held up her hand to stop him. She sighed as she kneeled next to his chair and put her hand on his forearm.

"We have to rise above the masses. We all want to see him pay for what he has done but we need to be held to a higher standard, not because we are better than other people but to show people that the right thing can be done even if it is the hard thing. This is a defining moment. This is what ruling is. We have to make the hard decisions' the one nobody else wants to make. Now is the time to choose whether to rule as a tyrant or a benevolent king, recklessly or with wisdom." She looked deep into his eyes. She wanted him to understand so badly. "The decision is yours to make. You have listened to your councilors. I have said my piece. What do you want to do?"

Lirith allowed his chin to drop to his chest as he thought about what everybody had said. "The law is clear," he said. "My uncle must be given a chance to speak. As much as I would like to jump to summary judgment and not have to face him again, I must do my duty to my country and to my people. They must see that no matter who you are or what you have done, you will be treated with justly." He raised his head and gazed back at his wife with eyes shining from passion and unshed tears. "Too long, we have lived in a world that has been corrupted by politics. It has become second nature to us. I'm glad you are at my side ready to smack me because you reminded me that my duty to my heart is second to my duty as king." He drew her face up to his and kissed her deeply.

"Tomorrow, he will stand before the throne. I will allow him to speak. The evidence is overwhelming, so he must die, but he will be allowed to speak first." Lirith rose from his chair and retreated to his private office, clearly in need of some privacy to prepare for the trials ahead.

The guards walked the regent forward. The once confident, suave, debonair man was disheveled and shrinking away from the hate in the eyes of those around him. He chafed his wrists as though they had been bound and his feet shuffled in an uncertain fashion.

Arlaya's nostrils flared at the tangible fear rolling off of him in waves. This was the foul man who had tried to kill her, tried to kill Lirith, and killed Ruadana. Her eyes narrowed as she studied him. The regent blanched under her scrutiny.

The lead guards halted at the base of the dais. Lirith's uncle stood as far away from his nephew and Arlaya as possible. Quint took a step forward with an axe in his hand. If any rescue attempt occurred he was ready to put it, and the regent, down.

"Hello, uncle," Lirith said coolly into the oppressive silence. The regent flinched and started shaking. "You have been brought before me today to answer for your crimes against the crown." He paused before continuing. He knew the people around him would be upset with what he said next. "I am not a despot nor am I without mercy." He paused again, this time for the effect. "Therefore," he continued, "I will allow you to defend your actions. Explain yourself, if you will."

A gasp rippled through the throne room. Soon there was a roar as the people comprehended what he just said. Quint turned to stare at the Lirith. He couldn't understand how he could forsake Ruadana. She had died for their mission and the three of them had sworn vengeance over her still warm corpse.

Lirith nodded silently at his friend, acknowledging his internal turmoil. Quickly, he gestured toward the hoard now surging forward to extract justice before their soon-to-be king had his way. Quint turned and signaled the guards to form up their lines. They did not draw their weapons because they didn't want any of the civilians to get hurt but they also did not let anybody get near the former regent.

"Please," Lirith's voice rang out. "We must hear him out. If we kill him without letting him explain his actions, it will be tantamount to murder."

"*He* is a murderer!" one woman screamed and many cheered at the sound of her voice.

Arlaya stepped up to speak but Lirith waved her back. There was the light of determination in his eyes. He would convince them that this was the proper course of action. It would take civility to overcome the hardships of the past few years and especially of the past few weeks.

He raised a hand and spoke again, "He is a murderer but we are better than that. The laws of our people say that any man can defend himself against any accusation. Let us not turn from our laws and our traditions simply because emotions got the best of us. I know better than most, the consequences of this man's actions." He pointed at his uncle amid boos and sneers. "Let us have silence and hear him before the sentence is carried out." Obediently, his subjects quieted to the point that only a few grumblings could be heard. Lirith waited a moment more and gestured to their captive to begin his tale.

"I am innocent of these charges, nephew," he said shakily. There were shouts and from somewhere a shoe flew through the air and hit him on the arm.

"Stop!" shouted Lirith with his hands held high. When the room was quiet again, Lirith looked at the regent, "I suggest you choose your words carefully," he said in a gruff, quiet voice.

"It is true that I wanted you to wed my daughter," the now cringing man said. "I wanted you to cement our families closer together. When the Lady Arlaya appeared suddenly, it was like the gods were playing a trick on an old man." As he spoke, the regent stood up straighter and his voice became stronger. "I was certain she was trying to deceive us. There is no way any member of the Rivell family survived, or at least that is what I thought. After speaking to

213

the two of you on your birthday and hearing her story, I came to accept her. I still resented her but the story was convincing enough for my skeptical mind to believe.”

There was silence as he took a deep breath. “I still resented her. My daughter would have been the perfect match for you. She has experience as a leader and in politics. She has known this city her entire life and the people love her. Besides, she has had a hand in making all of the policies in the last few years. Yes, she was the perfect wife for you. But I did not let that resentment get to me. It would pass in time, I thought.”

He chuckled and looked down at the floor. “When she disappeared, I thought maybe there was a chance for things to go as planned. Then, the rumors started flying. Every servant, stable hand, even lord or lady I ran into would abruptly stop talking as I entered the room. My friends started to put more distance between us. In the three days that she was missing, I came to realize the perilous position I was in. I had to protect myself because clearly everyone thought I was responsible.”

“I left a note to you on your mantle, which you clearly did not receive. In that note, I told you that I was going to depart for the summer residence. I felt that I would be safer there and that putting distance between myself and the situation here would allow me some perspective on who the real culprit may be and remove my complicity from the equation.” His hands started shaking and he visibly forced himself into motionlessness.

“On my way out of the city, I was accosted and kidnapped. I have no idea by whom, but I have been locked in a cellar since the day you found Arlaya. I never saw the faces of my captors. They fed me through a slot in the door by the floor. Yesterday, I heard shouting and fighting. Suddenly, the door opened and the light of day blinded me as the guards manhandled me out of the cellar and to the palace.”

He dropped to his knees with his hands held open at his side. “I could have had nothing to do with the attempts on your life or the death of your friend,” he said quietly. “I know there is nothing I can do to make you believe me but know that even with my death there will still be a traitor in your midst."

Lirith stepped down from the dais toward his uncle. "I am sorry, but the evidence against you is too great. Tomorrow morning you will meet the executioner and you will join our ancestors in the afterlife." He kept his distance from the condemned man but there was a sadness in his eyes and a desire to have things turn out differently. A cheer whipped through the throne room as the guards escorted their ward from the presence of the prince.

Lirith turned back to Arlaya and just looked into her eyes. She knew exactly how he was feeling. His uncle had been too clear and concise in his tale. There was no doubt in her mind that, even if parts of his story had not been true, his statement about a traitor still existing in their midst was fact. Her shoulders almost wanted to slump forward in despair at the thought that this treacherous time in her life was not yet over. She did not allow herself that moment of pure emotion. She needed to present a strong front to not worry her subjects. She was a good actor, but she could not help feeling that, for once, she wanted to be a simple person again with the ability to curl up and cry if she wanted to, hug another without thoughts of the political consequences, or not constantly look for assassins over her shoulder.

Lirith had once told her that this life would get her in the end. She had done what few other spies or assassins had ever been able to do. She had found a life to fall into that did not involve putting one's neck on the line on a regular basis. As queen of Belevis, she would no longer go on missions and only occasionally would she decode her own messages. Calden would continue performing as spymaster and he would pass on anything she needed to know.

She turned to look at her former employer, her friend, her mentor, adopted father of her love and almost flinched at the look of disgust and pure hatred on his face. He was staring at the door to the throne room which was just thudding shut behind the former regent. Nobody else was watching him and Arlaya was sure he was unaware of her gaze. His open look of fury was dreadful on such a handsome man. She quickly turned away and hoped he wouldn't realize she had seen his expression.

She stepped down next to Lirith and whispered in his ear, "Let's go to a quiet place where we can talk things over."

He nodded and offered his arm. Together, they walked to the royal suite. Their guards fell in around them and a hush descended on the hall as the lords, ladies, and any city dwellers who had been able to attend bowed them out. Quint and Calden followed them silent as shadows.

As soon as they entered the royal suite, Arlaya and Lirith turned to enter the office. They had worked diligently since moving in to prevent the ability to spy or listen to their conversations. The wall was two feet thick with stone and there was no access to the room over their heads. There wasn't even a fireplace. They would make due with stones heated in the sitting room fireplace during the winter.

"He was lying," Quint said into the silence. "He had to have been lying."

"I'm sorry, Quint," whispered Arlaya.

"No! He was lying!"

"Quint," Arlaya placed a hand on his arm, "there is someone else out there; a partner that he worked with."

Quint snatched his arm away from her and turned to leave.

"Sit down," ordered Lord Calden in a menacing but calm voice.

Quint glared at the man and stood a moment longer facing the door. He nodded as though coming to a decision and his shoulders fell in half surrender. Slowly, he walked toward a chair, giving every other person in the room a very wide berth. Lirith held out his arms to Arlaya and the two sat together on the settee as Calden chose to lean against a bookshelf.

"If there is another out there, how do we find him?" asked Quint.

"I don't see what we can do," said Calden.

"We cannot just sit here and wait for Ru's killer to come for us!"

"That is precisely what we have to do," Calden said in a cold and logical voice. "We must wait for whoever it is to make a mistake."

"Quint, Calden, we are getting nowhere with this conversation," Lirith said. "We agree that there is another enemy out there but we are too close and too emotional at this particular moment. We must come to terms with this revelation before we can come up with a plan to eradicate our demons." Quint nodded choppily and left the room hurriedly. Calden stayed a moment longer, staring at nothing before he too departed.

"What do you think, darling?" asked Arlaya.

"I think that we must be careful who we trust," replied Lirith. "My own uncle betrayed me. Who will be next?"

"I think that Syril's text may hold some secret we need," said Arlaya thoughtfully.

"Come again?"

"The old book that I study when I have a spare minute. It was written by the first king and talks about the political intrigue at the beginning of the government. I think that once I discover who the original enemy was it will bring the modern enemy out of obscurity."

"I still don't understand, love."

Arlaya sighed and snuggled deeper into her husband's arms. "There has been a history of assassination and attempts to gain control of the crown through deception and playing the political game. It all started with the violent deaths of my ancestors. Perhaps if I can identify the man who perpetrated those crimes I will find his progeny and that may lead us to the enemy of the now."

"It is definitely an interesting thought."

"It is also something more than sitting around waiting for a mistake to be made." Arlaya let silence fall as she decided how to phrase her next request. She cleared her throat.

"Arlaya, whatever it is, please, don't be afraid to tell me," Lirith said and kissed her hair.

"I don't think we should tell Quint or Calden," she replied quickly.

"You don't trust them?" asked Lirith.

"You said yourself that we cannot trust anyone. I feel that we must keep this idea close to our chest. It is the only way to ensure that I am able to discover who we must be wary of." Arlaya sighed again. "I don't like it any more that you do, but it is for the best."

"Let's put aside intrigue and grief tonight, little bird," he whispered in her ear. "We have been married for an entire week and have not yet had our wedding night. I almost lost you and tonight I want to have you forever." He kissed her neck and rang for servants.

The servants came in with candles and covered dishes of food. Lirith guided Arlaya to a seat at their private dining table. He sat in his own chair and saluted her with his goblet of wine. She couldn't help herself, she giggled and touched his glass with hers. Although both were tired and grieving, they enjoyed just spending time together. They laughed and joked and teased one another. Finally, they were out of food and Lirith was gazing at his beautiful wife. The glow of the candles took her sensual features to an entirely new level.

Arlaya felt her heart skip a beat as her love looked at her. She hadn't considered this part of their relationship.

"If you are not ready after what happened last year, I will understand," Lirith said delicately, "but I want to be completely honest with you, Arlaya. I want to make our marriage real tonight." He sipped his wine to give her time to process.

Instead of saying anything, Arlaya stood up from her seat. Lirith's expression fell for half a second. Then, she reached down and took his hand. Gently, she led him toward the bedchamber. If Lirith noticed the slight shake in her hand or that she was sweating faintly, he gave no indication.

Before they crossed the threshold, Lirith wrapped an arm around his wife's waist and whipped her up into his arms. She laughed and nuzzled against his neck. He felt anticipation rise as she kissed his skin. He laid her gently on the bed and helped pull her gown off, even as she helped to undo his trousers and pull his shirt over his head. Once they were undressed, he kissed her. He was hesitant at first but hesitation quickly turned to passion.

Arlaya gasped and pulled away. "I love you," she whispered in his ear. "I've never done this before," she said.

"Don't worry, darling," he whispered back, "we will figure it out together." He kissed her again then shifted he weight so he was lower. He left a trail of kisses down her chest and stomach. Finally, he kissed her between the legs.

Arlaya gasped in surprise and entwined her fingers in his hair as his tongue quested around her. She had never felt anything like this. She felt her temperature rise with her desire and felt Lirith's lips turn up as he smiled at her reaction. She arched her back in pleasure and he raised his head to grin at her.

Lirith raised himself so that his face was even with hers once more and kissed her while stroking her breast. Arlaya wrapped him in her arms and pulled him closer. She felt all of her insecurities from the past year melt away. She slid one of her hands down and started stroking his erect penis. He shook with restrained excitement.

Arlaya, still stroking, adjusted her body beneath his. "I want you," she whispered hoarsely.

Lirith didn't need any other invitation, he pressed himself into her. Arlaya felt a pinch then her flesh parted and all was right with the world. He lost himself in his carnal desires and he took her right on with him.

Some time later, Lirith rested on his elbows and gazed down at the most beautiful woman in the world. He loved her so much and he could see that she felt the same. In this treacherous time, how could such a miracle be true? He felt the comfortable hands of sleep pulling on him but he didn't want to look away.

"I love you," he whispered as he rolled off of her.

"I love you more," she whispered back. "I love you to the ends of the earth and back and no matter what happens, I want to show you that every night." She kissed his chest and laid her head against him. In no time at all, they were both sound asleep.

Today, I weep for my best friend, a man who is more of a brother than a friend, is dead. His entire line was slain in the night. Not a child was left alive. Sorrow does not even begin to describe my emotional state. Lord Caldenaria has come by again to provide support and to discuss his daughter once more. Before long, he will ask me to choose her as my son's future wife. For now, I will simply avoid that particular conversation.

Arlaya rubbed her eyes and yawned. She had gotten nowhere in her studies of the text. *Lord Caldenaria may be an ancestor of Lord Calden. The title might have been shortened over the centuries.* She could not get rid of a nagging feeling that Caldenaria was important to the story of why her ancestors had to die.

After stretching and rolling her shoulders out, Arlaya bent to the next entry and her songbook.

We have been unable to discover the identity of the perpetrators of the mass murder. There remains no justice for the Rivell family. I have gotten word that one young man did survive the carnage. He holds within him, the spirit of hope. My friend lives on in his young son.

Arlaya wanted to scream in frustration. With every new passage, Arlaya felt a new spark of hope. Conversely, every time that hope was dashed, her nerves were frayed. She swiped everything off of her desk in a fit of vexation as she determined the next passage was about Caldenaria once more maneuvering for a union between his daughter and the prince.

"Sweetheart, come take a break. It is late and sleep will help." Lirith was standing at the door with a thin smile. He leaned against the doorframe and crossed his arms over his chest. Arlaya smiled as she knew that he would not let her say no.

She stood carefully and bent to clean up her papers and books. "I must not leave a mess," she said to excuse her delay in complying.

Lirith laughed and took his wife up in his arms. Carrying her to bed, he kissed her on the forehead and slid her under the covers. "Don't even try to seduce me tonight, little bird. You need your sleep. You have been working entirely too hard." He chuckled softly. "Who knows? You may have already discovered the culprit but were too tired to see it."

Arlaya's eyes drifted closed and she barely noticed when Lirith laid down next to her. Within moments she was fast asleep and her husband watched as tranquility took over her expression. He knew how she had been hunted her whole life. All he wanted to give her was the peace of mind that she would no longer be pursued. He wanted her to feel secure in their life together.

***

There was a crash of thunder as she ran through the woods. Her breathing was labored and the bottoms of her feet were slick with blood. Her skirts kept getting snagged on bushes and she cut her hands as she brushed branches out of her way.

There was something or someone chasing her. She could hear the beast growling and her heartbeat quickened. Thunder crashed again and lightning flashed, illuminating the gnarled tree limbs blocking her path. The trees moved as the wind screamed. In the bright flashes of light, the trees looked like shadow figures reaching out to grab her.

Arlaya found herself in a clearing, running toward a tower. There was a single grove of trees at the base. She called for help as loud as

Arlaya sat bolt upright in her bed with a gasp. Her heart was pounding in her ears and she was drenched in sweat. The bindings she had felt on her legs were her blankets, twisted around her body from her struggles. All she heard in the darkness of the room was the calm relaxed breathing of her husband. Having Lirith next to her was comforting and she felt her heartbeat slow down as the echoes of the dream faded.

The family Caldenaria had hunted her ancestors down through the centuries but they didn't exist anymore. The Caldenaria line had died out ages ago. She could feel the panic ebbing as she pondered the problem. The descendants of the line in other families must somehow have picked up the standard of the old feud.

She rubbed her eyes and felt a headache coming on. *The family Caldenaria,* the menacing dream voice whispered in the dark. *Calden...*

Arlaya drifted to sleep again with her head on Lirith's chest, the steady beat of his heart soothing her nerves. She woke the next morning with only a hint of fear from the dream. The rest of her sleep had been dreamless and uneventful, if not fitful.

She felt the sun streaming across her face as Lirith pulled the curtains back to reveal a beautiful cloudless day. It was the perfect day for the coronation. She rose and stretched with a yawn while walking over to join him. The sunlight of the new day reflected off of the newly fallen snow, winter's last attempt to maintain its hold on the world.

"Good morning, my darling," whispered Lirith in her ear. She could hear the smile in his voice and his proximity sent shivers of delight down her spine. There was just one thing preventing her from acting on the carnal visions filling her mind at that moment.

Caldenaria, the voice whispered, sending shivers of loathing and fear to replace those of love, anticipation, and warmth her spine had just felt. Lirith was stroking her shoulder and paused when he felt the shiver. He gently placed his hand under her chin and turned her face toward his.

"What is wrong, little bird?" he asked softly.

"Nothing," she replied quickly, "it's nothing. It's just the remnants of a nightmare."

"It's more than that," he pressed. "If you can't trust me then we are done for."

"I trust you completely, dear heart," Arlaya replied with a sensual kiss. "It's simply that I haven't figured out what is going on. I don't know who our mystery enemy is and I don't know how to keep you safe until you are old and grey." She sighed and turned to start dressing.

"I will be fine, darling. We have taken every possible precaution against the inevitable attack." Lirith reached out and grabbed his wife's shoulders. He squeezed gently in a reassuring fashion. "What will come will come. We just have to trust in our friends and our own very formidable skills."

"I'm not the sort of woman who can sit around and wait for the world to happen to me. I had a thought last night. I want to spend the day in the Hall of Records. I believe there might be something in the histories of the families that will provide some clue as to what is happening." She strapped her wrist braces on under her flowing long sleeves.

"Ari," Lirith whispered.

Arlaya turned to face her husband. He had unshed tears in his eyes which were wide with concern.

"I will be safe, Lirith," she whispered back. "I'm the best you've ever seen, remember?" Her small smile sparked one of his little grins that she loved so much.

"I know I shouldn't be worried about you. It's just who I am." He stroked her face. "Don't forget to leave yourself enough time to prepare for tonight. It's a party celebrating me so I fully expect you to look stunning." He winked, pecked her on the cheek and left their bedroom.

Arlaya carefully and quietly left the room by a separate door. She moved swiftly through the corridors to a part of the palace most people don't visit. Her senses were on high alert. Every face she passed in the hall was mentally cross checked against everyone she had met or seen since her first day in the complex.

Arlaya realized that she was simply working herself up into a frenzy of worry and stopped in her tracks. The first day that she met Lirith, he told her that one day; the paranoia would encompass her life. She knew that it was one of the perils of the job as much as she knew that this was the worst possible day for the paranoia to take hold.

After a few deep, settling breaths, Arlaya settled into her former role of Phoenix. It was Phoenix that survived the attack on the outcasts, the trial by battle among the assassins, the kidnapping, and the attack a week after her wedding day. Arlaya had been playing politics for weeks but Phoenix had been playing intrigue for most of her life. Since she was a child, she had been trained for this one moment, this one day of such great importance.

After she had carefully sorted her thoughts, Phoenix straightened her shoulders, set her emotions aside and walked at a more sedate pace to the Hall of Records. In her calmer frame of mind, Phoenix felt her muscles relax and a headache that had been building simply fluttered away like a leaf on a light breeze.

She closed the door to the Hall of Records with a quiet click and inhaled the scents unique to a place of learning and history, that of vellum, parchment, and ink. Books lined the shelves from top to bottom and sunlight flowed through the windows at the top of the outer walls. Arlaya stood perfectly still and watched the dust motes float through the light.

Slowly, her gaze shifted to the large desk in the middle of the room. Behind that desk sat a young man with his long nose nearly touching the paper to which he was applying his ink. She watched his quill dash up and down and ink splatter his fingers and that nose.

Not wanting to startle the poor young man, Arlaya cleared her throat gently. She needn't have bothered worrying about startling him because he seemed to be more than a bit squirrely and jumped at even that small noise that she made. His ink well overturned and stained his sleeve and his eyes went wide as he stabbed his finger with his quill. Arlaya simply stood waiting, inspecting her fingernails, until the archivist regained his composure.

"H-how c-can I h-help you, ma'am?" he asked.

She looked up and smiled. "I'm sorry to disturb you, but I was hoping to spend some time looking at the histories of the leading families of the kingdom. If you could point me in the right direction, I will let you get back to your work."

"Of course, ma'am, right this way." The young man gestured toward the back of the cavernous room.

Together, they entered a smaller room with twelve bookshelves with unmarked books. Each bookshelf was marked at the top with a brass plate bearing the name of one of the founding families. Arlaya stopped and stared at the books for a few heartbeats before she realized that the archivist was still standing with her.

"Thank you, I appreciate your help." Arlaya turned and nodded to the young man in an appreciative manner and strode into the heart of the room. She quickly found her own family's bookshelf and felt her heart fall. There was one single book on one single shelf. The other empty shelves were obviously carefully cleaned as there was not a speck of dust on any of them.

After regaining her control, Arlaya turned to find her desired bookshelf. She read each plaque in turn until she found Caldenaria. Once more, she felt her heart drop, this time in despair. Each shelf was crammed with volume upon volume. *Where do I begin? I have so little time before the coronation.*

By virtue of needing a starting point, she pulled a random book off of the last shelf and sat at the small desk provided for the uncommon historian who perused these volumes. Upon turning to the first page, she found that it was a registry of the members of the family. She quickly flipped to the final pages of the book. The last member of the family included in the registry was a man who had died many decades earlier without ever having married or had legitimate children.

"That's no use to me. Who could it be?" she whispered to herself.

She sat pondering for many minutes. "No legitimate children," she muttered meditatively.

She sat up straight in her chair. "No *legitimate* children!" she said more forcefully. "What about illegitimate children?" She sprang to her feet and rushed to the next book on the shelf.

It was exactly what she was looking for, a list of all progeny not just the direct line. She flipped through to the last page and scanned the names. The people in this book had died many decades before and their children were also already dead. Arlaya felt confident, however, and moved on to the next book. It was a continuation of the list and Arlaya knew in her gut, she would find her answers here. She flipped to the last entry and scanned for a familiar name.

She read out loud, "Last in the Caldenaria line, while illegitimate, is the Lord Calden, born of the Daughter of Oldara, Christialla, and heir to the title of Oldara." She sat back stunned. It took her quite a long time to put all the facts in order. "Calden…" she whispered.

"Yes, little bird?"

Arlaya jumped to her feet. "I didn't hear you come in, sir." She turned to face her former employer and friend with an expression of complete calm. Her training took hold and she would not let anything slip past her mask.

"I'm sorry for startling you but we've been trying to find you. Aren't you supposed to be getting ready for the coronation, child?" he asked in a concerned, fatherly sort of way.

"I was just trying to calm my nerves," Arlaya explained. "We all know that our mystery foe is going to strike tonight. He or she cannot afford to let Lirith be crowned." She carefully picked up the books and slipped them onto the shelves for her family. "Instead of focusing on that, I wanted to spend some time learning about my own ancestral roots. There isn't much here. Not like these other shelves." She waved her hand around the room. "If I am going to die tonight, I just wanted to know where I come from."

Calden wrapped his arm around her shoulders and started steering her out the door. "Worry not, little bird," he said in her ear, "you and your love will be safe tonight."

It was all Arlaya could do not to shiver at his touch and his breath on her neck. She needed to play as though she did not know of his treachery. He was her mentor and teacher and he knew most of her tricks. What she needed to do was reach her husband and warn him of the impending doom. There might be enough time to change their strategy of protection. Calden had been instrumental in making the plans for Lirith's safety.

"Let me walk you to your rooms so you can get dressed. There isn't much time." Calden's smile never changed as he pulled her gently through the shelves to the corridors. Arlaya consigned herself to her escort. After she got dressed, she would be able to warn her husband.

It seemed like an eternity before she was finally able to close her suite doors behind her. The solid barrier between Calden and Arlaya, allowed her to breathe more freely. She carefully got dressed in her coronation outfit. First was a pair of tight fitting scarlet trousers, followed by scarlet and gold skirts in layers and a tight bodice. Over the bodice, Arlaya pulled a tunic with flowy sleeves. She then put on her extra hidden weapons; knives in her boots, daggers in her wrist sheathes, her fans in her belt.

She noticed something odd about her fans. After pulling them out of her belt, Arlaya balanced them in her hand. The balance was off and the weight was not quite right. These were not her fans. *He switched them,* she thought. It was a good thing she had stored all of her other fans in a secret cache. She quickly rifled through her other fans and found two that would complement her dress of silk fire quite nicely and slipped those in her belt instead.

There was a knock at the door.

Arlaya strode to the door, confident in her ability to act calm and give her enemies no indication of her knowledge. Any slip at this critical moment would cause the death of the only man she had ever truly loved and the only man she would ever call brother. Lirith and Quint had changed her life and she would do everything in her power to keep them in her life. The knocker was none other than Quint and with him, Calden and Lirith.

"Are you ready, Ari?" Quint asked.

"I am ready, Quint." Arlaya reached out and grabbed the hand of the brother she chose. Carefully, so as not to attract anyone's attention, she squeezed. Quint shot a glance in her direction but took his cues from her face and squeezed back.

I know who our enemy is, she squeezed. It had been a while since she had used this method of communication so she squeezed the code slowly.

Who? Quint asked.

Calden, Arlaya replied but she kept squeezing as she felt Quint stiffen. *Do nothing. If we act now, we will lose the people. Calden is loved and respected.*

How can we do nothing?

Please, she begged him silently. *Please, understand. It's the hardest thing I will ever ask of you. Do nothing so that we may save everyone.*

But, he killed Ruadana, Quint protested.

And he will pay, Arlaya promised.

Quint nodded slightly and Arlaya dropped his hand. He dropped back behind the royal couple. "I need a few minutes if you don't mind," he said carefully.

"Quint?" Lirith asked with concern.

"I haven't been in there since…" Quint's voice trailed off.

"Of course," whispered Arlaya, "of course, you can have a moment. Take all the time you need." She hugged him and turned back down the hall.

Lirith nodded to his friend and joined his wife. He slipped an arm around Arlaya's waist. He squeezed reassuringly. "What is going on, darling?" he whispered.

"The two of them were in love. Quint was sure he would never find that in this line of work but he did and now she is dead. Of course, he would need a few minutes to prepare himself before entering that room," Arlaya explained, hoping he wouldn't probe any further.

It was a waste of hope. "What about your project from this morning? Did you find the information you were looking for?" her husband asked.

"No," she lied.

"That's too bad," Lirith muttered.

"Shall we, Majesties?" Calden asked.

"Yes, My Lord," Arlaya agreed.

They reached the double doors to the throne room and paused. Lirith stepped forward and held out his arm to his wife. Tradition dictated the prince entering the room alone but he was breaking from the tradition. Lirith wanted to start his reign with his wife on equal footing. They would rule as partners rather than King with his Queen following one step behind and so they would both be crowned on this day.

The plan for preventing an attack called for Calden guarding the door. He would stand in the doorway as the royal couple moved down the aisle toward the dais, thus giving his blessing on the coronation. A member of the Order of Dirige would waited with the simple circlet of gold inlaid with diamonds that would act as Lirith's crown and a delicately wrought circlet of gold leaves inlaid with sapphires that would act as Arlaya's crown. The dais would be surrounded by trusted men, both guards in uniform and in civilian clothing.

A fanfare cut through Arlaya's thoughts. No matter how she reviewed the plans they had in place, nothing could work now that she knew who the enemy was. The doors opened smoothly and slowly and Lirith started forward. Arlaya paced next to her partner for life knowing full well that their life together would most likely end in the next few minutes.

The people in the throne room were on their feet and watched as the couple went by. There was a collective gasp as they realized the significance of the break in tradition. The common folk at the back of the hall burst into spontaneous cheers and Arlaya's heart swelled with pride. She felt her spine stiffen and felt Lirith respond the same way. A slight smile touched his lips and he squeezed her hand.

They finally reached the dais and the couple knelt on the cushions provided there. The monk stepped forward and started intoning the ceremonial words of coronation. The words had been changed slightly to include Arlaya as an equal. She knew that this was one of the biggest moments in her life, however, all Arlaya could do was wait for the hammer to fall. Her more passive mind was focused on the ceremony so that when it came time for her ceremonial response, she replied in the proper words. "I solemnly swear to uphold the laws of Belevis and protect the people of the Kingdom until my dying breath in the presence of all the gods of all the people of the land." She felt the circlet's weight upon her brow and the more substantial weight of responsibility on her shoulders. Carefully, she remained on her knees but shifted her position so her weapons would be immediately accessible.

A palpable silence fell as the monk turned to Lirith. Not a single muscle moved in that vast room as all of the citizens witnessed their king being crowned. It was in this room of calm and hush that Arlaya projected her senses. The slightest shift, rustle of cloth, or even clearing of a throat could be a signal of the start of the fighting. Because of this she almost missed it when it happened.

The whistle of an arrow broke the quiet. Rather than being followed by the grunt of a man being hit by the projectile, the arrow sank into the wood panels at the back of the room. Arlaya was on her feet quicker than a thought standing at her husband's back with two daggers drawn. The men hidden through the crowd stood and circled the royal couple and, suddenly, there was a wall of men between the king and any perceivable threat.

Arlaya glanced at the monk. His hood had fallen back but he continued to perform the ceremony as though nothing had happened. As she turned back to the rest of the room, Arlaya froze. The monk was Syril.

"I solemnly swear to uphold the laws of Belevis and protect the people of the Kingdom until my dying breath in the presence of all the gods of all the people of the land," swore Lirith as the first wave of attackers struck.

The cries of pain almost drowned out the cries of fear from the legitimate guests of the coronation. A third of the men in the outer ring were dead or dying, yet no enemy had reached the royals. Thus far, even though Calden had been principal in the planning, the king was safe.

"May I present to the people, our king, King Lirith of Belevis!" Syril's voice could barely be heard over the din. He then produced his own weapons to protect the king.

Lirith stood and turned Arlaya to face him. He enveloped her in a deep embrace. "Let's kick some ass and save our people, little bird," he whispered. He kissed her and she felt the tears running down his cheeks.

"I love you," she whispered and he nodded. He was unable to respond.

They both turned back to the battle at hand. Time lost all meaning as they fought for their lives. Slowly the men surrounding them fell. One by one holes opened up in their defenses but Tiger and Phoenix had been training all their lives for this. The king and queen were blurs as they moved. Phoenix did not notice as she lost three of her four daggers and fought with her last dagger and a knife. She had yet to draw her shukusens but she knew that would change soon. Tiger had claimed swords from their fallen compatriots and now dual wielded them in a whirl of steel and death. Syril fought at their back protecting them from unseen advances. How a man of his age moved so well, Arlaya would never know but she was glad he did.

Finally, the fighting stopped. Arlaya straightened and took her first deep breath. There were moaning men scattered throughout the throne room and even more men who lay in the perfect stillness of death strewn through the mess. Her hand started shaking and she dropped one of her blades.

A warm comforting presence grabbed her now empty hand. "We did it, darling. We survived." Arlaya looked up into her husband's eyes and saw his relief but her gut said that the relief was premature.

"Your Majesty!" rang an oddly muffled voice from the corridor.

Lirith and Arlaya quickly turned to face the speaker. They saw a man in a black mask, cloak and hood, with black fighting gear underneath. He held a bare broadsword in one hand and a short sword in the other hand.

"You think you have won," he said. "You are wrong. As we speak, my men are surrounding you. You have no chance of walking out of this alive. Accept your situation and throw down your weapons. It will be quick."

"Calden," Arlaya whispered.

Lirith looked at her in surprise. "Calden?" he asked.

"That's what I found out in the Hall of Records," she responded. "Calden's family is the one that slaughtered mine. He's the bastard son of the last member of that family."

"He's the one man I thought I could count on." He raised his voice to be heard by the man in black. "We will never surrender. You will have to kill us."

"That was going to happen anyway," said the man with a chuckle as new fighters entered the hall. Arlaya scooped up her fallen blade and spun into action. At all times, she kept one eye on Calden. He hadn't engaged with anyone yet, he simply stood and waited for the defenders to be whittled down.

Man after man was wounded or killed. There were more enemy deaths than defenders but it wasn't too long before Arlaya, Lirith, Syril, and two other defenders were the only ones standing.

Calden held up a closed fist. A dozen more men entered the throne room and lined the back wall on either side of the doors.

"Calden, what has gotten into you?" demanded Lirith. "We worked together for years. You taught me to be a man and how to lead. Why are you fighting me now?"

The man in the mask started laughing. "You got close, little bird. You almost figured it out." The laughter continued as Arlaya and Lirith stood breathing heavily and shaking from exertion.

"Almost…" muttered Arlaya.

Two men dragged a third in from the corridor. "Here is your friend, Your Majesty. Unfortunately, you and he will no longer be playing chess or having late night discussions about political intrigue." The masked man flicked his hand forward and the two men dropped the body of Lord Calden, the Shadow Man, at his feet. He had a deep wound in his chest and his throat had been cut.

Lirith stiffened, his body full of tension. "You killed one of the greatest men the kingdom has ever known." Anger rolled off him in waves.

"A great man whom you thought had betrayed you up until a moment ago," the mask shot back with another laugh.

Lirith was suddenly flying through the room, charging the enemy. With a roar, he swung his sword up into a striking position. The masked man dodged and spun. His dagger slipped through Lirith's defenses and into his side. Arlaya gasped as her love fell to his knees.

"I'm not going to kill you, yet, boy. First I am going to make you suffer," the masked man stated in a haunting voice that carried across the room. He turned to look at Arlaya. "I'm going to take care of your darling wife first." He shoved Lirith over onto his side and strode toward the dais.

Carefully, Arlaya adjusted her grip on her weapons. The hilts of her blades were slick with sweat and blood but she knew that the next few moments depended on her holding on to her weapons. Her husband needed her, her kingdom needed her and she was not about to let either one down.

At a finger twitch from her enemy, Arlaya's head whipped toward the back of the room. A lone bowman loosed an arrow and Arlaya forced herself to remain stationary as the projectile approached her. It wasn't until the last fraction of a heartbeat that she realized the arrow was going to miss her. There was a grunt and a solid object hit the floor behind her.

Arlaya turned to see her old friend and mentor on the ground with the arrow protruding from his chest. Syril had been the target of the bowman, not Arlaya. She quickly turned back to her advancing enemy and found him only a few feet away.

"What do you say, little bird?" he asked.

"What do you mean?" she shot back.

"Well last time we fought, you won. Today, you will lose." He laughed and raised his sword. "Let the best man win, little bird."

She barely parried the blow with her daggers. Instead of engaging with this obviously stronger foe, Arlaya danced backwards making space.

"You can't win by retreating, little bird," taunted the man.

"Stop talking and start fighting. And stop calling me that!" she snarled as she closed the space. Instead of rushing into an attack, she rolled across the floor and off the dais. There was something irritating her about this man. Obviously, they knew each other and there was something familiar about his voice, though she was having trouble placing it around the distortion due to the mask, and the way he moved.

"Quint," she hissed.

"Ah, she finally figured it out," Quint growled and ripped off his mask. He struck at her in quick fluid movements. It was all Arlaya could do to hold him off. She lost one dagger, then another, and was finally standing breathing heavily with Quint's sword point at her throat.

"I have never been anything but a friend to you, Quint. I counted you as a brother," Arlaya whispered. She felt a tear roll down her cheek.

"Sentiment, Arlaya?" Quint jeered. "I wouldn't have expected it of you but it means that I did my job right. My ancestors would be proud to know that, once and for all, the Rivells are finished."

"Your ancestors? Calden was the last in the Caldenaria line."

"Yes, he was the last recorded descendent. There was, however, one other, my mother. She was persecuted and fled her family, and the royal family, and even the Oldara family. My mother's rightful place was on that throne wearing that circlet of gold." He ripped the crown off of Arlaya's head and threw it across the room. "I will have to rule in her stead," he snarled.

Arlaya felt the tip of the sword bite into her neck and suddenly she felt like all the energy in the world was flowing through her veins. She turned her head and felt the blade cut shallowly toward the back of her neck. While she twisted, she pulled her fans from her belt and snapped them open. With a flick of her wrist, the fabric of Quint's tunic fell away from his stomach and a quick slash from her other fan caused a line of scarlet to appear across his belly. There was a strong metallic scent as Quint's innards pressed against the wound..

Quint quickly ripped up what was left of his tunic and tied it tightly around his wound. Arlaya took the time he gave her to catch her breath. Once his makeshift bandage was in place, he reengaged her. She found herself fending off more earnest attacks from her former friend.

Each time she blocked his sword, she felt her arms shake and give a little. Quint didn't appear to be weakening even though he was wounded and a shadow of doubt entered Arlaya's mind. She didn't think she would make it through this fight in one piece, let alone alive.

"Why, Quint?" she gasped. "You killed Ru."

"No!" he screamed. "You killed her! She wasn't supposed to take an arrow. She took one that was meant for you! She died because of you!" He took a deep breath as he parried one of her fans. "He promised Ru would survive. I would help rule the kingdom and she would be at my side. I'm glad Lirith had him executed. He broke his promise." Quint was almost hysterical. Arlaya stumbled over the body of a guard and fell and he raised his sword in a two-handed overhead chop to end the fighting.

A blade abruptly appeared in Quint's chest causing him to hesitate in his attack. He screamed in rage as Arlaya took advantage of the momentary pause to jump to her feet and slice her fan across his throat. He grunted and crumpled as she was bathed in his blood. Arlaya dropped her fans and fell to her knees. Lirith's face swam in front of her eyes as she began to weep.

"I'm fine, darling, I'm fine," he whispered while stroking her hair with one hand while the other kept pressure on his side wound to stop the bleeding. "We are both alive."

It took a long time for Arlaya to regain control. "I'm sorry, Lirith," she whispered.

"You have nothing to apologize for. You could not have known about Quint. Somehow, my uncle got to him and convinced him to do this.."

"He was like a brother to me. He was a mentor to me at the Citadel. He was there for me in one of my weakest moments! How could he do this? How could he make me kill family?" wailed Arlaya. Her voice broke in the torrent of grief.

Lirith had no words. He could only hold his wife as she dissolved into hysterics. Finally, her breathing slowed and the sobbing stopped. Lirith looked at her tearstained face and saw the fear and the despair finally falling away.

Hawk came running in followed by two dozen men. "We just broke down the lines of the rebels outside. Are you alright?" She skidded to a halt as she took in the carnage. She saw Calden lying in a heap and the king holding his grieving wife. She turned and ordered half of her men to guard the room and the other half to ensure the enemy men were dead.

"Syril," Arlaya whispered, "we have to bring him out and bury him." She slowly stood and walked over to her mentor. The body was in the middle of a circle of bodies. Arlaya hadn't realized how many men had stood up to protect their beloved king. She felt so drained of emotion that she could only look at the dead with regret.

Gingerly, she reached down to turn her friend over from his stomach to his back. His eyes were closed and it looked as though he was sleeping. Her exhaustion and desire to see Syril alive made her almost imagine that he was breathing. She carefully cut the arrow out of his upper chest. The wound bled sluggishly as Arlaya carefully cleaned him up.

Lirith slowly walked up to the pair. He did not like seeing his wife in such anguish. She had survived so much in her life and he wanted to protect her from any further losses.He knelt next to her and pushed her hair out of her face. "Darling, we need to let the physicians check you over," he whispered as he placed a cloth over her bloody neck.

"Lirith," she whispered and looked up into his face and he could see the doubt in her eyes, "I hope I didn't lose the baby."

"What?" Lirith gasped.

"Sweetheart, I'm pregnant."

Lirith gathered her up in his arms and kissed her deeply. He tasted the salt of her tears but he didn't care. His heart suddenly felt light and love replaced grief and despair.

"As much as I like the sentiment, children," said a voice right next to them, "we should probably do as you say and see the physicians."Syril laughed at the stricken look on their faces and dissolved into a coughing fit. Arlaya fell on top of him in a hug of relief. "Child, you are heavy," he said with a laugh and gently nudged her off of him.

Lirith and Arlaya helped him stand and half walked half carried him from the throne room. Although they still felt the impact of all of those deaths, for a brief moment they were happy. The royal couple were expecting a child and one of the men who had treated Arlaya like a daughter was not dead.

***

The physicians were not happy that Arlaya, in her pregnant state, had fought. They expressed surprise that she hadn't had a miscarriage and they kept tutting that strenuous activity could cause problems for the baby. Arlaya just shook her head thinking *these people have no idea what went on in that room.*

Lirith had little scrapes and bruises but the dagger thrust into his side caused enough damage that he was restricted to bed rest until it healed properly. Syril's arrow wound was more of a concern. He was lucky that it hadn't hit a major blood vessel. The arrow nicked smaller vessels which caused the wound to bleed pretty heavily. The surgeons cauterized the wound as they pulled the arrow out. They could work fast because Arlaya had cut the tip and the fletching off.

Arlaya snuck away from the others to walk through the carnage of the throne room. She silently said prayers over the dead men who had protected her family, thanking them for their service and pleading with whatever deities may exist to let them have a peaceful afterlife. She carefully laid out all of the bodies of the loyal on one side of the room and piled the enemy soldiers on the other side of the room. She must have been there for hours because dusk slowly dimmed the lights in the majestic hall before she looked up from her work. She realized that the palace servants had come in to help clean up the mess. None of them had said anything to her, they just simply started working.

Furniture that had been damaged or broken was whisked away for repair or to be made into firewood. The blood soaking the floor was being carefully scrubbed so that not a single spec would be left. Arlaya took a deep shaky breath and grabbed a broom to start sweeping the smaller debris into manageable piles. With the fourth or fifth pile, she hit something metal and it scraped on the floor. The sound was grating to her ears, so Arlaya looked down and picked up the offensive item.

It was her circlet that Quint had thrown across the room. It had apparently hit something heavy and strong because it was bent into an unrecognizable shape. The queen sighed and straightened, running her fingers over the intricate metalwork that made the leaves. The sapphires twinkled at her in the shifting light of the candles that the maids were lighting.

One maid lit the candle nearest Arlaya and stopped. She stood there waiting for her queen to notice her. Arlaya felt her presence and looked at the maid. "Ma'am," the maid said quietly, "we can take care of the rest. Dinner has been set out for you and His Majesty in the royal suite. "

Arlaya felt anger. *This girl dares to order me around?* She felt a flash of pain in her hand and looked down. She had clutched her circlet so tight in her fury that the metal bit into her skin. She silently watch the drops of blood well up slowly through the cuts in her skin and let her anger flow away. It wasn't the girl's fault that she got angry, the maid was expressing concern over Arlaya and it was as simple as that. She nodded at the girl and calmly walked from the room to join her husband for dinner.

It would take some getting used to, but it finally looked like Arlaya would live a relatively normal life. Certainly, after so many attempts on her life at such a young age, she had earned peace. Besides, nobody would dare come after them once the stories started to circulate.

The sun peeked through the gap in the curtains. A solitary ray snuck across the room to illuminate a portion of Lirith's face. Arlaya watched his chest rise and fall and gently stroked his arm absorbing his strength and warmth. *It's over*, she thought.

Lirith's eyelids fluttered as he felt her watching him. "It's early yet, dearheart. They won't expect us to even leave our suite today." His eyes opened as he spoke in a husky voice.

"That's why I have to go out today," she replied. "We have to show that the royal family is intact and willing to pitch in."

Lirith propped himself up on his elbows with a slight hiss of pain. "I think you took care of that when you practically cleaned the whole throne room by yourself. The people saw that you weren't afraid to get your hands dirty and that you respected the lives of your subjects."

"I feel as though I should do more," she said.

He rolled over so that he had her pinned under him. "I know what we could do," he teased then kissed her.

Arlaya started giggling then pushed him off of her. "I can feel you shaking. Are you sure you're up for this?" she asked as she straddle him.

"Oh, I'm sure," he laughed and the two fell passionately down the rabbit hole together, forgetting their cares and fears and embracing their love.

***

It was two days before the king was granted permission to walk around by the physicians. Arlaya had planned out a leisurely day of walking the gardens to help Lirith build his strength back up. Lirith, however, was tired of being cooped up inside and wanted to leave the palace grounds entirely.

This was how, an hour after sunrise, Arlaya found herself walking down a city street beside Lirith and Hawk. They were wearing common clothing and had left the palace without a guard. It had taken some convincing for the head of Lirith's personal security detail to agree but he was finally able to walk the streets as Tiger once more. He wasn't without protection, after all.

The group walked very slowly, taking in the sights and sounds of normal life going on around them. It was almost as though there hadn't been an attack recently. Except that every gathering of people surrounded somebody recounting what they had seen or heard. As they moved deeper into the city and further away from the palace, the stories became more and more outlandish. At one point, they passed a marionette show depicting the coronation and all the events that followed.

Eventually, Hawk stopped and looked her companions up and down. "What is it?" Arlaya asked her curiously.

With the most serious look on her face, Hawk answered, "From the way they tell it, you and Tiger should be about ten feet tall and breathe fire." Then she couldn't hold her expression anymore and started laughing. The other two joined in and they started attracting attention but they didn't care. It felt really good to laugh. It was a release and they relished in their ability to let loose after being so vigilant for so long. After a while, the laughter subsided and the three made their way back to the palace.

There was to be a royal procession through the city and the surrounding countryside in the next few weeks to show all the people that the royal family was safe and well, but first Lirith need to heal up fully and start undoing the damage his uncle had done to the kingdom.

Epilogue

Arlaya stood in the throne room and smiled at the roaring crowd. She was very tired but to every eye she looked nothing less than radiant. Lirith stood next to her as both her husband and as her very real physical support. Together, they held their new babies. Arlaya had given birth to twins the night before and the babies were being presented to the kingdom.

The herald knocked his staff on the floor and the people quieted. "I have the pleasure of announcing, His Royal Highness and Heir Apparent Prince Calden first born of King Lirith and Queen Arlaya and Her Royal Highness Princess Ruadana!" His voice rang off the walls of the chamber and was answered by a new cheer from the crowd.

Lirith looked down at the prince in his arms and smiled. Arlaya watched her husband and knew that no matter what had happened in the past, she was happy and living a good life. The baby in her arms cooed up at her mother. Arlaya shifted the baby's weight carefully and stroked her chubby baby cheeks and she felt a tear run down her own cheeks.

A strong calloused finger plucked away her tear and Lirith whispered in her ear, "You have done something amazing, little bird." She smiled at him so full of love that her heart felt like it was going to burst.She had also taken over the kingdom's spy network and no longer needed to worry that the people close to her were going to die. Their kingdom was safe and she had a family.